Older, Wiser ...
HAPPIER

10 Choices for Rebooting
Your Life at 50+

P. Clay Carter

ISBN: 1453609660
ISBN-13: 9781453609668

Contents

Figure 1 – 10 Choices

Introduction

Older, wiser, and happier. The people who can make this claim are likely to have made several positive choices in the list to be considered in this book. Those who cannot make this claim can be comforted in knowing that it is not too late to make some of the most important choices in all of life.

The first premise of this book is that happiness is a result of choices. At first, this may not be welcome news. We can all think of things we meant to do and didn't, things we wish we had done differently or not at all. If our choices are to blame, then we can feel deeply saddened at how we have made a mess of life.

However, when the truth sinks in we see that life is shaped by choices, and that includes from here on out. If it is our choices that have had most to do with the form and substance of our lives, that means we have power to keep on doing just that: making choices that shape our lives.

That is where the second premise of this book comes in. We can make choices now that make life good. At whatever time we make the good choices, it is as if we have hit the reset button or rebooted ourselves.

Rebooting is a good image to keep in mind. A new start of sophisticated machinery is not simply a cop-out when we cannot think of anything else to do. In fact, the restart actually allows elements to adjust their alignment so they can function normally.

At various stages of life this fresh outlook is precisely what is needed. We get into routines, maybe even ruts. Then something happens and the previous satisfaction wanes or vanishes completely. Minor adjustments do not work. It's time to reboot, restart, and get a fresh run at life.

The ten choices are here because they have unique affect on people's lives. There are many choices that make life more pleasant or convenient, but these ten choices are about more profound issues. They go beneath the surface layers of education, culture, economics, and plain old luck of the draw. These are choices that are as important for one person as another.

Even though I have presented the choices as either/or, each choice is like the difference between hot and cold, the two options being separated by gradual degrees. The closer we get to one or the other extreme, the more we feel the effect of the difference between the two.

Throughout the book, an appeal will be made to see that it is easier to make and implement good choices if we keep company with people who have made a habit of happiness. As we consider each choice, it will benefit the reader to scan your personal history until you find people who embody the descriptions on the page. You may be surprised to see that some of the experts have neither rank nor fame. They are distinguished by their habits of attitude and behaviors. We are enhanced by keeping company with them.

At the end of each chapter, study questions are provided to help readers make the topic more personal. You will benefit from answering them for yourself. You will benefit even more if you discuss the answers with other trusted people.

Also at the end of each chapter is a list of possible commitments to action. In order to try out some of the ideas in the chapter, choose one of the commitments or write one of your own. You can decide how long to focus on what you select and when to try a different commitment.

Another question is designed to get at what keeps you from making the most positive choice.

Certainly there are external obstacles to each, but perhaps even more crucial are the hidden obstacles that arise from inner resistance. Your success at making a good choice and sticking with it may depend on how willing you are to see the inner resistance to what is best for you.

CHOOSER OR VICTIM

Making Choices or Feeling Powerless

I sometimes respond to the casual greeting "How's it going?" by saying, "Any way it wants to." I'm just aiming for a smile or an interruption of ritual greetings that are not meant to be taken seriously, much less literally.

"Any way it wants to" could also be a slogan for people who feel that that most of their lives are shaped by circumstances beyond their control. "A victim of circumstances" is a familiar way of saying that we have very little choice about the way life unfolds.

BENEFITS OF VICTIM ATTITUDE

Making a habit of seeing ourselves as hapless, helpless victims of circumstances has certain benefits. If every situation is entirely someone else's fault, then we are never accountable for anything. We can never be expected to act with more maturity, boldness, kindness, wisdom, or efficiency. If we are not satisfied with life, then it is because we have been neglected or actively mistreated. As a victim, we are blameless, and all the responsibility lies with those who have power and resources.

Another benefit is that some people may respond to victims with sympathy or pity. I saw an extreme example of how this benefit can be used when I made a trip to India. I was walking in New Delhi with a friend, and we were suddenly confronted by a man holding out his hand, asking for alms. In his other arm, he cradled a small child whose legs were so badly twisted that he would obviously never be able to walk. Naturally, I was moved to make a generous gift. As we walked on, my friend, who had lived in India, smiled sadly and told me that beggars often broke their children's legs in order to gain sympathy and better donations.

A stunning reality. And yet, people in every culture sometimes resort to appearing weak and ineffectual in order to get more help than they might if they appeared strong and able.

VICTIM OR CASUALTY

When I worked in residential treatment centers, I learned quickly that recovery usually depends on a person's willingness to shift from the victim mindset to an attitude of hopefulness and strength. Most people I encountered in those programs were casualties of significant mistreatment. Almost all the women and about three-fourths of the men had been severely abused as children. Most of the abuse was done by older family members. They suffered many of the same symptoms of soldiers who are called psychiatric casualties. (see the book *On Killing*, by David Grossman) ~ *collateral damaged*

Yet, maintaining an image of self as a helpless victim tends to shape the rest of life. In victim thinking there is meager hope for change. Since this mindset grants primary power to forces and people outside of ourselves, the best we can do is hope for good luck or unanticipated pity from those who have all the resources we need.

A casualty is someone who has suffered. However, a person who has been damaged physically or mentally does not have to become a permanent victim. It matters how we see ourselves.

CHOOSERS

The way we think affects our choices. The most important habits take place right between our ears. Dr. David Burns, researcher and teacher, says: "You can change the way you think about things, and you can also change your basic values and beliefs. And when you do, you will often experience profound and lasting changes in your mood, outlook, and productivity."[1]

This way of seeing ourselves was proposed by Abraham Lowe, a physician in the 1930's, and was refined by Albert Ellis, a psychologist in the 1950's who developed rational emotive therapy as an approach to helping people find satisfaction and happiness. Today it is widely known at cognitive behavior therapy or rational emotive behavior therapy. The contribution of this perspective is that we can see sense in how we are reacting, and further, we can exercise choice about how life unfolds.

The cause-and-effect chain looks like this:

Beliefs cause **Emotions** cause **Attitudes** cause **Behaviors** cause **Consequences.**

Most of us have had mixed success with self improvement or making ourselves feel better. We muster our best intentions, but we often simply do not get the job done. Experience has shown us how difficult the direct approach can be.

The reason we often fail in this apparently sensible approach is that we often try to get results without knowing the crucial realm that calls for a choice. In the following discussion, we will see that choosing is effective, IF we choose in the realm that has the most effect on our situation.

CONSEQUENCES *assigning "blame"*

Let's start with consequences because they are what we see every day. The Scottish author Robert Louis Stevenson said: "Everybody, soon or late, sits down to a banquet of consequences." Not everyone believes it. Some people seem to think that our life situations are a result of luck and fate. Others think that life is predetermined by direct, unpredictable control of some higher power. In both cases, people seem to think that they have had little or nothing to do with the way their lives have turned out.

If we look carefully at our lives, we see signs that we had something to do with where we are right now. If we want to put the blame on people close to us who let us down, we must discount the evidence that we either made choices about the relationships in the first place, or we had chances to modify the relationships after we found out they were causing us harm. If we want to put the blame on the actions of toxic strangers, we must discount the evidence that we chose to be at certain places at certain times. If we want to put the blame on the inequities of society, we must discount the evidence that we had choices about how we reacted to the same obstacles that other people faced more effectively. Certainly there are factors and people who contribute to our difficulties, but if we are completely honest, we finally admit that we have been active players in our own destiny.

physical How does this relate to the inevitable progression of years? Even though we cannot stop or reverse the aging process, we *can* decide how wisely we will act as we age. For example, several physical aspects are worsened if we choose to be sedentary. Among them are blood pressure, cholesterol levels, bone density, cardio-vascular conditions, and the immune system. Aging brings a tendency to be less active, but at the same time, good health requires a certain level of physical activity. We may identify with the statement I overheard recently: "I'm not in good enough shape to work out." Even as we smile and agree, we know that if we give in to the tendency to be physically lazy, then we are choosing the menu for our own banquet of unpleasant consequences.

social Many of us become socially lazy. Granted, we have lost contact with people who have been so important to us that they will never be fully replaced. It is not unusual for us to begin tunneling in socially when we start losing our network of important relationships. Also, health issues may make social activity inconvenient, or may cause us to be self-conscious about our declining vitality. The consequences of giving in to isolation are profound. Isolation results in loneliness and boredom, which are bad enough. In addition, medical studies indicate that social isolation and loneliness also lead to poor physical health.

Most of us know someone personally who has gone into hiding. I knew a woman who had been active in church and other social groups all her life. She drove her own car and was a ring leader in organizing vacations, shopping trips, and card parties. Then in her seventies, she developed Parkinson's disease. Although the symptoms did not prevent her from doing most things she had been doing, she gradually withdrew from every social group. She dropped out of church, which had been a primary network for most of her life. She stopped meeting with her card-playing group. She initiated a move into her daughter's home in a distant city, away from her support system, and she quickly became totally dependent. Even though her doctors kept encouraging her to become more active, she stubbornly maintained her isolation and inactivity. As a result, she became depressed, and that caused a whole new set of unpleasant symptoms, such as sleeplessness, poor appetite, and the natural side effects of those tendencies. Even though she had a measure of real health issues, most of her discontent was caused by her choosing to drop out of living. Consequences.

Another set of dangerous consequences occur if we neglect our spiritual growth. Spiritual issues become even more important as we get older. It is not about which church is better, or the subtle differences in doctrine, or how closely we comply with someone else's picture of goodness. At this point in life, we need to have an inner sense of balance. We need spiritual security to deal with the challenges that we cannot avoid as we age. We need a quiet center that helps us answer the big questions: What is most important in my life? What does my life mean to me....to the people close to me? How have I related to people? Have I achieved what I wanted in my deepest self? Have I lived well? How will I deal with my failures? Have I learned what life could teach me? How will I close it out? What comes next? If these questions are not answered satisfactorily, we will have no serenity. Instead, we will find ourselves unsettled, anxious, worried, restless, fearful, and dissatisfied.

Write the situations that interfere with your serenity. As you do, think about how you may have contributed in some way to these situations.

Seeking serenity

1. Dwindling family
2. Loss of some friends
3. Close friends are far away

> **Exercise:** Write situations that interfere with happiness.
> Example: I have physical conditions that restrict my activities.
> Example: I have financial pressures that cause me to worry.
> Example: I do not know where to turn for spiritual guidance

Beliefs cause **Emotions** cause **Attitudes** cause **Behaviors** cause **Consequences.**

BEHAVIOR

Behavior is not merely random actions that are unconnected and without purpose. Rather, our behavior tends to follow patterns, and those patterns take us to predictable places. We may not be aware of our habits, even though they become physically embedded in our brains. It is biology's version of the old story of a sign on a frozen, muddy country road: "Choose your rut with care; you will be in it for the next 10 miles."

Since behavior is the direct cause of consequences, and we can make decisions about behavior, this is the aspect that we do well to look at carefully. I remember clearly when this became clear to me. I had left a career in which I had been somewhat disappointed that I did not get as much recognition as some of my peers. Part of my transition involved group therapy, and it that process I became aware of how my habitual behavior had been contrary to what would have given results that would in turn have gained more affirmation. I had gotten what I deserved and had the kind of life that I had worked to create.

I realized that my life had been primarily shaped by my own behavior, rather than the capriciousness of other people. The hopeful awareness was that I could make better decisions that would make my life turn out more like I wanted.

Write the behaviors that interfere with your serenity in aging, such as the examples provided.

> **Exercise:** Write actions that Interfere with well-being
> Example 1: Since I have less energy than before, I conserve my energy whenever possible.
> Example 2: Since I have fewer enjoyments than before, I indulge myself with as many foods as possible.
> Example 3: Since I don't hear as well as I did before, I avoid social situations.

Beliefs cause **Emotions** cause **Attitudes** cause **Behaviors** cause **Consequences.**

ATTITUDES

Behaviors flow naturally from attitudes. Attitudes are states of mind that affect the way we see the world, ourselves, and other people. The following are pairs of contrasting attitudes:

Abrupt – Deliberate

Arrogant – Humble

Aggressive – Passive

Bossy – Collegial

Closed – Open

Critical – Appreciative

Demanding – Unselfish

Demeaning – Affirming

Dominating – Submissive

Evasive – Forthright

Deprived – Grateful

Harsh – Gentle

Inconsistent – Reliable

Indecisive – Decisive

Judgmental – Encouraging

Malleable – Stubborn

Manipulative – Honest

Methodical – Spontaneous

Negative – Positive

Oblique – Direct

Rejecting – Accepting

Resistant – Responsive

Rigid – Pliable

Rude – Polite

Sad – Happy

Selfish – Generous

Sullen – Cheerful

Suspicious – Trusting

Unreliable – Trustworthy

Vindictive – Forgiving

It is easy to see how attitudes will determine the way we react. Take any of the pairs listed, apply each to the same situation, and you can see how different the behavior will be.

Reality is what happens to us. Attitude is how we interpret what has happened. A soldier is wounded and says, "I was lucky to get out alive." Another soldier is wounded and says, "Why me?"

Parents lose a child to an incurable disease and say, "We were fortunate to have had her for those few years." Other parents lose a child and their inconsolable grief destroys their marriage.

An elderly person complains, "I have outlived all my friends." Another exclaims, "I have met so many interesting people!"

We are familiar with obvious attempts to create a shift in attitude. Maybe you have seen a friend displaying a long face and you said, "Cheer up. Smile and you will feel better. Look on the bright side." Such advice is based on the assumption that attitude is something we consciously choose, and is therefore something that we can shift at will.

Attitudes change when we get information or have experiences that change the way we feel. An example. Recently I stopped at a drive-through restaurant. The young woman who took my order was brusque, and when I stopped at the window, she handed my order to me without saying a word. Her sullen attitude had a negative effect on me and made me reluctant to stop there again.

If her supervisor told her to "Cheer up, be friendly," I doubt it would help much. She seemed to be showing the effects of negative emotions. I do not know what they were. Maybe she was angry at her supervisor for having changed her schedule. Maybe she was feeling frustrated by having a low-paying job when she is qualified for something else. Maybe she was worried about a health problem with one of her children. What would give her a different attitude? If something happens to change her emotional climate, then her attitude will also change.

At any given moment, we all have several emotions going on, but we usually have a dominant theme. When the strongest emotional state is positive, then we are likely to display positive attitudes. When our emotions are predominately negative, then we are likely to display negative attitudes. When we notice ourselves being caught in the same negative attitudes, we can look at the emotions that are dominating us. It will probably be anger, or resentment, or fear, or shame, or frustration or some combination of several negative emotions. Bad attitudes come from bad feelings. *Patterns*

Using the examples already provided, write the attitude that interferes with your serenity in aging. Add more items as you think of other attitudes.

Exercise: Write attitudes that hinder good relationships.
  Example 1: I am quick to see the faults in people and situations.
  Example 2: I feel cheated if others get more than I do.
  Example 3: I must use all my declining resources to look after myself.
  Example 4: I don't have time or inclination to think about others.
  Example 5: I never forget a wrong done to me.

Beliefs cause **Emotions** cause **Attitudes** cause **Behaviors** cause **Consequences.**

EMOTIONS

Emotions are the result of what we believe to be true, whether or not we are correct in our perception. Some psychologists have said that there are only four basic emotions: Joy, Anger, Grief, and Fear. *(For a fuller description of these four major emotions, see the chapter on Awareness.)* Every other emotion is derived from one of these, or is one of these in lesser intensity. For example, we often insist that we are not angry, we are only frustrated. They differ only in degree. We say that we are uneasy or nervous, not afraid. Again, the difference is only in the level of intensity. When we look at shame carefully, we realize that it is based in fear. Joy includes many variations, such as love, awe, contentment, and hope.

Emotions set the tone for our lives. A useful exercise is to occasionally sit quietly and take a careful inventory of all the emotions we have in that moment. We may be surprised at how many different emotions we have, and even more surprised that some are positive and some are negative. For example, a person at a funeral of a loved one will be feeling grief at the personal loss. He may also feel confusion (a form of fear) at what comes next in life, especially if the deceased is a mate that he depended on. And there may also be joy at having the loving support of people whose presence makes him feel stronger.

Another example: a religious person may feel satisfaction in her religious life, and feel energized by worship experiences. Both of these are a form of joy. In ~~resentment~~ addition, she may feel resentment because her husband does not relate to family members as she wishes. And further, she may be afraid to express her feelings openly lest her image as a saintly person be compromised, and perhaps because she is afraid to risk divorce and the financial uncertainty that would bring. And she may feel grief about the loss of personal self esteem and freedom that went with a career that she gave up to be a fulltime homemaker. This complex mix of emotions can cause a person to be basically unsettled and uneasy, and she may not know why. —anxiety → loss of identity

We do ourselves a favor when we are as vigilant about our emotional health as we are about our physical well-being. By paying attention to our emotions, we can alter the tone of our lives and get what we want and need.

Using the examples already provided, write the emotions that interfere with your serenity. Add more items as you think of other emotions.

> **Exercise:** Write emotions that interfere with happiness.
>   Example 1: Shame
>   Example 2: Bitterness
>   Example 3: Fear

Beliefs cause **Emotions** cause **Attitudes** cause **Behaviors** cause **Consequences.**

BELIEFS – perception ⟶ response to stimuli

We come now to the element that is the first link in the chain: the way we think. The process begins when our beliefs trigger our emotions. If you question this linkage, look at some examples.

Suppose you have been standing in the concession line at the movie, and suddenly feel a push in the back that propels you into the person in front of you. What emotion do you have? It all depends on what you believe is happening. If you believe someone was being either careless or purposely rude, you would probably be angry. However, if you heard a mixture of sounds that made you be- lief someone was having a heart attack and fell against you, you would probably feel concern or anxiety.

Suppose you are at a party, and you notice a friend talking to someone, point- ing in your direction and laughing. If you believe the friend is saying something derogatory about you, you will likely feel anger or shame (a form of fear). But if you believe the friend is repeating a clever joke you told and giving you credit, you will probably a warm feeling of pleasure. It all depends on what is in your mind about the situation.

Our beliefs about our situation are crucial. If we believe that we are losing some vital aspect of life, or that most of the good in our lives is already behind us, then the emotional response will likely be a mixture of fear, anger, and grief.

Unless we are among the rich and famous, aging increases the likelihood that we will have experiences that make us feel that we are gradually becoming in- visible in the eyes of younger people. In fact, even some of the rich and famous have felt nudged out of their privileged positions as they get older. The feeling of slowly diminishing, even while we are still here, creates a visceral feeling that can only be traced to fear. *No*

If we believe that we are being disrespected and displaced, we probably get angry. We may call it something else, like frustration, or being hurt, or irritation, but all of these terms are merely forms of anger. We may feel this when we are forcibly retired from work, even though we can still do the job and prefer to keep working. We may feel it in churches when we are no longer asked to serve in important roles, but instead are enlisted for committees that do things that do not matter very much.

The belief that we are less valued and that we have little more to contribute will likely produce grief. Our culture, including family and younger friends, may tell us, "You've earned your retirement. Take your rest, take it easy, relax….etc." For some, the relief from work-a-day pressures is so welcome that we may enjoy coasting for a long time. But many of us will feel a great loss when we can no longer do something we consider important.

Beliefs that create all these negative emotions set in motion a chain reaction. They create emotions that lead to attitudes than are expressed in actions which lead to natural consequences. To achieve serenity, we must confront the process at its source: our deeply held beliefs.

Write the beliefs that interfere with your serenity. Then write what the changed belief would be.

Exercise: Write beliefs that interfere with happiness.
    Example 1: My worth is tied directly to my physical capacities
    Example 2: Pity is a useful tool for getting attention.

The connections between beliefs, emotions, attitudes, actions, and consequences are often hidden from our awareness. It is much like one of the running jokes in the old TV series, The Beverley Hillbillies. When the countrified Clampets heard the door chimes in their new California mansion, one of them would start toward the front door and say, "There're those bells again. I guess we'd better go to the door. Seems like every time they go off, somebody shows up."

HABITS

Habits make life easy for us. They make it possible to drive around the block and talk to a companion at the same time. Or to eat while watching TV. Or to find our way home while we are thinking about an upsetting conversation we had earlier in the day. The gist of habits is that when we start on a familiar series of actions, we can stop thinking about them and complete them without conscious thought or attention.[3]

Recent research has shown that when we repeat thoughts or actions, we are creating connections in the brain that are called neural pathways. The more a certain thought or action is used, the more firmly the pathway is set. It is easier to go over familiar territory than blaze new trails. Furthermore, the brain treats the first step of a habitual pattern as if it is the entire sequence of thoughts or actions.[4] Thus, habits become a kind of mental shorthand.

An apt analogy for the physical character of habits is the footpaths that show where people have cut across grassy areas. The first trip across the yard will not be seen the next day, but after several trips across the same route, the path gradually becomes more visible. After a while, the grass surrenders. Habit has prevailed.

Purposeful

The effect, of course, is that habits make life simpler so that we can do more things at once and many things with less effort. But first, there is purpose. We repeat the thoughts and behaviors that do something important for us.

And so we establish careful study patterns because we enjoy learning new things and perhaps the praise for getting good grades. We practice good hygiene because we like the way we feel and the way people relate to us. We regularly do our duty because we like how we feel about ourselves and the way other people respond to our behavior. Good habits have positive payoffs that are easy to see.

The Good in Bad Habits

What about habits that have negative impact on us and people around us? For example, the pattern of overeating or eating to relieve emotional uneasiness. Or not paying our bills on time even when we have the money. Or letting our expression of anger be the "fly-off-the-handle" variety. Or smoking even when doctors tell us we are endangering our lives. Or constantly feeling sorry for ourselves. Or seeing only the negative in every situation. Or always overtly agreeing with people even when inwardly we do not agree. Or gambling even after we are dangerously in debt.

Even with habits with lots of negative side effects, we are still tightly linked to the positive side effects of the treasured habit. Compulsive eating gives temporary pleasure that distracts us from unpleasant thoughts or feelings. Addictive substances like nicotine and caffeine give physical and mental feelings that cause us to view their temporary rush as worth the long-term risk. And besides, we intend to quit...someday. Blustery anger tends to intimidate people and helps us get our way. Adopting a victim role transfers responsibility to others so that we do not have to be depended upon. Looking for the negative gives us credibility with other complainers, and together we avoid committing to positive outcomes. And gambling provides excitement that we do not want to do without. So, even habits that are apparently negative have benefits that we have come to depend on.

Quitting a Habit

To quit a habit we must deal with two obstacles. One is that we are trying to give up something that gives us a desirable benefit, whether we are fully aware of it or not. With aging, we become familiar with losing aspects of life with no choice whatsoever. So, when we are faced with doing without something and we have some choice in the matter, we may decide that whatever the risk is, it is worth the continuing pleasure.

We also get into the mode of thinking that it is too late for us to change, and we are more than a little relieved at not having to make the effort. We decide that what is shall be. Younger folks may view this as loss of mental acuity or physical energy. It is more a surrender of the will to explore new options.

We may not realize how powerful our inner dialogue, or self-talk, is in shaping our lives. For example, when we detour from a path we want to follow, we may say to ourselves, "There you go again. You always do that. You're never going to do it right." And we believe it, and we carry the negative message with us when we get ready to try again. The more times we hear the negative message, the more we doubt our ability to break out of the old pattern.

The real question is how to deal with fearfulness and its effects. If negative messages work against us, then it makes sense to start giving ourselves positive messages. At this point, we must admit an annoying reality: we have messages that we repeat to ourselves, and they seem to be written into our minds in indelible ink.

For example, we may address our feelings of loneliness by intentionally saying, "I am an interesting person that people like." And then the persistent qualifier that slips in from some dark corner, unbidden, "Yeah, but I say dumb things that turn people off."

Or, "I like this time in my life." Then the qualifier, "Yeah, but I've had to give up some things I wouldn't swap if I had a choice." In this way we sabotage our best efforts at encouraging ourselves.

Research psychologist Shad Helmstetter developed a strategy for overcoming the insistent negative messages.[5] He recorded positive messages on a cassette player and then replayed them to himself while he was getting ready for work each morning. He said that an even better option is to have some other person record them, so that the voice is not your own. Hearing the messages spoken aloud frequently has more impact because the negative qualifiers are not being heard in the same way as the positive messages.

The strategy is to gradually replace negative messages with positive messages that are grounded in reality. Instead of saying to myself, "I always eat the wrong things," I can repeatedly hear the message, "I am eating food that makes me healthy and happy." Instead of saying to myself, "I am always too tired to exercise," I can hear the message repeated, "I enjoy the benefits of being physically active." Instead of saying to myself, "I don't have any friends," I hear the refrain, "I am doing things that will bring me into contact with people who share the same values that I have." By reshaping our inner conversation, we affect our attitudes and our behavior. But we must first determine to give up the benefits of what we have been thinking and doing.

The second obstacle to changing habits is also in our heads…literally. As previously mentioned, our brains have established patterns (the neural pathways) that make it physically easier to do what we've been doing rather than something else.

And then the most difficult part: getting rid of the neural pathway that makes it so easy to slide back into the old thinking and behavior. Which brings us to the key truth: **it is easier to start a new habit than stop an old habit.**

Forming a Habit

The good news is that our brains are still making new pathways. For many years we thought that the structure of the brain and its functioning was pretty much fixed early in life. In the last twenty years, new technology has enabled scientists to study the brain with more precision. They have found that many long-standing assumptions about the brain and body were entirely wrong.

For example, it was once thought that if you had a stroke and part of your body lost functioning because of brain cell damage, you just had to live with it. New research has shown that new neural pathways will form if given a chance. Actual cases have shown that a stroke victim who has lost control of the right arm can regain full use of that arm by limiting the use of the left arm. By restraining the good arm, the brain is forced to create new neural pathways around the damaged part of the brain, and the affected arm will regain use. If, however, the good arm is not restrained, no new neural pathways are formed, and the ones that remain dissolve.

This means that the physical tracks that habits run on do not have to be permanent. But they do remain **unless** they are left unused for a period of time. One estimate is that it takes about twenty-one days for an unused neural pathway to dissolve. This estimate is not coincidentally about the same as the traditional estimate for breaking a habit: about 30 days.

It does not take a pessimist to observe that this does not happen with great frequency. An elderly gentleman who was being interviewed on television was asked if people tend to get grouchier or sweeter tempered with age. The old fellow pondered a moment and then said with a twinkle in his eye, "We just get more so." It is the stuck-in-the-same-rut theme, but in real life, it is being stuck in the same neural pathways.

The answer to changing life is the same as getting out of a muddy rut: we need help. Every person I know that has made significant, lasting change was part of some ongoing group. The group may have been a twelve-step group, a therapy group, a Weight Watchers group, a military unit, or some informal group of friends that met regularly and were faithful and honest with each other. Private self discipline works for some people sometimes, but it's easier to detour from your goal when you do not feel accountable to another person. Individual counseling with a trained therapist is often needed to get out of some disabling situation, but the normalization of life calls for a community of fairly normal people.

We have innate ability to mimic the behavior of other people. Medical research has discovered a group of brain cells called ***mirror neurons.*** These cells enable us to understand each other and copy the behavior of other people. Our brains do more than merely notice outward behaviors in a way that we go through similar motions. Rather, our mirror neurons enable us to actually feel with the people we are watching, so that matching their behavior is not merely superficial copying, but is something we feel at our deepest levels.[6]

The implications for ongoing groups are powerful. This means that we can choose the people whose behaviors we want to copy, and by being close to them on a regular basis, we can absorb motivations and perspectives that made changes in them. *no, I will create my own.*

We have experiences that prove that this is possible. We can all think of people we know who affect us profoundly. Just by being around them, we feel affected by their quality of life. Sometimes they are positive, optimistic people who make us feel enlarged and empowered. Sometimes they are negative, pessimistic people who make us feel fragmented and exhausted. But either way, we absorb their influence in ways that are more profound than we even know consciously.

So, we change our behavior by choosing the kind of people who will support the life we want to live. They do not have to be perfect in every respect. We just need for them to be committed to the path that we want to travel, and to be kind enough to keep drawing us into their company. We are creatures who respond to community. We get to choose the community that is going where we want to go. Within an authentic community, we can feel the increased influence of power that we may choose to ascribe to just the people, or we may be convinced that the power comes from a Higher Source. And thus we move on.

STUDY QUESTIONS ON CHOOSER OR VICTIM

1) What benefits do you get from habits that you consider negative?
2) Have you had success in starting a new habit? Stopping a habit?
3) What part did other people play in starting or stopping a habit?
4) When did new information change the way you felt about something?
5) What is a negative message about yourself that you say to yourself frequently?
6) What is a positive message that could replace this negative message to yourself?

EXPERIMENTING WITH BEING A CHOOSER

Make selections to try or write your own.

- ☐ I will notice my choices and how they are related to consequences.
- ☐ I will notice each day's attitude and how it shapes the outcome of the day.
- ☐ I will notice which emotions result in attitudes that create satisfaction and which create dissatisfaction.
- ☑ I will spend time with people each week whose attitudes and behavior I admire.
- ☐ I will make a list of my habits that have a negative effect on my life.
- ☐ I will make a list of my habits that have a positive effect on my life.
- ☐ I will write down the names of people who embody positive habits I would like to have.
- ☐ I will make a list of the negative messages I say to myself most frequently.
- ☐ I will make a list of positive alternatives to the negative messages I have listed.

OBSTACLES TO HAPPINESS

1) What makes it difficult for me to be a chooser rather than a victim?
2) Is the obstacle a
   ☐ Thought or belief   ☐ Emotion   ☐ Attitude   ☐ Behavior
   ☐ Consequence/situation?
3) What would I have to do to make a different choice?

ADAPTABLE OR RIGID

Adapting to Life's Stages and Circumstances
or Being Captive to Futile Habits

LIFE SITUATIONS

We human beings have an inherent need to make things happen. From the time we can interact with our world until we are ready to leave it, we find pleasure in exercising power. We like to control things.

Toddlers delight in knocking over toys, pushing anything that will move, and throwing their food. All of these are ways to make things happen, not only with things, but also with the adults who are watching over and picking up after. One theory about why kids like to hear the same story over and over is that once they have learned it, they know what is coming next, and can even say the lines themselves. It's like they are making the story happen. **Causing stuff.**

Teenagers thrive on finding ways to outsmart adults and do what is dumb, dangerous, and often illegal. They relish their skill at being separate human beings in the face of all efforts to make them copies of those who claim to be wiser. **Changing the world.**

Adults feel a sense of achievement when they manage their families, homes, and jobs with competence. Much of adult talk is about how we are doing a better job at something than others are, and we feel good about our starring roles. **Being competent.**

We feel happier when we are making the decisions that shape our lives. We do not want someone else telling us what to eat, whether we can drive, and where we must live in order to lessen the worry of other family members. **Still kicking.**

Having significant impact is rewarding. It causes us to feel that what we are doing matters. It makes us happy because it makes us feel that we have a certain amount of control.[7]

Recent studies show that control is more than a momentary feel-good. The feeling of control – whether real or illusory – is one of the wellsprings of mental health.[8] In fact, it may affect physical health as well.

In one study, researchers gave residents of a nursing home a house-plant. They told half the residents that they were in control of the plant's care and feeding (high-control group). They told the remaining residents that a staff person would take responsibility for the plant's well-being (low-control group). Six months later, 30 percent of the residents in the low-control group had died, compared with only 15 percent of the residents in the high-control group.[9]

Researchers then arranged for student volunteers to pay regular visits to nursing home residents. Residents in the high control group were allowed to control the timing and duration of the student's visit ("Please come visit me next Thursday for an hour"). Residents in the low-control group were not ("I'll come visit you next Thursday for an hour"). After two months, residents in the high-control group were happier, healthier, more active, and taking fewer medications than those in the low control group.

At this point, the researchers concluded their study and discontinued the student visits. Several months later they were chagrined to learn that a disproportionate number of residents who had been in the high-control group had died. Only in retrospect did a possible cause of this tragedy seem clear. The residents who had been given control, and who had benefited measurably from that control while they had it, were inadvertently robbed of control when the study ended. Apparently, gaining control can have a positive impact on one's health and well-being, but losing control can be worse than never having had any at all.[10]

The application is obvious. Maintaining the ability to exercise power is vital for our total well-being. We need to exert our will to make things happen that are important to us.

The crucial issue is how we cope with limits of control. Being flexible may not sound important at first, but in reality our capacity to adapt has an enormous effect on our health and happiness.. At this point, a prayer that is often used in ongoing groups can be a good reminder of vital balance:

> God, grant me
> The serenity to accept the things I cannot change,
> The courage to change the things I can,
> And the wisdom to know the difference.[11]

This is often called the serenity prayer. It is a succinct statement about the need for both control and flexibility. Our happiness depends on our ability to know when to exert control and when to be adaptable.

DEALING WITH LOSS

A major aspect of maturing is dealing with various kinds of losses. We lose people that are vital to us. Spouses die, or leave, or have their awareness impaired by debilitating disease. Old friends move away, or die, or lose their ability to be active friends. Our children become preoccupied with their own lives.

We lose status in the community when we can no longer do the most highly valued jobs, or display physical beauty and health, or be a part of activities that value strengths we no longer have.

We lose self-esteem as treasured parts of our lives gradually decline or disappear altogether; when we cannot remember as quickly, or move as easily, or respond to stimuli the way we once did.

We lose faith in the possibility of fulfilling treasured dreams. Aging prompts us to measure what we have, to reflect on what no longer is, and to face what will never be.

Talk to any elderly person and ask if they know what it means to be not noticed. It's almost as if we are gradually fading from sight, becoming less and less visible to people who once would have smiled, and chatted, listened to our views, and valued our company.

When these losses occur, grief begins.

STAGES OF GRIEF

People grieve in ways that fit our personalities and lifestyles. Still, there are some stages of grief that are common to most, even though the sequence may vary from person to person.

1) *Feeling emotionally numb* is often the first reaction to a loss, and may last for a few hours, days, weeks, or months. This is the stage when we cannot really believe that the loss is real and permanent, or when we cannot fully realize the profound effect it will have on our lives from that time forward. The death of a beloved person, the loss of access to people who are important to pleasurable living, the loss of a treasured physical ability, the loss of a capacity to function in a way that has been crucial to one's life; all these may at first seem unreal. People may look calm during this stage because we have not absorbed the full significance of the loss.

2) The numbness is often replaced by *surges of powerful emotion*. We may have a deep yearning for what is no more. We may feel agitated or angry, and find it difficult to concentrate, relax or sleep. We may also feel guilty, dwelling on what we did or did not do that contributed to the loss. We may replay the missed chance to help the person who died, or wish for another

chance to change the decision that led to lost access to loved ones, or rue the delay in getting the medical test earlier that might have prevented the disease, or think of how the career could have been extended. We may look for people to blame and may plot vengeful actions. We may rage, fume, or wander about restlessly.

People may think we are just being cranky, and may assume that is an inevitable part of aging. As we get older, we may have more empathy for the cranky aging woman, Weezie, in the movie Steel Magnolias. She said, "I'm not crazy. I've just been in a bad mood for forty years." Being caught *Sometimes* in a negative mood is often a signal that we are stuck in unfinished grief over some aspect of life.

3) The periods of powerful emotion usually are followed by **bouts of intense sadness**. The yearning may be so powerful that it feels like physical pain. During these times, we may withdraw from family and friends. We are more prone to see reminders everywhere of what has been lost. We may think we see people who really cannot be there. We may be overcome with sudden outbursts of weeping.

   During these painful stages, we may look for distractions from the pain. We may use drugs or alcohol, or sexual activity, or compulsive buying, or anything else that occupies the mind and gives the pleasure centers of the brain a much desired jolt.

4) In the next stage, **_normalcy begins to return_**, and we may begin to see life from a larger perspective again, and may begin to hope for future happiness. Even during this stage, there may be sudden lapses into deep sadness.

5) The final phase of grieving is to let go of the person, or capacity, or identity that was so vital to our self image, and **_move on with life_**. Gradually the sadness is less frequent and life takes on new patterns that have their own satisfaction. Sleeping patterns and energy levels gradually return to normal.

Many patterns often attributed to aging may be signs of unresolved grief. In people middle age or younger, these symptoms would be noticed for what they are, but as we age they are often misdiagnosed, if they are noticed at all.

LIFE'S STAGES

The process of aging tends to throw life out of balance. Our Western culture values youthful beauty and vigor, and we quickly get past the peak of physical powers. Our culture also tends to reward people who can deliver a valued product, such as entertainment, or business skills, or a service that people are willing

What about self-value?

to pay for. People who cannot perform a marketable service, or have not accumulated wealth that can be used to benefit the community, are generally valued less. Thus, the emphasis on youthfulness and productivity and competition that makes our culture successful in so many endeavors is precisely the attitude that puts us at a disadvantage as we age.

Until recently, the medical field tended to support society's evaluation and perpetuated the myth that aging brought inevitable decline in all aspects of a person. Conventional wisdom claimed that the brain could not grow new cells and that once we get past school age, our ability to learn steadily declines. These conclusions were based on the belief that the physical aspects of the brain were fixed very early in a person's life.

Recent research has challenged those long-held, untested opinions. Recent studies at a variety of universities and medical schools have shown that the brain does *not* deteriorate with age, that the brain is constantly remaking itself in response to experiences, that new brain cells are formed throughout a person's life, and that the flexibility of the brain actually improves with age.[12] The current body of research says that even in our performance-oriented culture, older people still have skills that have intrinsic worth. The conclusion is that "Healthy older brains are often as good as or better than younger brains in a wide variety of tasks."[13]

In spite of this good news, aging brings significant challenges. First, aging increases the chances of a person developing some type of physical condition that can affect the brain's efficiency, such as Alzheimer's disease, or small strokes, or circulatory deficiencies.

Second, it is more important than ever for us to maintain good health habits in order to keep the body working efficiently. That includes diet, exercise, sleep, social activities, and the choices we make about expanding the mind.[14] When we were younger, the effects of neglecting body and mind were not so noticeable, but as we age, the effects are quicker in coming and have more impact on our total well-being. At a time in life when many of us might prefer to just relax and coast, self-discipline is more important than ever.

And finally, we live in a culture that has built-in factors that put older people at risk. The continuous inflation of the economy puts economic pressure on people whose earning peak is past, and even those who have planned carefully often have nasty surprises visited on us by our government and the world economy. The constant stress of worrying about survival and quality of life can affect us physically and mentally, and the stress can have myriad negative effects on a person's overall health.

Let us consider some of the ordinary challenges that are intensified as we get older.

LONELINESS

When we feel disconnected from a network of people we value and trust, we feel lonely. It does not matter whether we are living in austerity or luxury, in a crowded setting or alone, in a simple or complex life. We need to have access to people who know us and are personally interested in our welfare.

A part of the issue may be that we have not fully understood what constitutes an adequate support system. A proverb, widely thought to be of African origin, says, "It takes a whole village to raise a child." Some cultures utilize all the aspects of a community to help a person navigate through life's stages. In the Western culture, as an increasing percentage of us choose to live in urban areas, we have de-emphasized the importance of a person's larger community. Even if a person has a beloved mate and a supportive primary family, we still need a wider community of support. If we do not have it, and events occur that disable or remove family members, we will be vulnerable.

Mobility

A cultural pattern that has contributed to loneliness is mobility caused by employment. For decades it has been the norm in our county for working adults to change employers or to change locations with the same employer. A negative impact of this pattern has been that the older we get, the more likely it is that we have been gradually separated from our adult children, grandchildren, and friends and neighbors who knew us in early stages of life. We may find new friends in new locations, but the sense of shared history cannot be duplicated. We may develop a feeling of being out of touch with important elements of our heritage, elements that are vital to our sense of identity and worth. We have the feeling that our new friends can never see the full picture of who we are, no matter how many old photos we show them.

It is the kind of feeling expressed by a character in one of Agatha Christie's novels. Miss Marple, a senior citizen amateur sleuth, was surprised and puzzled at how distressed she was at the death of an aunt. She finally realized the reason: "She was the last person who remembered me as a child."

Seeking Ideal Locations

Another trend is the increasing tendency of people to sell the family home and get a new residence, often in a different region. This scatters long-time neighbors and severs our connection to place and personal networks. The feeling of extended family that some close knit neighborhoods have is lost, and the benefits are not easily replaced.

When we move away from family and friends, we put pressure on a smaller number of relationships. If we move with mates, then the mates suddenly have more responsibility for each other's total well-being. Where we may have had a wider community in the former home, we are now leaning more heavily on each other. The pressure of altered expectations may affect the relationship in ways that create disappointment in both people.

Following Family

Sometimes we move in order to be closer to other family members, most often our children and grandchildren. **Difficulties begin when we organize our lives around our children's families.** While this may be mutually acceptable in some situations, many families find it burdensome. Sometimes without being aware of it, we make our children's families responsible for meeting a broad range of social, emotional, and physical needs. Relationships change in ways that are not satisfying to us or our families. We become more dependent and our children's families feel responsible for aspects of life that we once looked after for ourselves. All too often, this causes significant damage to intimacy and good will within the families.

Illness

Another factor that contributes to loneliness as we mature is the increased incidence of illness, either to self or a mate. Visits to doctors' offices, empty time in waiting rooms, coping with surgical procedures and recuperation, keeping up with medical bills, following up on mistakes made in the billing process are activities that are exhausting, even for younger people. The burden can cause us to ignore social contacts that are just as important to our overall health as medical treatment.

Indeed, there is evidence that loneliness actually causes an increase in the incidence of illness. Studies have shown that people who are isolated and lonely have a higher incidence of health problems. A 1998 study of women found that symptoms of depression and lack of social support correlated with an increased number of heart attacks, open-heart surgeries and deaths from cardiovascular disease.

Longing for Community

The instinctive longing for community probably contributed to the popularity of the TV series, Cheers, which debuted in 1982. The weekly episodes took place in a local bar in a working class neighborhood in Boston, where regular customers and bartenders shared experiences and formed genuine friendships. The theme song contained these words:

> Sometimes you want to go where everybody knows your name,
>   and they're always glad you came.
> You wanna be where you can see our troubles are all the same,
> You wanna be where everybody knows your name.

Gary Portnoy and Judy Hart Angelo

The stories were about people who were related by choice. In spite of their glaring imperfections, mostly played for laughs, each was valued by the entire group, and each had a well defined role in the group. The popularity of the series owed a lot to the universal yearning to be part of a group that knows us and loves us for what we are.

This is a good model to remember. In our search for community and intimacy, we are not limited to family members. We can choose the people who comprise our circle of caring.

DEPRESSION

The point at which loneliness evolves into full blown depression is often hard to identify precisely. Depression among older people has long been ignored, but recently is getting more attention. A 1996 Senate hearing, "Treatment of Mental Disorders in the Elderly," dramatically increased awareness of illness. Senator Harry Reid (D–NV), whose father killed himself at age 58, used the event to call for more National Institute for Mental Health (NIMH) funding to study depression treatment and suicide prevention in the elderly. In 1999, the Surgeon General's report on mental health sounded a new note by calling for the de-stigmatization of mental illness. The report described depression as a condition that takes an inordinate toll on older citizens.

Symptoms that would signal depression in younger people are often labeled a natural part of aging. Because of this mistaken assumption, depression may go undiagnosed in four out of five people past middle age. Left untreated, depression may prompt suicidal thoughts. It contributes to the increased lethality of disorders that typically accompany aging, such as cardiovascular disease, an effect that arises at least in part because depressed elders tend to take poor care of themselves. This depression-driven deterioration is so common in nursing homes, says psychologist Donna Cohen of the University of South Florida, Tampa, that it even has a name: "failure to thrive," a term normally used in reference to infants.[15]

Symptoms of Depression:
- A persistent sad, anxious or "empty" mood
- Loss of interest or pleasure in ordinary activities, including sex
- Decreased energy, fatigue, feeling "slowed down"
- Sleep problems (insomnia, oversleeping, early morning waking)
- Eating problems (loss of appetite or weight, weight gain)
- Difficulty concentrating, remembering, or making decisions
- Feelings of hopelessness or pessimism
- Feelings of guilt, worthlessness, or helplessness
- Thoughts of death or suicide; a suicide attempt
- Irritability
- Excessive crying
- Recurring aches and pains that do not respond to medical treatment

Notice how many of these symptoms are often associated with normal aging. In reality, none of these is natural for us.

VARIETIES OF LOSSES

With age we accumulate more valid reasons to grieve. We have had multiple losses, not just with family and friends, but losses of functioning or lifestyle. Losing a part of your life that defined you is a powerful experience. It may seem that you have lost not just that treasured portion of your life, but the very essence of life as you have known it.

Losing a dream often makes us profoundly sad. So long as the dream is still out there in the future, and still an option, even though somewhat remote, we are partially defined by it. When a shift in life or our perceptions make the dream no longer possible, we feel a significant loss.

The roles of men and women are not as different as they were for generations. More women are the primary wage earners for their families, and more men are involved in the full range of care for children and other family members. Sometimes the untraditional path is taken by free choice to follow one's own vision, and other times because of uncontrollable circumstances.

Our ability to work is crucial because we have lived through eras of economic pressure. Being able to do productive work has been a way of meeting life's challenges and building self esteem. If we have been proud of our ability to do important work, then we may try to carry our career credentials forward as a way of making favorable impressions with new acquaintances. Introductions and conversations are filled with references to titles, positions, pay grades, and accomplishments. After a while, the loss of meaningful activity can no longer be salved by remembering past achievements. We need something more.

Caring for people who are important to us is often a crucial part of our self-image. In whatever ways we have given the care, it has been a source of satisfaction and pride. When the natural flow of life takes away our ability to give necessary care, we may suffer a severe loss of self esteem. The crucial point is that a person is losing value in his or her own eyes by no longer producing important results. The loss can trigger the grieving process.

Though some people get stuck in the grief process, for most people the process is time limited; we move on eventually. However, if the losses keep on accumulating, one after the other in rapid succession, a person may have difficulty ever finding a stable ground before the next loss hits. After a while, a person may begin to see grieving as the normal state. This misconception could cause us to cease our efforts to move forward to healthier attitudes and activities.

UNSETTLING SIDE EFFECTS OF AGING

The following check lists can help identify effects that interfere with our overall happiness.

Emotional Consequences

- ☐ 1) Loss of self-esteem
- ☐ 2) Loss of a dependable sense of reality
- ☐ 3) Loss of life goals
- ☐ 4) Acting against your own values and beliefs
- ☐ 5) Strong feelings of shame
- ☐ 6) Strong fears about the future
- ☐ 7) Strong feelings of isolation and loneliness
- ☐ 8) Emotional numbness
- ☐ 9) Emotional instability and changeableness
- ☐ 10) Suicidal thoughts
- ☐ 11) Attempted suicide
- ☐ 12) Thoughts about committing violence
- ☐ 13) Feelings of hopelessness or despair
- ☐ 14) Failed efforts to change your moods and attitudes
- ☐ 15) Feeling like two different people: living a public life and a secret, private life
- ☐ 16) Other emotional consequences

Physical Consequences

- ☐ 1) Acting in ways that endanger your safety and well-being
- ☐ 2) Significant weight loss or weight gain
- ☐ 3) Chronic physical ailments (e.g. ulcers, high blood pressure, headaches)
- ☐ 4) Physical abuse or injury by others
- ☐ 5) Involvement in potentially abusive or dangerous situations
- ☐ 6) Vehicle accidents (e.g. automobile, bicycle)
- ☐ 7) Self-abuse or injury (e.g. cutting, burning, bruising)
- ☐ 8) Sleep disturbances (e.g. not enough, too much)
- ☐ 9) Physical exhaustion
- ☐ 10) Other limitations related to aging

Spiritual Consequences

- ☐ 1) Strong feelings of spiritual emptiness
- ☐ 2) Feeling disconnected from yourself
- ☐ 3) Feeling disconnected from the world
- ☐ 4) Feeling abandoned by God as you understand God
- ☐ 5) Loss of faith in anything spiritual
- ☐ 6) Other spiritual consequences

Family and Partnership Consequences

- ☐ 1) Risking the loss of partner or spouse
- ☐ 2) Loss of partner or spouse
- ☐ 3) Increase in marital or partnership problems
- ☐ 4) Loss of respect for your partner
- ☐ 5) Loss of your partner's respect
- ☐ 6) Loss of or unwelcome reduction of sexual intimacy
- ☐ 7) Jeopardizing the well-being of your family
- ☐ 8) Loss of your family's respect
- ☐ 9) Increase of problems with your children
- ☐ 10) Loss of your family of origin
- ☐ 11) Other family or partnership consequences

Career and Educational Consequences

- ☐   1) Decrease in productive work
- ☐   2) Withdrawal of opportunity to be productive
- ☐   3) Loss of co-workers' respect
- ☐   4) Loss of your ability to work in the career of your choice
- ☐   5) Loss of the opportunity to work in the career of your choice
- ☐   6) Failing mental ability to perform productive work
- ☐   7) Failing physical ability to perform productive work
- ☐   8) Forced to change careers
- ☐   9) Not working to full capacity (underemployed)
- ☐ 10) Termination from job
- ☐ 11) Other career or educational consequences

After looking at our answers to these exercises, we begin to see the degree to which aging has interfered with our overall sense of well-being. If the inevitable, natural process has disrupted our achieving satisfaction, then we find ourselves becoming increasingly unhappy. The first step is admitting that it is so. Not everything that is faced can be overcome, but few things can be overcome unless we face them.

BENEFITS OF AGING

It is also good to admit that there are some benefits that come as we reach the mature stages of life. Here are a few:

- ☐   1) Willingness to be honest about what we think
- ☐   2) Saying what we really feel
- ☐   3) Freedom to delight in children, rather than having to parent them
- ☐   4) Relief from necessity to be orthodox
- ☐   5) Freedom to question
- ☐   6) Good excuse to avoid activities that we do not enjoy
- ☐   7) Don't have to put up with people we don't like
- ☐   8) Focus time on people we enjoy
- ☐   9) Having wisdom based on many years of experience
- ☐ 10) Freedom from planning a long future
- ☐ 11) Learning to recognize liars better
- ☐ 12) A longer list of heroes and heroines
- ☐ 13) Pleasure in doing nothing
- ☐ 14) Not responsible for other people

☐ 15) Thinking more about spiritual matters
☐ 16) Time to enjoy good music
☐ 17) Old photographs
☐ 18) Perspective
☐ 19) Pleasant memories

Admitting the good stuff is important. Otherwise, we can get into the self-pitying mode. Making a gratitude list on a regular basis can make us appreciate where we are.

WAYS OF RELATING

In his book, **Games People Play,** psychiatrist Eric Berne popularized a discipline called transactional analysis. It is a system for looking at the ways people interact with each other. He described three different modes that all people use to relate to each other. He called these roles parent, adult, child. Each has a primary mindset that is familiar. More recent development of Berne's approach can be found in books such as **TA Today,** by Ian Stewart & Vann Joines. The contribution of current books is that they emphasize the differentiations within the Parent and Child modes that were implicit in earlier works.

Everyone knows what each of these roles or modes feels like. We see toddlers "playing parent" as they parrot the words and mimic the attitudes of their parents. The little tykes are very entertaining as they experiment with being in charge.

Conversely, no matter how old we get, we feel the agony and ecstasy of being caught up in profound emotional experiences, which is the homeland of children.

And we all know those times when we are adult enough to admit the full truth about the present situation and what the implications of our behavior will be. In such times, we focus our attention on finding workable solutions and applying them.

Awareness of these different mindsets can help us understand the importance of adapting our way of relating to fit the situation.

PARENT MODE: BEING IN CHARGE

The term "parent" is merely a way of talking about the mindset when we are trying to control situations and people. It may be direct control (critical parent) or indirect control (nurturing parent), but it is control nonetheless. When we look at the focus, behavior, and language of the control mode, we may be surprised at how much time we operate from that attitude.

When we are operating from the **Critical Parent** mindset, our *focus* in on the following:

- Values
- Ethics
- Morality

- Rules
- What is right

Our attention is firmly fixed on our perception of what is right, and we compare situations and people's actions with the standard we have in our minds.

Our *behavior* is a natural extension of our mindset. Therefore, we tend to do some or all of the following:

- Blaming
- Controlling (directly)
- Correcting
- Criticizing

- Giving orders
- Ridiculing
- Shaming

All of the behaviors are intended to bring situations and people into alignment with our perception of what is right.

The *language* of the critical parent often includes messages such as:

- "You should"
- "You should not"
- "What were you thinking?"
- "Why did you do that?"

- "Don't make a mistake"
- "Who is to blame"
- "Who gets credit"
- "Why don't you learn?"

Being in charge can also be a kindly mindset, which is the way we function as the **Nurturing Parent.** The focus is still on what is right, but in this mode we add another concern: what is helpful.

- Values
- Ethics
- Morality

- Rules
- What is helpful

Because of this one shift in emphasis, the behaviors also change:

- Comforting
- Controlling (indirectly)

- Directing
- Protecting

The language of the nurturing parent often includes messages such as:

- Taking care of "I will help you"
- "I will do it for you"
- "You can't"
- "Are you okay?"
- "I forgive you"
- "You couldn't help it"

Parent Benefits

There are many situations in which the parent mode or mindset is beneficial to us and others. In this mode we challenge behavior that is hurtful or inappropriate or unkind. We challenge people, including ourselves, to do the right thing, to be responsible. We expect people to take the rightful consequences for their behavior.

A significant portion of the anger that many feel about the economic meltdown that began in 2008 is caused by the way that certain individuals and companies have evaded the consequences for their behavior. The parent mindset causes us to resist the idea that people can flaunt the standards of decency and then escape the natural consequences of their behavior. When we hear, "That company is too big to fail," it reminds us of instances in which a child of an influential person is given exemption from the standards that apply to everyone else. We know that violating the rules of justice is not good for anyone, including the escapee, and we rebel against the notion that anyone is ever too big or too influential to get what they deserve.

It is also the parent within us that looks on those who have done the right thing but are being neglected. We feel the impulse to take care of them in some way, to stand with people who are being mistreated. It is our nurturing parent instinct that is outraged on behalf of those who are innocent sufferers. It is this mindset that takes people into situations of danger in order to care for someone in need.

Parent Liabilities

One of the chief appeals of staying in the parent mode is that we like the feeling of being in control. It makes us feel important and valuable. By making others wrong, we are in the right, and being right gives us status in our own minds. We savor the feeling of power that comes with being able to point out other people's mistakes.

Attributing blame is another function of our parent mode. When circumstances violate our standards, a popular coping strategy is to use the being-in-charge mindset to look around for someone to blame. Even if we were not able to control events, the right to assign blame restores some sense of control.

It is in the parent mode that we feel the right to set expectations. The negative aspect of that is when we impose our "should's" on others regardless of their own wishes. And that leads to the next topic.

Super Ego

Coping with Perpetual Parents

Although being in charge is useful in some situations, it can create problems in relationships, especially when making other people wrong is one of our routine strategies. If you are habitually in the being-in-charge mode, then people tend to react in one of two ways.

Some people will go along in order to get along, like a compliant child. This method of coping causes us to hide differences of opinion in order to preserve surface harmony. The compliant person either becomes dependent or develops a secret life in order to have independence. In either case, the relationship has little real depth or intimacy. "Yes, Mother," or "Whatever you say, Daddy," often hide thoughts and actions that are not shared for fear of having to deal with disapproval and conflict.

Even if our intentions are completely unselfish, the habit of constantly being in charge interferes with true intimacy and trust. We make a habit of exerting direct or indirect control over our adult children, our mates, our friends, and everyone else we encounter. And most of the time we may get our way and conclude that our ways works quite well.

A good friend of mine, whose aggressiveness has been key to his life-long business success, was introducing me to his neighbor. The neighbor said, "Yeah, he's very famous around here. We have several streets named after him."

Naturally, I was impressed. "Really?"

"Yeah. One-way."

Getting our way does not mean that we are in harmony. It may just be that our relationships are two-tiered. On one level, the routines and rituals of the controllers are faithfully observed. On another level, the compliant people have other aspects of life that are never shared with the controllers. The person in the parenting mode wins control of the superficial encounters but loses the benefits of honest, in-depth interactions.

C. Parent

This may help explain why so many eventually feel isolated and lonely. We have lived long enough to feel that we have earned the right to give sage advice and tell people what they should and should not do. It is true that our breadth of experience gives us the benefit of perspective, and we may often know a lot about wise living. Because we think that we know what is right and wrong, we may try to impose conformity of thought on our families and acquaintances. Even if people give outward compliance, we will miss the exchange of thought that comes when people feel it is safe to be honest with us. The "Yes, whatever you say," may give the momentary illusion of control, but the truth is that we lose genuine companionship that we need.

Not every child reacts to parents by giving surface compliance. When some children reach the natural stage of developing their own identities, they openly resist unneeded or unwanted parental control. They rebel. "No, I don't want to do that!" "I can do it myself."

For some children, the rebellion is not a temporary stage that they grow out of quickly. They instinctively settle into overt resistance to controlling behavior wherever they encounter it, regardless of whether the form of the control is critical or nurturing. Parents who try to win the battle by increasing the pressure find the outcome with these children is escalated conflict and eventual permanent separation.

Constantly being in charge has the same effect on relationships as we age. **Unrelenting and unwelcome control forces people to maintain their freedom in the only way controllers permit: by creating protective barriers**. Adult children put emotional and geographic distance between themselves and parents who will not permit the relationship to become less over/under. In social settings, some people either express dislike for controlling people or avoid their presence. These people are not willing to sustain a charade of civility in order to protect the feelings of those who are trying to exert control over what others believe and do.

Probably everyone can think of at least one person who triggers resistance in us. It is difficult to say what causes one person to be flattered and grateful to a person who gives parent-like attention to us, and another person to be resistant to the point of being angry. The key issue is that we learn to avoid sabotaging important relationships that are important for our own well-being. For our own good, we must learn how to make our way of relating appropriate to the life situation.

CHILD MODE: IN THE MOMENT

There is within each of us an unfettered child. The focus of the free child is on emotions, action, and pleasure. In this mindset, we live without the overlay of rules, customs, and obligations. We are delighted and awed by people, nature, and experiences. We delight in being playful and exuberant. When we are expressing ourselves as the **Natural Child,** our *focus* is on the following:

- Feelings
- Excitement
- Action
- Pleasure

The **behaviors** that naturally flow from the child's focus include the following characteristics:

- Spontaneous
- Playful
- Noisy
- Unrestrained

- Energetic
- Enthusiastic
- Creating

The **language** has themes similar to the following:

- "Let's relax"
- "Let's try this"
- "Let's get going!"
- "Loosen up!"

- "Oh, no!"
- "This is fun!"
- "This might work"
- "What's the big deal?"

I learned about this child mode as a middle-aged man while I was in group therapy at the Gestalt Institute of Memphis. As part of our healing regimen, we went on a weekend retreat to give concentrated attention to the issues that were interfering with our serenity and personal growth. It turned out that one of my issues was an under-developed capacity for play. During our relaxation breaks, the group taught me how to enjoy simple games like drop the handkerchief and red rover, so that I could feel what it was like to be a child.

In a grown-up world, that may not seem important, but in fact the capacity to be emotionally involved in pleasure will affect our relationships with children, our mates, and friends. There are moments when the most loving action possible is to play on the floor with a child. An emotionally mature person has the ability to be fully involved in the emotion and action that fit a given moment.

Focusing on the fullness of the present moment is profoundly important. With the passage of time, we have a lot more history to think about, and we are tempted to pay attention to an endless series of remembered segments of our life story, so that our conversations are like snippets from old newsreels and TV shows. Living in the past causes us to lose the present, no matter how skillfully we select only the parts that illustrate our favorite opinions. We need to reclaim the child's ability to enter completely into this moment, to engage with full attention and feeling into this activity for its own sake. We cannot change the past. We only have the present and future to work with.

Another important part of being childlike is that we leave behind our habit of feeling that we know what is right, what is wrong, what should be done, and what should not be done. In short, we need to step outside the sense of knowingness that we cultivate as we get older. Reclaiming a child-like willingness to learn, to be surprised, to be delighted, to be spontaneous is vital not only to mental health but to simple enjoyment of life. We get a taste of this when we spend time with preschool grandchildren and marvel at the invigorating effect it has on us. It is an attitude that can be cultivated.

People are still mulling over the full meaning of one of the sayings of Jesus: "Unless you change and become like children, you will never enter the kingdom of heaven." (Matthew 18:2) Could it be that the attitude of openness, curiosity, full engagement, spontaneity, and exuberance is part of what any person needs in order to know existence at its fullest?

all facets can be adapted

Child Liabilities

The child mode also has a dark side. As an **Adapted Child**, we are more in touch with feelings with a more somber *focus*:

- Feelings
- Fears

- Crisis
- Survival

We can all remember the fear and dread that are part of every child's life to some degree. We can smile at those childish fears now, but if we let ourselves, we can still feel the awfulness that came from dangers that were real or imagined.

The *behaviors* reflect the absence of safety and freedom:

- Reacting
- Responding

- Complying
- Rebelling

Sometimes we reacted by being very compliant in order to make ourselves feel safer. When taken to the extreme, this instinct to make peace with the powerful can lead us into a lifetime of unhealthy compliance.

The *language* is both more plaintive and more resistant:

- "Please"
- "I can do this"
- "No!"
- "I won't do it!"

- "I don't like this"
- "Yes, Mother/Daddy"
- "I'm bored"

Think for a moment about the last time that an authority figure did or said something that triggered a fearful response in you. It may have been the police car that slid in behind you as you were driving along. It may have been the supervisor who frowned when you offered a comment on the task at hand. It may have been anyone who had some kind of power that could be used against you if the person chose.

All of us must cope with situations that cause the child response. The key is to not let the fearfulness that is natural to childhood become the controlling pattern of daily life.

Reg. Ego

BEING ADULT AND REASONABLE

In this mode, we are at our most reasonable. The *focus* is on the following:

- Thinking
- Information

- Analysis
- Clarity

When we are in the adult mode we are looking at limitations and circumstances and determining what is possible and what is not. In this mode, we search for the truth even if it is hard on our cherished values. We consider each option and where it will lead, and we do not spare ourselves the discomfort of seeing unexpected circumstances that call for an adaptable mind and a flexible attitude. We are trying to find out what works best rather than being preoccupied with imposing our will and proving ourselves right.

The *behaviors* appropriate for this mindset include:

- Solving problems
- Planning

- Developing Strategies
- Clarifying issues

Familiar *language* of this mindset includes the following:

- "Let's think this through"
- "What are the facts"
- "What is the best approach"
- "What is efficient"

- "What is practical"
- "What works best"
- "Where do we go from here"
- "What resources do we have"

Our happiness depends on our ability to be as realistic about our limits as we are certain about our opinions. This is who we are when we are being reasonable and practical. This is the mindset that enables us to suspend certainty in order to absorb new insights and get new ways of seeing the world and ourselves. Important breakthroughs are made when we are free enough to change in accordance with new reality. This is the adult state of mind.

Some seem to think that by the time we reach this stage in life we have already learned enough. People with this view seem to envision our latter years as the mental equivalent of a luxury cruise, where we just coast, lounge, and let the momentum of the journey take care of everything. Nothing could be further from the truth for most of us. Every new stage of life brings new reality, and we are happy to the degree that we adapt to our changing world.

In the Parent mode, we cling to the conviction that we can control people, events, and circumstances. Our failures put us into a constant state of frustration, not to mention the fact that they drive everyone around us crazy. In the Child mode we cling to fantasies, and we are deeply hurt when they turn out to be mere illusions. So, the adaptability of the Adult mode is indispensable for our well-being and happiness.

STUDY QUESTIONS ON ADAPTABLE OR RIGID
1) Have you lost any skill or ability that once was crucial in your self image?
2) Is there any change in your life to which you have not been able to adapt satisfactorily?
3) In what mode of relating (Parent-Child-Adult) do you find yourself most often?
4) Tell about a recent time when you were in the Parent Mode. What did you like about it? What did you dislike about it?
5) Tell about a recent time when you were in the Adult Mode. What did you like about it? What did you dislike about it?
6) Tell about a recent time when you were in the Child Mode. What did you like about it? What did you dislike about it?

EXPERIMENTING WITH ADAPTABILITY
Choose an action or write one of your own.
- [ ] I will permit myself to grieve over lost aspects of myself.
- [ ] I will permit myself to grieve over important people who are no longer in my life.
- [x] I will identify a time when it is appropriate to exert nurture for someone I care about.
- [x] I notice when I am being parental in situations that are not appropriate.
- [ ] I will consciously move from one mode of relating to another in order to be at my best.
- [ ] I will practice feeling like a Child.
- [x] When I am fearful, I will practice being Adult in my way of being.

OBSTACLES TO HAPPINESS
1) What makes it difficult for me to be adaptable rather than rigid?
2) Is the obstacle a
   - [ ] Thought or belief
   - [ ] Emotion
   - [ ] Attitude
   - [ ] Behavior
   - [ ] Consequence/situation?
3) What would I have to do to make a different choice?

AWARE OR OBLIVOUS

Fully Aware of Physical and Emotional
Realities or Hiding Behind Diversions

In this chapter, we consider with what kind of consciousness we typically interact with people and the environment. First, however, we will consider habits that affect our physical and mental involvement in life.

PHYSICAL HEALTH

Staying fully involved means doing good things for your body and mind. The AARP website published an article by Heather Boerner entitled *50 Ways to Boost Your Noodle*. The list includes practical things you can do. Here are some examples, arranged according to categories.

EAT TO LIVE WELL

I confess to being a recreational eater; that is, I tend to eat to because it is a genuine pleasure. The older I get, the more apt I am to get bad results from the habit of indulging myself. At the very least, I gain weight that puts strain on my body and may set me up for a variety of diseases from high cholesterol to high blood pressure to diabetes. I also set myself up for bad feelings about myself. At a stage of life when some of the finer points of physical appearance erode, I do not need to exacerbate the effect by packing on a bunch of extra pounds. The bulges and bulk interfere with the way I move and the kind of clothing that I can wear and still look good. I need to take some good advice about developing healthy habits.

1) **When looking for a sweet pick-me-up, choose a pear, apple, orange, or melon instead of candy or cookies.** The combination prevents elevated blood sugar that could impede brain cells from firing correctly. It also provides fiber and antioxidants that help scrub plaque from brain arteries and mop up free radicals that inhibit clear thinking.

2) **Instead of sweets, choose blueberries and almonds.** Fruits and nuts lower blood sugar. The omega-3s in the almonds and the antioxidants in the blueberries tend to make your brain function more efficiently.

3) **Instead of croutons on your salad,** try walnuts. Omega-3s in walnuts have been found to improve mood and calm inflammation that may lead to brain-cell death. They also replace lost melatonin, which is necessary for healthy brain functioning.

4) **If you use wine, choose red wine and sip judiciously.** Up to two glasses for women and up to three for men weekly delivers the powerful antioxidant resveratrol, which may prevent free radicals from damaging brain cells. But beware: Drinking more than that could leach thiamine, a brain-boosting nutrient.

5) **Drink two cups of gotu kola tea daily.** This ayurvedic herb, used for centuries in India, regulates dopamine. That's the brain chemical that helps protect brain cells from harmful free radicals, boosts pleasurable feelings, and improves focus and memory.

6) **Try some new tea.** Tulsi tea, made of an Indian herb called holy basil, and ginseng tea both contain herbs that can help reduce overproduction of the stress hormone cortisol, which can hamper memory. The herbs also help keep you alert.

7) **Swap your fries and burger for lean pork loin crusted in peanuts and broccoli.** The pork and peanuts are high in thiamin, a nutrient that reduces inflammation that damages brain cells. The folate in broccoli is good for keeping synapses firing correctly.

8) **Top rolled oats with cinnamon for a brainy breakfast.** The oats scrub plaques from your brain arteries, while a chemical in cinnamon is good for keeping your blood sugar in check, which can improve neurotransmission.

EXERCISE YOURSELF

We all need exercise that is strenuous enough to get our blood flowing, our breathing to deepen and speed up, and our muscles to be challenged. Sometimes aging brings physical conditions that make us far less physically active. When forms of exercise that we once did become too demanding, we must find alternatives. If we can no longer jog, we can walk vigorously or ride a bike. If we can no longer play tennis, we can swim. We may need to shift to some new activity that fits our physical limitations, but it is vitally important that we stay active. Part of the reason to exercise regularly and vigorously is to maintain good health, but also to get the feel-good effects of the natural endorphins that our body creates. Some suggestions from the AARP website:

1) **Take a walk**. Walking for just 20 minutes a day can lower blood sugar. That helps stoke blood flow to the brain, so you think more clearly.

2) **Try ballroom dancing**. Dancing is a brain-power activity. Learning new movements activates brain motor centers that form new neural connections. Dancing also relieves stress.

3) **Strength training.** Lifting weights regularly helps build older adult muscles and increase your metabolism, which helps to keep your weight and blood sugar in check. Ask advice from someone who has expertise in recommending the kind and intensity of exercises that will be beneficial.

4) **Stretching exercises** can give you more freedom of movement, which will allow you to be more active during your mature years. Stretching exercises alone will not improve your endurance or strength.

5) **Endurance exercises.** Any activity – walking, jogging, swimming, biking – can increase your heart rate and breathing for an extended period of time. Build up your endurance gradually, starting with as little as 5 minutes of endurance activities at a time.

6) **Pilates** is a new yoga-type exercise program that strengthens the body and improves balance. It does not involve high impact and can be learned at whatever level of ability a person has

EXERCISE YOUR BRAIN

1) **Volunteer** to answer questions at the library, arboretum, museum, or hospital. Playing tour guide forces you to learn new facts and think on your feet, helping to form new neural pathways in your brain. What's more, interacting with others can ease stress that depletes memory.

2) **Try video games.** New video games can be brain teasers that make you learn the computer's interface as you master the brain games. That's a double boost to the formation of new neural connections and to response time and memory.

3) **Eye exercises.** Stare straight ahead, and now—without moving your eyes— see if you can make out what's at the periphery. Do this regularly and you'll stimulate the neural and spatial centers of the brain, which can atrophy as you age.

4) **Read the news**. Keeping up with the world and local events activates the memory part of the brain, and also gives you something to talk about with friends and family. Interaction with other people about current events can activate multiple parts of your brain and encourage cell growth.

5) **Practice relaxation and meditation. Sit quietly, choose a word that calms you, and when your mind starts to wander, say the word silently.** This type of activity can reduce the stress hormone cortisol, which interferes with

memory. Meditation also helps lessen feelings like depression and anxiety. In addition, 10-minute sessions of meditation and relaxation increase our ability to concentrate.

6) **Continue education**. Research shows that taking courses, even just auditing them, reduces the tendency for early dementia. Get involved in book readings, seminars, and other educational events.

7) **Limit television time.** TV may provide a lot of stimuli, but watching too much can dull brain transmission. Instead, spend an afternoon listening to your favorite music. Music can lower stress hormones that inhibit memory and increase feelings of well-being that improve focus.

8) **Learn to play an instrument.** Learning to play an instrument creates unique brain functions. It also eliminates boredom, a brain state that can cause some thinking skills to atrophy.

9) **Take naps.** Most of sleep's benefit to concentration and memory happens in the first stage, so even a 30-minute nap can benefit your brain.

MENTAL FOCUS

We know that we are happy when we enjoy what we are doing. The error we make, though, is assuming that the enjoyment depends on finding the right things to do. The truth is surprising at first, but clear when we think about how our own experience verifies it. It is this: enjoyment comes as we do things with full focus of our attention.

So long as we think that enjoyment comes from the things we do, we are dependent on our ability to find the right thing and then being able to do it. However, if enjoyment comes from our own focus of attention on whatever we do, then we have unlimited opportunity to create enjoyment in everyday life, no matter what. It's all a matter of choosing our state of mind.[16]

Author and lecturer, Eckhart Tolle, gives an exercise to test the idea for ourselves. Make a list several ordinary activities that you do frequently, just routine activities like driving to work, or paying bills, or sorting mail, or doing the laundry, or cleaning the kitchen. If you are like most people, you probably do not find these particularly enjoyable, and may try to find ways to distract yourself from these familiar chores.

Now, as a conscious experiment, choose to be totally present in each of these activities while you are doing them. That means you do not do something else at the same time, something that distracts you from the chore. Give your full attention to the activity for itself. In this heightened state of attention, you may then become aware of a level of energy in yourself that is different from what you have usually felt while doing this routine chore. The pleasure that you get is not from the activity itself, but rather in your own sense of awareness and aliveness.

Another way to test this idea is to look at the way we feel when we go on vacation or visit new places. We savor the scenery because we are seeing it as new rather than a backdrop for routine activities. The new activities stimulate enjoyment, not because of the activities themselves, but because they are occasions for a level of attention that enables us to feel our own aliveness.[17]

DISTRACTION AND DIVERSION

A more familiar piece of advice we get when we are not enjoying our lives is to find distractions, a way of mentally avoiding familiar activities. Getting-away-from-it-all is a normal attitude when it applies to vacations or relaxing weekends. Even the most extraverted person needs some time to be quiet, and sometimes getting away is the only way to make it happen. Different people need different amounts of quiet time, but all of us do best if there is a rhythm of inward retreat and outward engagement.

The problem comes when getting-away-from-it-all becomes a pattern for dealing with the inevitable conflicts and pressures of ordinary life. When things are going well, the pleasure centers of the brain are stimulated naturally. We spend time with loved ones, and we feel the warm glow of affection. We participate in sexual relations, and we feel the excitement of giving and receiving pleasure. We succeed at work, and we feel the satisfaction of achievement. We eat, drink, rest, exercise, and we feel the pleasure of being in tune with our bodies. We participate in spiritual activities, and we feel the settling, energizing, enlightening effects of larger perspective. In all these experiences, we are naturally stimulating our brains to feel pleasure.

When things are not going well, we can hang in there until the natural rewarding experiences return. Or we can look for substitutes. We have found that buying new things can give us a temporary boost of energy and pleasure, so shopping may become an activity that is needed often in order to maintain emotional stability. We crave the good feeling that surges through us as we focus on our new stuff. The excitement makes us forget bothersome aspects of everyday life.

We have discovered that some kinds of food and drink affect our moods, so stimulants such as coffee or frequent snacks may become indispensable for maintaining comfort.

There are many behaviors that can provide an artificial kick to our pleasure centers: gambling, recreational drugs, unhealthy eating, an endless string of romantic attachments, or shopping sprees. All these can distract us from the discomfort we feel when our basic needs are not being met.

A mindset that is often underestimated in its power to distract us from every-day reality is the habit of focusing on drama. The most benign form is reading books that capture our imaginations and transport us to the world of story char-acters. As kids, the world of comic books and mysteries made us feel excited without ever having to leave our homes. Later, movies became the doorway into worlds beyond, and our favorites were those that made us feel part of their expe-rience. The entertainment industry is built on the human desire to rise above the ordinary world and enter worlds where idealized or fictionalized characters create excitement that we can share.

Drama is not limited to books, movies, and television. The car wrecks that other drivers slow down to see, the bad news of world-wide calamities, and the missteps of our neighbors are all exciting and become topics of animated conver-sations. In fact, the worse the situation, the more likely it is to be repeated with excitement. Trouble is more dramatic than stories about people who have been noble and efficient.

Focusing on drama, (i.e. excitement) can become a habit of living. Constantly watching other people's dramas can distract us from being and doing our best, and can thereby rob us from life at its fullest.

Tests for Substitutes

How can we know that we are leaning on substitutes? The first key is the matter of degree. How much and how often are we using something? We all need to eat and shop. However, we can usually tell the difference when we are using these activities to alter our moods and divert our attention from aspects of life that are either boring or uncomfortable. For example, if I am eating between meals to alleviate boredom, or to give myself respite from tension, then this is diversionary living. A signal will be that I am steadily gaining weight, or having to resort to frequent weight loss programs to maintain a healthy size.

A good example for me is the popcorn movie. No matter whether I am hun-gry or not, when I enter the theater and smell that unique odor, I feel impelled to complete the movie experience. Sitting in the dark theater, watching an interest-ing story, in the easy rhythm of alternating popcorn and sipping iced cola, caught up in a world that takes me out of my ordinary existence. The food is not for nourishment; it's for entertainment, and I am sorry when I have reached the point when I can eat no more. I am lucky if I avoid the Thanksgiving-hangover feeling.

If I am shopping not just to maintain necessary supplies, but I am accumulat-ing unneeded items, and perhaps even overspending my income, then I am using the temporary high of getting something new as a diversion. I can remember even now the smell of my first new car. I can almost feel the excitement of look-ing out over the glistening hood, learning the new terrain of the dashboard, open-ing the trunk and touching the jack that had never been used. We can all call up and relive the feelings of those first moments when we knew that a coveted object was finally ours. It is an undeniable rush, a high, a kick to the pleasure centers of our brains. If elements of life that would give profound satisfaction are missing or in short supply, the intoxication of new possessions can fill the empty place. When shopping is a substitute, it will be out of proportion to what is actually needed.

Another test is appropriateness. Does our activity fit the situation? Entertainment can make us enjoy relationships and refresh us for duty. But when things that excite us are used to avoid things that are essential to a well rounded life, then we may find that it takes more and more to make us feel entertained.

We sometimes need medicine to help our bodies deal with illness. But it has become almost routine to use drugs to fool the brain's pleasure centers so as to avoid the feelings that come with unpleasant life situations. All drug addic-tion begins with the drug being used to stimulate pleasure that was not being achieved in a natural way. After a while, however, the body adapts to the arti-ficial stimulation, so that the drug no longer gives extra pleasure. Instead, the body compensates for the artificial stimulant and the drug becomes necessary just to maintain what would have been the normal balance before the drug was used, and increasing amounts are needed to get the desired rush of pleasure. This kind of compensation is not activated with natural stimulants, such as lov-ing relationships, hard-won achievement, and the natural ecstasy of spiritual discipline.

We do well to consider how much we have used substitutes for life's natu-ral gratifiers, because distraction and diversion do not provide satisfaction at the deepest level. Activities or substances that are taking the place of experiences that give us what we need are never as effective or as long-lasting. As we get older, it makes good sense to do what works most naturally and gives the best results in terms of pleasure and satisfaction.

EMOTIONAL STATES

We live with awareness when we pay attention to the emotions that are basic to all the emotions that give rise to our reactions to life's situations. They are **anger, joy, grief, and fear**.

ANGER

Anger does not have a good reputation in our culture. If we view ourselves as good people, we may feel embarrassed when we lose our tempers. Being out of control is felt by many people as a period of weakness, a time when we are not ourselves.

However, if we think of anger as part of the natural package of human emotions, then we begin to consider what good purpose it serves. **Anger gives us the energy to do what needs to be done to protect ourselves or those we care about.** Without the energizing effect of anger, we would be unable to respond with power in the face of danger. We would not be willing to do the hard, costly work of maintaining justice.

Sometimes we fall into the habit of passivity and are not aware of things that deserve our anger. Some of the things that should trigger our anger are directed at us as individuals. When people treat us with less respect than others, and we have reasonable signs that it is because of our age alone, then we should be angry. In a culture that is generally agreed to be youth-oriented, the opinions of mature adults are sometimes only slightly considered.

An example: A woman was a life-long member of a church comprised of upwardly mobile, well-educated, successful people. She was a teacher of an adult Bible class made up of community leaders in a respected city near the eastern seaboard. She was on boards and committees that made the most important decisions of the church, including budget formation and selection of professional staff. She represented the congregation in community service and interdenominational activities. She served for several years in the highest roles available to lay people in their denomination.

As she went past middle age, her authority was gradually taken away. She was still mentally alert and had as much mobility as she ever had. She still drove her car and was socially active. In fact, she was more ready to give first-rate service than any time in her life. However, the church was eager to reach younger people, and the strategy was to present an organization that was driven by people closer to the age of their targeted prospects. She was still a member, but as she aged, her participation was reduced to attendance at services, giving her money, and serving on committees that made sure that fresh flowers were in every service and refreshments were served at the receptions for prospective new members.

An example: A man earned advanced degrees that prepared him to be successful in a company whose name would be recognized by almost anyone. He left the large company to be a founding partner in a new company, and based on the efforts of the two men, the company created inventions that are still being used all over the world. During his successful career, his opinions were high valued; people listened to him. After his retirement, he was asked to serve on boards of directors, and he looked forward to sharing his experience to help companies flourish in areas where he had valuable experience. He was surprised to discover that his advice seemed to be sloughed off. After a while, he backed off, having become frustrated with being more figurehead than mentor and advisor.

Another example: a man was a well-educated teacher who gained prominence in the educational circles in his region. His ability to devise creative teaching methods and his personal winsomeness made him uniquely popular with his students. After his retirement, he envisioned himself as a busy unpaid consultant for schools and college students. But the schools did not call, and only a few of the college students took advantage of his high quality tutoring. During hanging out time at the local barbershop, he lamented, "I have all this knowledge, but nobody seems to want it." The only thing that had changed was his age. ~~and~~ *his situation*.

Many who have faced similar scenarios do not get mad. We try to be philosophical, even agreeable. The squelching of feelings of outrage takes considerable effort, whether we know it or not. And when we have put down our feelings about being put down, it is likely we will feel mostly sad, perhaps even depressed.

Some of the things that should trigger our anger are directed at us as a demographic group. Our culture is more inclined than most to treat older people as a group that is gradually becoming irrelevant, and to believe that we will quietly accept whatever is given to us. In a time when mature adults are becoming more numerically significant, we have more opportunity to make our voices heard. After all, we have been contributing to the growth and success of institutions and organizations. We are the shoulders that the present generations are now standing upon. It is only fair to expect support as we face challenges that will eventually face everyone. By expecting what we need, we can again blaze the trail for generations who have no choice but to follow.

GRIEF

Grief is a feared emotion, and not just because it signals the loss of a cherished person, or dream, or aspect of life. Grief is intimidating because we may be unsure how well we will endure its testing. It is helpful to realize that grief has certain predictable aspects that may seem overwhelming when we are in the midst of them, but which are part of what we humans feel when we lose something important to us.

Earlier in this book (Chapter on **Adaptable**) we looked at the stages of grief. We merely name them here, keeping in mind that people grieve in ways that fit our personalities and lifestyles.

1) *Feeling emotionally numb* is often the first reaction to a loss, and may last for a few hours, days, weeks, or months.

2) The numbness is often replaced by *surges of powerful emotion*. We may feel deep yearning for what is no more.

3) The periods of powerful emotion usually are followed by *bouts of intense sadness*.

4) In the next stage, *normalcy begins to return*, and we may begin to see life from a larger perspective again, and may begin to hope for future happiness.

5) The final phase of grieving is to let go of the person, or capacity, or identity that was so vital to our self image, and *move on with life*. Gradually the sadness is less frequent and life takes on new patterns that have their own satisfaction.

Well-meaning loved ones often try to shield us from unpleasant emotions. Doctors prescribe sedatives that give temporary numbness, but actually only delay the pain until the healing rituals are over and the sympathasizers have gone on about their lives. Then the awakening person is left to cope alone or to find other means of avoiding what needs to be faced.

Since dealing with losses is a relentless part of life, and accelerates as we age, we must live fully into grief. Otherwise, we miss so much of what enriches and deepens us. In the grieving, we find out that true blessings may be temporary, and yet they are worth the price we pay. We learn that healing of the mind and spirit takes time and we cannot hurry it. If we are fortunate, we let honest people enter into our experience, and then feel the lift of human connection. And perhaps most important, we discover that we will not die from an emotion. We are in danger only if we underestimate our durability and adopt desperate means to avoid pain that will eventually pass, if only we are patient and faithful to the natural processes of living through it. And finally, we learn that we are fortunate to grieve, because it means we have loved someone or something deeply enough to feel deprived when we are separated.

FEAR

The adrenaline rush created by scary movies and bungee jumping is entertaining for some people. There is a difference, though, in manufactured excitement and the paralyzing, stomach-churning, mind-numbing, smothering effect of real fear. Waiting for the result of a biopsy makes time stretch almost beyond our ability to bear it, while we try to shut out dire imaginings. Being in the path of a wildfire creates primal terror of an agonizing death. Getting news of a layoff notice arouses survival panic about whether we can keep on getting regular food, clothing, and shelter.

Uncontrollable Circumstances

As we mature, fear comes calling in new guises. Suddenly having a symptom that you believe is the precursor of a fatal or disabling disease. Hearing a doctor describe the loss of some vital function as "normal for your age." Realization that you can no longer afford to buy a medicine that your doctor said is necessary. Seeing signs that people whose company is vital to you have reallocated their time, and you are now a lower priority. Watching as loved ones follow careers to locations that are beyond your reach. When frightening circumstances like these first arise, the fear may be a hot rush of panic. As we have to live with it long-term, the fear may fade into the background to some degree, but it then becomes an undertone of dread that affects the way we see every aspect of life.

Situations with Options

Fear is not only caused by external circumstances. We can cultivate habits of thought that keep us in a stressful mode. The actress, Anne Bancroft, said: "I rarely fear for my life. My greatest fear is failure: failure to live up to everyone's expectations."

This reminds us that our greatest anxieties may arise from fear about reaching a level of performance that we can accept for ourselves. Usually such perfectionism is based on our fear that we are not important to people unless we are making a constant good impression. Security lies in knowing that we have worth to people because of who we are, not just for what we can do.

As hard as it is to realize when we are feeling stricken, fear is actually an ally. It is a vital warning system that alerts us to people who might damage us and situations that are unsafe. Fear urges us to prepare and cope, to prepare for imminent danger. When we envision the possibility of unpleasantness, we can choose do whatever we can to create a better future.

Sometimes the wise action is getting away from people or situations that are beyond our power to neutralize. As long we are living fearfully, and do not admit even to ourselves that we are imprisoned by intimidation, we cannot find serenity.

For example, sometimes people stay in pathological marriages because they are afraid of the consequences of making changes. And so they endure everything from lovelessness to unfaithfulness to a variety of abuse, all because they fear the unknown. Abuse is often denied by the victims because we fear what might happen if we take action to protect ourselves. Out of fear, we may squelch our natural instincts for self preservation, and may thereby refuse to heed one of our vital warning systems: fear.

Everyday situations can also be detrimental to a person's total well-being. People who use fear as a strategy for supervising people, either in the home or workplace, are in the habit of imposing constant stress on the people under their supervision. This style creates chaos that keeps people off balance. Those who are being directed never know what mood will be shown today, and they live in fear of being humiliated or severely punished. Bullies in the home or workplace think that they are maintaining control and thereby guaranteeing the successful implementation of their wishes. In reality, they lower the performance level of people, because creativity and excellence do not flourish under negative pressure. When we are put into the survival mode, then that is precisely what we are concerned about: survival. We need a measure of security in order to rise to higher levels of achievement.

yep!

Physical Effects

Fear works against us physically. When we feel stress, the body's response is somewhat like an airplane readying for take-off. Virtually all systems are modified to meet the perceived danger. Our adrenal glands release adrenaline (also known as epinephrine) and other hormones that increase breathing, heart rate, and blood pressure. In a life threatening emergency, this is a useful assignment of the body's resources. However, when stress is prolonged, the imbalance overworks the parts of the body that have been pressed into perpetual panic mode. The very mechanisms that protect us can, if turned into a habit, harm us in many secret ways.

When the body goes into emergency mode brought on by stress, some hormones shut down functions that are not necessary during a brief emergency. Sexual dysfunction may occur and the reproductive system may show a variety of problems from impotence to inability to conceive. The immune system is slowed and we become more likely to get sick and if we do, to be less able to heal ourselves. The blood supply to surface areas, such as the skin, is reduced, and this can lead to skin ailments like shingles or hives. The digestive system is not given the body's usual high priority, and a range of problems can arise, from mere heartburn to ulcers that threaten our lives.

Chronic stress also affects our brains. Crisis diverts energy producing glucose away from the brain in order to prepare for physical action. When the emergency response is activated regularly, this can actually affect the size of the hippocampus, that part of the brain that creates new memories. Studies have shown that elderly people with smaller hippocampuses have less effective memories.

Studies done at the University of Kentucky suggest that one cause of short-term memory deficiency in older people is a life-time of chronic stress.

We lessen our stress when we become aware of our fears and then develop actions that fit the situations we fear. The action of preparing for the worst drains off the numbing effects of dread. Probably everyone has felt relieved, even in the worst of times, when we bring the fear out into the open, talk with supportive people about options, and begin to take actions designed to deal with the threat. No matter what the situation, we are better once we start taking actions that challenge the dominion that the enemy that has over us.

It is vitally important to know our fears.

JOY

Joy is being keenly aware of an aspect of life or another person. The resulting sense of aliveness has been described as a lightness of being. We feel certain buoyancy that is missing when we are weighed down by mere distraction or displeasing circumstances. We actually feel a difference in energy when we are joyful.

The feeling of joy is something that is never explained fully, yet we have no doubt when we feel it in ourselves, and are fairly adept at discerning it in others. We often allude to it obliquely as we mention what we "en · **joy**." In the chapter on spiritual living we will give more detailed attention to creating joy.

Although people's lists of joy producing experiences will vary greatly, the categories are familiar. Most will fit within one of the following:

- Spiritual exultation,
- Religious practice, if the actions lead to new or renewed experiences of spiritual delight,
- Service, when done with the right attitude,
- Being part of a cause larger than oneself,
- Freedom to express our personal inclinations in words and actions,
- Seeing noble behavior,
- Intimacy in personal relationship.

Joy does not get the respect it deserves because it often comes to us in the everyday garb of contentment, or satisfaction, or fun, or a general sense of well-being. Joy encompasses the whole range of positive feelings that are the different faces of celebration.

It is important for us to be aware of joy in all its guises, so that we can choose to give the highest priority to what is worth celebrating. That may seem so obvious as to be trite, and yet we see people who spend most of the time and attention on the things they deplore. Being fully aware of our joy can help us pay more attention to the things that create positive feelings. This approach can make life better for us, and by extension, all the people who relate to us.

One of the benefits of aging is that we give ourselves more permission to choose. In part, it is because of increased wisdom; in part, because we do not want to waste precious time on people and experiences that do not give some form of joy. Life has taught us that there are some people and experiences that neither value nor warrant our precious time. In fact, we probably have stories that would illustrate how we have been harmed when we didn't pay attention to the warning against giving our best to people who were insensitive and unappreciative.

STUDY QUESTIONS ON AWARE OR OBLIVIOUS

1) How do you avoid unpleasant reality? *Try to change it or make it tolerable*
2) How often do you put yourself out in order to experience joy? *Daily*
3) What forms of joy do you experience most often? *Personal connection*
4) What things in your life that have gotten your full attention? *Writing*
5) How do you stay up to date on current events? *Read*
6) What have you done recently that intrigues you? *Began new OLLI Team*
7) What do you do to stay physically active? *Will walk*
8) What do you do that gives you joy? *Writing — loving someone connecting w/ others*

EXPERIMENTING WITH AWARENESS *Use this next week →*

Choose any write one of your own.

☐ Each day I will look at a familiar place as if I am seeing it for the first time.

☑ Each day I will note the various emotions that come and go throughout the day.

☐ I will notice how much time I spend processing the past and anticipating the future, and compare that with the time I spend focused on the present.

☐ I will reduce the amount of distractions that interfere with my concentrating on any one activity or person.

☐ I will increase the proportion of time that I am totally in the present moment without distractions.

OBSTACLES TO HAPPINESS *— Being willing to risk for belief*

1) What makes it difficult for me to choose to be aware rather than oblivious?

2) Is the obstacle a
   ☐ Thought or belief   ☐ Emotion   ☐ Attitude   ☐ Behavior
   ☐ Consequence/situation?

3) What would I have to do to make a different choice?
   Change situation

PURPOSEFUL OR ADRIFT

Having satisfying purpose or drifting in search of pleasure

Dr. Tal Beh-Shar, professor of positive psychology at Harvard University, has been teaching a highly acclaimed course on happiness. Its basic premise is that happiness comes from having a consistent balance between pleasure and purpose.[18]

PLEASURE

Pleasure comes from positive emotions that we have in the present. Pleasurable experiences can be either physical or mental, but most are likely a mixture. We eat a good meal and enjoy the reaction of our taste buds. In addition, we may be flattered that someone cared enough to prepare it for us. We may also feel grateful that we can afford an expensive meal. And we are reminded of other good times when we had similar feelings while eating, and the recollection of those times is in itself a new and different pleasure.

We go to a musical concert and hear sounds that are pleasing to our ears. We also feel the warmth of being included in a group of people who are also responding positively, and may resonate on an emotional level with the music and lyrics. Pleasure is, therefore, more than sensory satisfaction; it is also emotional satisfaction.

We read a good book or see a good movie and feel caught up in the story. A good story stirs our emotions and senses. It reminds us of treasured beliefs or surprises us with new insight. It helps us have mental images of evil and goodness, bravery and cowardice. The unwavering popularity of good stories proves the profound pleasure they give to all kinds of people.

We can even find pleasure in the midst of bad situations. When a death occurs, a family may be stricken, and their extended family and friends rally to give comfort. People bring food to the home, and the family members have moments of pleasure in eating tasty food. The sympathetic attention helps lessen the negative feelings and may even give brief moments of relief from the emotional stress. That is why you often see people smiling, even chuckling, in the midst of sad events. They are being soothed by comforting actions, and the real pleasure of interpersonal warmth lessens the intensity of negative emotions.

Being happy as we go through transitions requires the ability to have positive emotional experiences that give us pleasure. Unfortunately, some transitions include some kind of limitation, such as loss of a physical ability or skill, or an unwelcome change in appearance, or loss of an important relationship. When that happens, we may find ourselves with a pleasure deficit. Unless we can find new positive emotional experiences, the overall experience of life will be thrown out of balance. Regular pleasure is a necessity for happiness because it is one of the original needs from our childhood. We never outgrow it.

Here are some activities that give us pleasure:

- Attending church
- Attending theater performances
- Boating
- Browsing used book stores
- Collecting
- Continuing education
- Cooking
- Crafts
- Creative writing
- Drawing or painting
- Eating out
- Exercise as a social activity
- Exercise to experience nature
- Exercise to feel invigorated
- Exercise as a meditative activity
- Games of chance
- Games of skill
- Gardening
- Helping someone in need
- Historical research
- Interior decorating
- Listening to music
- Playing board games
- Playing cards
- Playing physical sports
- Reading books that create a feeling of being in a different time period
- Reading books that give new information about current events and situations
- Reading books that give new information on the past
- Reading books that give subtle insights into character
- Reading books that revive memories of places
- Reading books with unpredictable plots
- Reading newspapers and magazines
- Relaxing on the beach
- Sewing
- Shopping
- Stitching
- Swimming
- Talking on the telephone
- Traveling
- Visiting with friends
- Visiting with relatives
- Watching movies for amusement

- Watching movies for excitement
- Watching movies for mental or physical stimulation
- Watching movies to anticipate plot development
- Watching movies to experience places beyond our own reach

- Watching television
- Winning any kind of mental contest
- Winning any kind of physical contest
- Working crossword puzzles
- Yard work

PURPOSE

Most people are well aware that regular pleasure is necessary to a happy life, but many are not aware of the unique importance of purpose. George Bernard Shaw said, "This is the true joy of life, the being used for a purpose recognized by yourself as a mighty one." Sometimes we perceive our primary drive; sometimes it remains at subconscious levels. Either way, purpose affects the choices that chart the course of our lives.

Having a self-chosen purpose causes positive emotions that are pleasurable, but it is different from enjoyment that is sought directly. That is why being pampered or protected does not bring long-term satisfaction. Ease and entertainment cannot eliminate the nagging restlessness we feel when faced with a future that has no worthwhile purpose.

It is up to each of us to discover a meaning in life that is satisfying. It may be a family role, such as mother, father, or family wise-person. It can be a job, such as teacher, nurse, police, or politician. Aging often steals the roles that enable us to feel worthwhile. Even if we are still permitted to sit at the family table, or volunteer in a function we once were paid for, or remain on the rolls of organizations that once depended on us for survival.....when we become mere figureheads, something vital goes out of life.

In a televised conversation with Joseph Campbell about achieving bliss, journalist Bill Moyers said: "You're talking about the search for meaning in life."

"No, no, no," Campbell answered. "I'm talking about the experience of being alive!" [19]

To have our life's meaning stolen, even if by well-intentioned, sympathetic younger generations, is to have the feeling that we are no longer fully alive. All of us, no matter what our age, need to be doing something that we consider important. And the larger truth is that our culture desperately needs the accumulated wisdom of people who have learned well from difficult experiences.

BENEFITS OF PURPOSE

According to Harold G. Koenig, professor of psychiatry and behavioral sciences at Duke University Medical Center, "People who feel that their lives are part of a larger plan and are guided by their spiritual values have stronger immune systems, lower blood pressure, lower risk of heart attack and cancer, and heal faster and live longer."[20]

This is another in the long series of scientific studies that show health benefits to well-lived lives. Among other well known virtues to which recent studies attribute measurable health benefits are healthy relationships, staying physically and mentally active, avoiding constant tension and aggravation, having the hopefulness that is inherent in spiritual faith, being regularly involved in voluntary service, and being part of a benevolent community.

Having a worthy purpose gives, as one mature person put it, "a reason to get up and get dressed." Purpose is what makes life satisfying. It fits who we are and makes us feel completed.

ROLES

You become most powerful in whatever you do if the action is performed for its own sake rather than as a means to protect, enhance, or conform to your role identity. Every role is a fictitious sense of self. Roles stand between people, so that from either side, we are unable to interact with integrity. When we are in a role, i.e. an artificial self, we corrupt whatever experience we are having in the moment. Most of the people who are in positions of power are identified to an unfortunate degree with their roles: politicians, TV personalities, business leaders, and religious leaders.

Sometimes our habits of thinking and acting are so prominent that our basic character is hidden from others, maybe even ourselves. We get our habits from our backgrounds and our inherent personalities. Letting habits rule requires the least amount of effort in the moment, so it's not surprising that this is the way that many people live most of the time. It is essentially doing what is most familiar.

PERSONALITY

An obstacle to living purposefully is letting our inherent personalities have full control. Most people are only moderately aware of deeply ingrained personality traits that have regular effects on the way we interact with people and our environment.

Studying personality type is one way of understanding ourselves better. In the 1920's, Swiss psychologist Carl Jung developed categories for understanding the ways we tend to react. Although he was a brilliant psychiatrist, he was not studying mental health, but merely the patterns that people instinctively use in everyday functioning.

The crucial fact to remember is that personality type does not take into account everything about any individual. It does not include intelligence, mental health, family history, personal experience, cultural influences, socio-economic levels, and many other factors that make each person unique. Rather, personality type focuses on a limited number of functions that all humans have in common, and then seeks to determine how preferences about these few functions create a style of reacting and behaving.

In the 1960's Katherine Briggs and her daughter, Isabel Briggs Myers, published the Myers-Briggs Type Indicator to measure categories that Jung conceptualized.[21] It has been carefully studied and verified by many kinds of experts, but the most significant verification has been by millions of people saying, "Yes, that's who I am!"

PERSONALITY SYSTEMS

There were other attempts at identifying personality patterns prior to Jung and Myers and Briggs. The Enneagram is an ancient system of personality type that emphasized healthy and unhealthy modes of behaving within each of nine types. The modern version of the system has nine distinct types with two sub-types in each of the major types, which results in eighteen different styles of personality.[22]

In addition to these complex systems for understanding personality, there are several models that have been developed more recently, such as the one which identifies four social styles: Analytical, Driver, Expressive, and Amiable. [23]

RELEVANCE TO SELF UNDERSTANDING

All these systems help us understand our natural tendencies to perceive and react in certain ways that fall into patterns. Becoming familiar with our habits of perceiving, deciding, and interacting helps us see our strengths and weaknesses. However, the goal in studying them is not to find an excuse for our behavior, but rather to gain more ability to choose what is best in spite of our natural instincts in a specific moment. Doing what comes naturally may not serve us well in the long run, and may even confound the best aspirations of the higher self. The goal is to look past our habits to the desires of the best self, and then to live in harmony with that essential self.

In the space shuttle explosion in 1986, we see an example of how personality tendencies can work against us. It is now well documented that prior to the explosion, engineers were aware of problems that they thought were dangerous and needed further attention. However, they were overruled and the launch stayed on schedule.

The desire to maintain orderliness and timeliness is a predictable drive in certain personality types. In many situations this instinct can be useful, perhaps even most apt to lead to success. However, in situations such as the space shuttle launch, timeliness is not as important as being open to any new information and the willingness to reform schedules. The instinctive schedule-keepers were in charge, and their habit of maintaining orderliness resulted in speeding up and overriding people who knew things were not being done safely. The stated goal was to have a successful space program, but bondage to the inclination to make timeliness the most important factor undermined the entire enterprise.

Personality tendencies are so ingrained that we may not even be aware of them, but they affect us just the same. And they may not always serve us well. Doing what comes easiest is not always the wisest course of action for ourselves or those around us. We do better if we learn what our instincts are, rather than being in blind bondage to our habits. Then we are freer to choose actions that will support our highest aspirations.

ESSENCE

A satisfying purpose will always fit with our essential being. Therefore, the obvious first question is, "What is our essence?" Here we are thinking of essence as that which is most basic to each person's individual nature. We share some traits with all humanity, but each of us is a unique combination of elements that are as individual as fingerprints or DNA.

Some of the areas that will differ are birth order, intelligence, education, personality, physical health, mental health, family background, socio-economic setting, gender, race, historical setting, etc. Added to these variables is the cumulative effect of our conscious and unconscious responses to life situations. And added to all this is that part of us that we may refer to as our best self or our higher self. Our essence is simply a term for referring to the part of us that is beyond casual observation, that part of us which is deeper than we can fully explain.

The next question surely is, "How can we know our essence?" Perhaps this search is like trying to see in the dark. As a boy, walking home to the outskirts of the lighted parts of town, I learned something by accident. A noise or movement would startle me and I would turn to see what it was. I could see only darkness, and the longer I stared the more blurred my vision became. I learned to turn my head slightly and not look directly, but to use my peripheral vision, just at the point where I was almost not looking at it at all. That way I could see better.

Only much later did I learn that there is a physiological explanation for this trick of night vision. It happens because the retina has two kinds of cells, one that sees color and one that sees shapes. In the center of the retina, there are more cells that differentiate color, and on the edge are more cells that differentiate shapes. So, at night we can actually see better by using peripheral vision.

This may be a good metaphor for looking at our essence. Rather than gazing directly at the part of us that is often hidden from view, we will be more successful if we look at the effects created by our essence.

In the late 1960's and early 1970's psychologist Ira Progoff developed a journaling process (*Intensive Journal,* and *At a Journal Workshop*) that was designed to help people discern the patterns and decisions we use to shape our lives.[24] The method is an integrated system of writing exercises for accessing your feelings and experiences in an organized way. People who use the process discover that we have been moving through life according to an inner self that has been hidden from our conscious awareness.

One of the journaling techniques was paying attention to states of consciousness that we all know about but seldom put to practical use. For example:

> The key to Twilight Imaging lies in the fact that it takes place in the twilight state between waking and sleeping. We find that by working actively in that intermediate state of consciousness, we are able to reach depths of ourselves with which it is very difficult to make contact by any other means.[25]

By using the simple technique of journaling while we are just waking up or going to sleep, we get some insights that we do not get when we are fully awake to the external world. Even if we do not use the entire journaling process, we can benefit from the realization that there is more to us than anyone, including ourselves, sees by casual observation. With that in mind, let us notice some hints about our essence.

One hint can be found by answering the question, "When did you first feel different?" For most people, that awareness is usually rather early in life. For many people, the remembrance is unsettling, because it often causes us to relive an experience when we felt we were being treated unfairly. We recall knowing that we were more worthy than we were being given credit for, and we were being viewed and treated as if we were identified with some superficial part of us. We knew our essence was being violated.

Another hint: notice how many young people go through a period of time when they are "trying to find themselves." It is so common that it has become a cliché, and one that is often ridiculed by people who have no difficulty deciding what they want to do and be. The uneasiness often revolves around a person's feeling that the future seems to have been chosen by others, and yet it doesn't seem to fit some deeper instinct about the way he/she wants to go. The "finding myself" is the effort to discern why there is a feeling of discord.

Another hint: pay attention to the frequency that we hear about someone going through a "mid-life crisis." This is another cliché that is often ridiculed, and it is often assumed that its cause is the mere fear of getting older. In some cases, it may be that simple. But for many people the uneasiness is caused by realizing that a significant portion of life has already been expended and they suddenly feel that life has not turned out well. The part of the self that is rebelling may not have been noticed before, but now it is causing the person to feel unsettled and unsatisfied.

The Jacksonville zoo is the new habitat of a magnificent adult leopard. He has a large area, designed to resemble his natural habitat, all to himself. I saw that he was obviously well fed and healthy and free of the risks that come with living in the wild. And yet, he was restless. He would lie on a tree branch for a few minutes, and then he would leap down to the worn paths and resume his pacing. As I watched, I imagined that his instincts were so strong that they could not be quieted by routine security. His inherent nature wanted to come out.

It reminded me of the human restlessness captured by song writer Bruce Cockburn.

> Sometimes you feel like you've lived too long,
> Days drip slowly on the page.
> And you catch yourself
> Pacing the cage.

There is growing evidence that as we mature, we begin to pay more attention to messages from the deepest self. For some people, it may result in significant changes. Some may make radical detours from paths they chose in order to make a living.

I met a man in the mountains of North Carolina who had been a successful business man in New York City. When I met him, he worked as caretaker in a retreat center. He looked after the buildings and grounds, took people on hikes, and gave talks on all the plants and creatures surrounding the natural retreat site. I was living in the New York area at the time, so I was keenly aware of the pressures that buffeted business people. He said that he came to a point when he decided to live in a manner that brought contentment. He left his high paying job and the accoutrements of success and moved to the North Carolina mountains. He studied the plants and animals of the region until he was an expert. His favorite activity was leading city people through the trails and helping them learn to appreciate the trees, ferns, and animals. He was contented.

For others, reaching maturity may merely be giving greater emphasis to what is already being done. The fact is that we know intuitively that living in harmony with this deeper self gives serenity.

This is not an either/or issue. Rather, we find ourselves struggling somewhere between habits and essence. Some days we do well; other days, not well at all. We probably have some sense of where our general status is in this matter of character.

SIGNS OF SUCCESS

There are some signs that we have begun to live in accordance with your essential character. One of them is a feeling of "Eureka!" or "I have found it!" We all know the feeling of discovering something that fits us perfectly, whether it is a pair of shoes, an article of clothing, a piece of furniture, or a music album. The feeling is what we want to notice, the sense of rightness. The same sense of having found the right frequency can come when we are living ordinary life in a way that fits our essence.

Another sign is that we function with ease and proficiency. Not only do we know it, but others watching us can see that we operate with an economy of effort. The term, "She's a natural," is an expression of the obvious fit of person and action. We may push ourselves into a variety of lifestyles in order to get rewards, and we may not even know that we are going against our essence. But when we find the true self, life flows with naturalness and ease that makes everything else seem awkward in comparison.

For example, people who are gifted administrators have a knack for organizing tasks and seeing how to break them into manageable portions that can be distributed to various people. People who are gifted counselors have the ability to establish rapport with a wide range of people, and the resulting trust causes other people to tell their stories and listen to advice. People who are gifted as leaders have the instincts for assuming authority and knowing how to delegate tasks and authority. People who have the gift of wisdom have the capacity for seeing things in a more complete context than most people, and because of this wider vision, they have the ability to perceive likely results of actions. People who are gifted in service have the capacity for humility and unselfishness that is devoid of any resentment or obligation. People who are gifted in hospitality have the ability to share their energy and space without begrudging the effort, but rather savoring the company of their guests.

A third sign is that we have unlimited creativity when we are living out of the true self. We do not have to worry about knowing what to do; it comes to us as instinctively as the involuntary processes that keep our bodies healthy.

A fourth sign of finding our essential character is self-disclosure. We actually come to know ourselves fully only as we make ourselves known to a significant degree to at least one person. So long as we keep ourselves hidden from everyone, we are to an important degree hidden from ourselves. As we let others see us, we see ourselves more fully than ever before.[26]

Self-disclosure is not something that comes easily to many people. One of the reasons is that we have been so immersed in the roles that define our lives, such as wife, husband, mother, father, business person, professional person, church member, and all the other roles that we have taken on in the course of living. We know the characteristics that define these roles. To the extent that we do not meet them, we have disguised our deviations from the norm. We may not even be conscious of the way the roles cramp us and stifle us.

I have often been surprised in groups where conversations went beyond the trivialities of routine existence. When we begin to talk about topics of substance, we invariably say things that not only surprise other people, but often even ourselves. In the flow of conversation, connections are made that seem new and startling. Perhaps all of us have had the experience of pausing and saying, "I hadn't thought of this before, but...," and then sharing the insight that has just occurred us to about ourselves.

In the end, we must admit that finding the best place for the true self to be expressed is a mystery that we solve on our own, if at all. And yet, it is something that we can do if we desire it. The mystery and possibility are balanced in us.

To realize your true nature, you must wait for the right moment and the right conditions. When the time comes, you are awakened as if from a dream. You understand that what you have found is your own and doesn't come from anywhere outside.[27]

THE TRUE SELF EXPRESSED

The initial thought may be that we would all enjoy living with noble, worthy purpose but we are hindered by difficult circumstances. Among the obstacles often cited are keeping body and soul together, coping with extreme situations, poor health, and aging.

Even as you read these words, your mind probably goes to stories about people who have managed to do something worthwhile in the face of obstacles that cause others to settle into subsistence living. People who are living from paycheck to paycheck often find ways to share something with people who are either in the same boat or maybe even worse off. Sometimes it is food or shelter; sometimes it is hope and wisdom.

Soldiers put their own lives at risk trying to protect or rescue a buddy. Firefighters and police go beyond mere duty in order to protect and serve. Health workers risk infection in order to give treatment. A well-to-do person voluntarily partakes of the painful existence of the poor or powerless.

The routine progression of life, with its responsibilities and obligations, often causes us to drop out of purposeful living. But then we are challenged by those who continue doing things they consider important far beyond the time when others have shifted into neutrality.

The difference lies in the way we see things. This was the lesson learned by Viktor Frankl, an Austrian psychiatrist who was imprisoned in a German concentration camp in 1942. As he watched the way different people reacted to the most extreme circumstances, he saw that people who had an internal vision of purpose not only behaved more nobly, but even thrived in ways that people who lost their sense of humanity did not. Out of that awful experience, he developed the belief that meaning is the essential thrust of our existence.[28]

We are often distracted from a sense of purpose as we give attention to transitions from one stage of life to another. The busy-ness of moving from one kind of existence into a different one can occupy us so completely that we neglect to think about purpose.

AWARENESS OF PURPOSE

Serenity comes when we move from confused floundering to being aware of our purpose. In 1915, Robert Frost published a poem about the haunting memories of pivotal choices.

The Road Not Taken
By Robert Frost

Two roads diverged in a yellow wood,
And sorry I could not travel both
And be one traveler, long I stood
And looked down one as far as I could
To where it bent in the undergrowth;
Then took the other, as just as fair,
And having perhaps the better claim,
Because it was grassy and wanted wear;
Though as for that the passing there
Had worn them really about the same,
And both that morning equally lay
In leaves no step had trodden black.
Oh, I kept the first for another day!

Yet knowing how way leads on to way,
I doubted if I should ever come back.

I shall be telling this with a sigh

Somewhere ages and ages hence:
Two roads diverged in a wood, and
I—I took the one less traveled by,
And that has made all the difference.[29]

Who has not wondered whether we chose the right path? Sometimes the questioning thoughts may surface in unexpected moments. When we recall a decision about a relationship, we wonder if we listened too much to temporary emotions. When we think of what we did about education, we wonder if we followed our true priorities. When we remember what we did to earn a living, we wonder if it was the best way to invest years and energy. The "road not taken" is the untold story of what might have been.

As we mature, we often become more aware of how each person needs the satisfaction of doing what we consider good and important. A segment of Charles Schultz's Peanuts comic strip had Linus asking Lucy, "What do you hope to accomplish in your life." Lucy glared at him and shouted, "Accomplish? Accomplish? I thought we were just supposed to keep busy!"

Psychologist Rollo May pointed to a disturbing trait: "It is an ironic habit of human beings to run faster when we have lost our way." Much of life is spent on routines that give meager satisfaction. We learn that the good life is not making big impressions or surviving a long time. It is being directly involved in what we care about deeply.

In 1987, just months before his death, Joseph Campbell was interviewed by Bill Moyers for a Public Broadcasting System television series.

BILL MOYERS: Do you ever have the sense of... being helped by hidden hands?
JOSEPH CAMPBELL: All the time. It is miraculous. I even have a super-stition that has grown on me as a result of invisible hands coming all the time – namely, that if you do follow your bliss you put yourself on a kind of track that has been there all the while, waiting for you, and the life that you ought to be living is the one you are living. When you can see that, you begin to meet people who are in your field of bliss, and they open doors to you. I say, follow your bliss and don't be afraid, and doors will open where you didn't know they were going to be.......
Wherever you are – if you are following your bliss, you are enjoying that refreshment, that life within you, all the time.[30]

We have seen this illustrated in people whom we admire. We have seen that the difficulties and apparent monotony of pursuing one's passion in life do not detract from the joy. Ultimately, life at its best is living in harmony with a purpose that is connected to our deepest self. Whether we find and follow that purpose is up to each person. But where do we look?

FITTING

Many have described in various ways the human drive toward finding that pattern in life that fits so well that it seems designed for us alone. Abraham Maslow said, "A musician must make music, an artist must paint, a poet must write, if he is to be at ultimate peace with himself. What a man *can* be, he *must* be. He must be true to his own nature." [31] ✱ *Yes, yes!*

The *must* is not always realized, of course. Many people either do not find their purpose, or in finding it, fail to live it. Or we may let other people convince us that at a certain age we must retire from doing what makes us feel whole. In fact, we never outgrow our need to be doing what gives us a sense of being true to our nature. One important thing we can do for each other is to cheer each other on in living what we feel designed to do. Our prayer and meditation keeps us knowing what it is and how to do it.

I hear about some who stay on their path. I think of a woman who has worked hard and learned hard lessons. Finally, all the strands have woven together neatly and she can take her ease. Yet, she seeks out people who need something that is natural to her: listening, respecting, and caring. She finds her way to people who are stricken with Alzheimer's and befriends them. By her innate kindness she soothes their troubled spirits, conveying to them that perfectly functioning memories are not prerequisites for receiving respect and tenderness.

I have seen the twinkling eyes of a man who has retired to enjoy the payoff of his successful career. That is not what makes him smile. He goes into high schools to teach youngsters who need someone with the right blend of intelligence and patience; else they will miss their chance to find more than they have seen modeled. He is invigorated by being a mentor to young editions of himself in a company that is smart enough to call him back to share things that can never be put into a training manual.

I think of people who link up with pre-school children from abusive homes. Their wounded psyches seem to feel safer with people who are older, and the surrogate grandparents are enlivened by their contact with these children who are hungry for what mature adults have to give in abundance: loving kindness.

I watched as a successful business woman shifted her focus to an infant granddaughter. As the child grew, so did the grandmother's pleasure. They seemed connected by a mystical bond as they frolicked through endless imaginary scenarios that involved stuffed toys, hiding places constructed from any piece of furniture not too heavy to move, and story lines that expanded to Suess-like proportions. It is easy to believe that the child will have a unique ally in all situations. Clearly, the new role of life mentor would keep the grandmother forever youthful.

The purpose of life is embedded in our intrinsic character, and when we find ways to express ourselves fully and honestly, we shall then be of most pleasure to ourselves and those around us.

BALANCE

For life to be at its best, we need pleasure and meaning to have equal weight, not only when we look at the entirety of life, but when we look at any small segment of time.

When purpose overwhelms pleasure, life can become burdensome and hectic. Think about the glimpses we get of the intern period of medical doctors. We have seen television series, and perhaps had personal contact with real medical trainees, and we know that diminished capacity occurs when duty occupies every waking moment.

Think about periods when parenthood consumed every molecule of energy and every moment of attention. Recall how the joy got crowded out by constant responsibility and life became a grind. Even the noblest purpose can drag us down physically and mentally if there is no pleasure.

Recall times when work demanded so much that there was nothing left over for relationships, relaxation, or leisure. No matter how necessary or important our jobs may be, complete immersion in them is dangerous to all aspects of a person's well-being.

On the other hand, recall times when indulging pleasurable impulses was so overdone that the pleasure seemed to evaporate. Leisure that is constant becomes boredom. Consumption to the extreme becomes satiation. Perpetual entertainment ends up in something akin to channel surfing, i.e. diminishing satisfaction that drives us to increased activity that results in even less satisfaction, etc., etc. We never outgrow our need for balance between meaning and pleasure.

STUDY QUESTIONS ON PURPOSEFUL OR ADRIFT

1) Divide the pleasures into categories. (E.g., physical, emotional, intellectual, spiritual, etc.)
2) What patterns do you see in your experience of pleasure? (E.g., Do you have a wide variety or is most of your pleasure derived from one category?)
3) Are you having as many pleasurable experiences as you did a year ago? Five years ago?
4) What patterns do you see in your meaningful activities? (E.g., Are you less involved in activities that you consider important than you were a year ago? Five years ago?
5) Do you have adequate opportunities for meaningful activity in categories that you prefer?
6) What were you doing when you felt most free of other people's expectations or pressure?
7) What were you doing when you enjoyed yourself and felt most competent?
8) What in your life are you most proud of?
9) What have you done that has given you excitement and pleasure?
10) What activity makes you feel energized?
11) What would change if you let people see your true self?
12) Who knows this part of you?

EXPERIMENTING WITH PURPOSE

Choose an action or write one of your own.

☐ I will make a list of activities that will include at least one pleasure in each of the categories of pleasure. (E.g., physical, emotional, intellectual, spiritual, etc.)

☐ I will make a list of aspects of life that give me a sense of meaning and purpose. (E.g., family, country, career, church, community, etc.)

☐ I will notice what proportion of time is spent in activities that give pleasure and what proportion is spent in activities that give a sense of purpose.

☐ Each week I will write down something that describes my essence.

OBSTACLES TO HAPPINESS

1) What makes it difficult for me to choose purpose rather than being adrift?

2) Is the obstacle a
   ☐ Thought or belief   ☐ Emotion   ☐ Attitude   ☐ Behavior
   ☐ Consequence/situation?

3) What would I have to do to make a different choice?

FULFILLED OR SURVIVING

Taking Care of One's Own Basic Needs

Whether we are aware of it or not, we all have certain basic needs that must be met if life is to be fully satisfying. If any of these needs is neglected, wittingly or inadvertently, then life will be like a melody played on a piano with one broken key. Most psychological systems give lists of basic human needs, with different names for the same needs. We are indebted to psychologist Abraham Maslow for suggesting how human needs are related to each other.[32] The ascending steps in Figure 2 suggest that typically the needs are met initially in a certain sequence, moving from lowest to highest. Keep in mind that one of the needs may become the primary focus again if something interferes with having the need met satisfactorily.

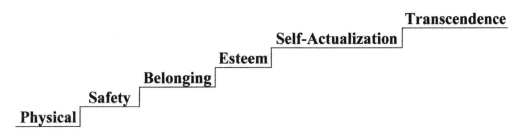

Figure 2 – Hierarchy of Needs

PHYSICAL NEEDS

Our bodies feel a need for air, water, food, sex, and sleep. When we do not get enough of any of them to satisfy the felt need, we feel sickness, irritation, pain, or discomfort. We feel impelled to get what we need as soon as possible in order to establish a feeling of balance. Until these needs are met, we feel that they are the highest priority in our lives. Once a measure of balance is restored, then we can pay attention to other needs (see the higher steps). We can see this principle at work in our development from infancy to adulthood, as we move from one kind of focus to another. We can also notice that interference with a basic need may cause a person's focus to move back to that need and give it more attention again.

As we age, the physical needs may regain primary importance during any period of physical or financial crisis. If my level of income drops so low that I fear I cannot afford the necessities, then I am likely to give most of my attention to these matters. Much of the tunneling in and withdrawal that happens as we age may be related to worry about having enough food, water, and shelter to keep going.

SAFETY NEEDS *physical — emotional —*

If we feel relatively confident that our physical needs will be met regularly, then we can turn our primary attention to a set of needs that we can describe as the safety needs. We need enough physical security and social order so that we do not have to live in constant fear and uncertainty.

With regard to aging, safety needs may become our first priority when things happen to undermine our physical well-being. Illness can do it, or just the gradual decrease of strength and flexibility. Losing strength and mobility can make us feel vulnerable in situations where we were once confident. Physical limitations that are often linked to aging can make routine activities seem intimidating. We feel handicapped in comparison with other people. We cannot move as quickly or with as much stability as we once could, and therefore feel that people who are moving too fast for us may jostle us. In order to avoid the feelings of being at risk, we may postpone or avoid shopping, going to the movies, going out to be with friends, and visiting with family. In order to feel safe, we may give up some other needs that are vital to overall happiness (look again at Figure 2).

Even though physical pain may not seem to others a valid reason for limiting important activities, with age it may be something that happens gradually, either consciously or subconsciously. If merely walking across the floor, or walking up three or four steps, or getting in and out of a car, or carrying a small load aggravate pain that is already with us, we may make a habit of holding back unless something is necessary. Avoiding only one or two activities is probably not crucial because we can assert ourselves if something is important. But reticence and timidity can become a pattern. We may begin to lose contact with aspects of life that are vitally important to our overall well-being.

We also need emotional security. If we are in situations where we are treated disrespectfully, we lose our sense of safety. Sometimes it is having people speak to us in irritable tones, or treating us as if we have minimal intelligence, or verbally brushing us aside, or ignoring us altogether. With advancing age comes increased frequency of being treated disrespectfully. Even if there is no threat of physical force, we may still feel unsettled. And the uneasiness may undermine our overall confidence.

Another threat to safety is the restriction of our ability to care for ourselves. We may worry that our increasing number of physical limitations will take away our independence. Mandatory retirement, regardless of experience or competence, gives the message that reaching a specified age renders us no longer capable. The ability to make enough money to care for ourselves is part of feeling safe. While some have enough retirement income that they do not feel anxious, many do not. Having reached a stage in life when our skills and energy have decreasing market value, we may begin to worry that we will not be able to live with dignity. The threat of descending into a lifestyle that makes us feel deprived is a significant source of anxiety.

BELONGING NEEDS — to love — to be loved —

If both the physiological and the safety needs are met regularly, then we focus on the need for love, affection, and belonging. We seek to meet this need by having friends, mate, or children. It is what makes us stay connected to extended family. We also yearn for inclusion in groups that we consider admirable, whether formal or informal in nature. "Peers"

The need to love and be loved can be so strong that we may choose to endure danger and physical discomfort. It is worth noting that we usually view those who put others before themselves as heroic and noble. For some, unselfish actions may be their way of being connected. It may be as much for their own good as for the people they help.

The first group that is important to us is our primary family. The interactions of that group remain important to us throughout life. If the acceptance was clear and easy, then we can build on that early self-confidence. If our first caring group did not function effectively, then we must find ways to come to terms with the early setback to our self-esteem.

Beyond that primary family group, we choose the individuals and groups whose acceptance is important to us. We may enter into a relationship with a mate. We may become part of academic groups, formal or informal. We may join religious organizations. We may be part of groups organized around some life style or mission. All of the relationships we choose do something to assuage our deep need to belong.

No matter what our age, we still need ongoing demonstrations that we are loved. We need relationships in which we are chosen and highly valued. Long-term relationships can give us the most of what we need because people can remember us at the peak of our powers. People who knew us then tend to see us with more than objective vision. They see the effects of natural aging, but they also remember us when we were younger, and they tend to relate to us with our history in mind. There is a sense in which we are always young to those who have known us through many stages of life.

Medical research shows that belonging is not just something that makes us feel good emotionally. It is also vital to our physical and mental well-being. Studies have been done of explorers, sailors, prisoners in solitary confinement, and brainwashing victims. After extended periods of isolation, people had problems with concentration, attention span, restlessness, and anxiety. Their thoughts became confused, they didn't eat properly, they had hallucinations, they had trouble sleeping, and their muscles became weak. Many of them experienced despair and eventually depression.[33]

Do these symptoms sound familiar? Of course. We have heard them used to describe older people who have become disconnected from activities and people. We have heard people say, "Well, those are just the natural effects of aging." Certainly there are some kinds of organic conditions that can cause the symptoms mentioned above, but they can also be seen in people who have merely been cut off from people and activities that are part of normal living.

There is clear evidence that every system in our bodies is affected by belonging.[34] Our minds and bodies function properly only when we have the nourishment of connections to people and activities that allow us to be fully human.

We humans take note of the instincts of animals. We know that lions naturally group in prides and each animal functions as part of that unit. We know that elephants have a definite social order that governs the normal development of each animal's health and survival. We have studied gorillas, whales, and migrating birds. And yet we have tended to ignore evidence that we humans have a powerful need to be part of groups, and that being deprived of interactions with other people, we will suffer great damage to mind and body.

As we age, we are more at special risk for isolation, especially in our Western culture. (Review the section on Loneliness in the chapter, Adaptable) We are more apt to end up living at significant distances from people who would provide social and emotional nurture. Many of the systems for caring for aging and ailing people are designed primarily for addressing the most crucial physical needs, such as food, shelter, safety, and medical care.

Belonging ensures that living a long time will be a pleasure and not a burden.

ESTEEM NEEDS

The next set of needs has to do with esteem. Unless a person has some kind of pathology, we all feel a need for the good opinion of ourselves and the good opinion of people whom we respect.

Some people are not healthy enough to love.

The first kind of need has to do with what we think of ourselves. There is the desire for strength, achievement, adequacy, mastery and competence, confidence in the face of the world, and independence and freedom. We can see that even young children quickly develop a need to see themselves as being competent. Their saying, "I can do it," or "Let me do it myself," reveals their need to see themselves as competent and capable.

When we see a person whose competitive instinct is out of control, it is likely that the person has not achieved a stable level of positive regard for self. Once we have answered for ourselves whether we are competent, we will not feel a constant compelling drive to develop new evidence.

With advancing age, this need can resurface in its importance. Even if we have gained consistent positive regard for ourselves, the aging process often causes us to reevaluate ourselves. If we based our positive self-image on levels of performance that are no longer possible, then we may loose valuable self-respect. For example, if a woman's confidence was based on physical beauty, the natural aging process can cause a great deal of insecurity. Or if her sense of worth came from her role as mother, the independence of children may be a threat rather than a satisfaction. If a man's self-esteem was based on his physical vigor, the limitations of aging can change his good opinion of himself. If his confidence came from his earning power, then retirement may take away the very evidence he needs to feel powerful.

The second kind of need has to do with the opinions of others. We have the desire for good reputation, or prestige and status, fame and glory, dominance, recognition, attention, importance, dignity, or appreciation. The most stable and therefore most healthy self-esteem is based on *deserved* respect from others rather than on external fame or celebrity. If we think that our good reputation is based on false standards, no amount of adulation satisfies the inner need. Throughout our lives, we choose the people and groups whose good opinions are important to us.

No matter what our age, this need does not disappear. Conversations about the past have frequent references to former accomplishments and social levels. For some, it may be merely nostalgia, but for others it is an effort to establish a level of status that enables a person to feel comfortable.

It remains very important to be doing something we consider important. All through life, worthwhile labor is important. We may have thought that merely making enough money to stop working is enough. But to some degree, everyone knows better.

Being listened to indicates that we have wisdom and experience that add up to something important. It can be extremely disappointing to see signs that the mere fact of aging lessens our authority in matters in which we were once considered wise.

Being responded to as a desired dinner companion, an astute political conversationalist, or a wise spiritual advisor is important.

SELF-ACTUALIZATION

Even if all the other needs are satisfied, a new discontent and restlessness may eventually develop if we are not doing what we are intrinsically suited for. People tend to agree that musicians must make music, artists must paint, and poets must write if they are to be ultimately at peace with themselves. Even people who are not in artistic vocations are pulled to satisfy their true nature. Psychologist Abraham Maslow used the term self-actualization to describe this desire to become everything that one is capable of becoming.

Maslow made the following points about self-actualizing people.[35]
- They embrace the facts and realities of the world (including themselves) rather than denying or avoiding them.
- They are spontaneous in their ideas and actions.
- They are interested in solving problems; this often includes the problems of others. Solving these problems is often a key focus in their lives.
- They feel close to other people, and generally appreciate life.
- They have a system of morality that is fully internalized and independent of external authority.
- They judge others without prejudice, in a way that can be termed objective.
- They can distinguish what is fake and dishonest from what is genuine.
- They realize that the means and ends are different, and thus the ends do not always justify the means.
- They enjoy being by themselves, but they also have deep relationships.
- They tend to be autonomous, relatively free from physical and social dependency.
- They have a sense of what is true beyond their culture and are highly resistant to pressure from the culture to fit in.
- Their humor is never a threat, and they often joke about themselves.
- They tend to be spontaneous and simple in their nonconformity while also having a certain humility and respect for others.
- They have freshness, a creative spirit and are original in their thinking.

Different traditions have pointed toward this drive to completion. In the Christian tradition, the intrinsic nature was referred to as a gift, literally a *charisma*. The gift was that capacity to do something with ease and instinctive wisdom, and in the doing, to feel a sense of satisfaction. The earliest congregations organized themselves, not by offices or official roles, but rather by letting people lead in areas where their innate gifts gave them functional authority.

Self actualization is coming into our own as we mature. We expect to learn lessons that make us into wiser, better people. We have lived long enough to witness trends, not only in our own lives, but also in institutions and nations. This broader perspective helps us make wiser decisions about a wide variety of issues. *Only if we mature emotionally →*

TRANSCENDENCE

The final level of need and development is what has been called transcendence.[36] The experiences in which a person is convinced of being in contact with something beyond one's self are often called "peak experiences."[37] Many people believe that during peak experiences they are in direct contact with a divine being. Others believe that the experience can be explained in natural terms. However a person accounts for peak experiences, it is generally agreed that the experiences are different from all that comes before in human development.

Peak experiences make you feel as if you are outside of yourself. They can make you feel very tiny or very large. They give a feeling of being a part of the infinite and the eternal. Many people actively seek these experiences. A peak experience has some (but not necessarily all) of the following characteristics:

- Very strong or deep positive emotions akin to ecstasy
- A deep sense of peacefulness or tranquility
- Feeling in tune, in harmony, or at one with the universe
- Feeling a sense of unity and harmony with all people
- A feeling of deeper knowing or profound understanding
- A sense that it is a very special experience that would be difficult or impossible to describe adequately in words (i.e., ineffability)
- A resulting sense of purpose in life
- Capacity for personal growth

Peak experiences may happen to the mature and immature alike. The best use of them is to view the temporary experience as a flash of insight into the nature of people and the universe, and to use that insight. For example, having once felt tranquil, a person might then fashion life in ways that eliminate things that keep us in constant tension and turmoil.

Another example: having felt the unexplainable nature of peak experiences, a person might become less driven to have all events explained in logical terms.

And once having felt that life is purposeful, a person might then become focused on activities that contribute to an ongoing sense of useful purpose.

As we mature, we reach the time to develop aspects of the self that we may have neglected in our younger years. Some view this as either irrelevant or too much trouble, and choose to relax and enjoy the basic comforts of life. Others report a nagging feeling that something vital is missing, even if they have all their basic needs met. For them, happiness lies beyond meeting basic physical and social needs. For such people, self-actualization and transcendence lead to profound satisfaction in living.

LIFE-LONG NEEDS

In recent years, the medical field has understood that just because a person has surgery does not eliminate the body's need for exercise. And if we do not get it, we are at risk for developing pneumonia or circulation problems that may be as dangerous as the condition that originally required medical treatment. For that reason, doctors now have surgical patients up and walking the day after surgery.

It is similar with regard to our human needs. The fact that we are aging does not eliminate basic human needs. Aging people and their caregivers sometimes focus only on the more obvious needs, such as food and medical care, and forget about the full range of human needs that, if ignored, will create as much unhappiness as any of the issues that we usually associate with aging. If we want to be happy, we must continue to address the needs that go far beyond mere food, shelter, and medical treatment.

STUDY QUESTIONS ON FULFILLED OR SURVIVING
1) What do you worry about most frequently?
2) What basic need is being threatened?
3) Are there any basic needs that you have started worrying about in the past few years that you didn't worry about previously?
4) Are there situations in which you now feel uneasy about your safety?
5) What groups have you belonged to in the past? In the present?
6) What have you done in the past that made you feel good about yourself?
7) When you consider your life so far, is there anything that you have left out that you wanted to be included?
8) What can you do from this point on to include elements that would make you more satisfied?

EXPERIMENTING WITH FULFILLMENT
Choose an action or write one of your own.
☐ I will determine where I am in meeting my basic human needs (Fig 2 – Hierarchy of Needs).
☐ I will identify a person that appears to have met a basic need that I have not yet met.
☐ I will talk with a person that appears to have met a basic need that I have not yet met.

OBSTACLES TO HAPPINESS
1) What makes it difficult for me to choose fulfillment rather than mere survival?
2) Is the obstacle a
   ☐ Thought or belief   ☐ Emotion   ☐ Attitude   ☐ Behavior
   ☐ Consequence/situation?
3) What would I have to do to make a different choice?

REAL OR ROLES

Disclosing True Self or Presenting
Acceptable Impressions

Few things interfere with happiness as much as unsatisfying relationships. We cannot fully understand how to have good relationships until we look at some patterns that tend to stick with us all through life.

CODEPENDENCE

In the past twenty years or so we have heard much of the term "codependence," though most people would feel awkward trying to give a clear, succinct definition of what it is. We have heard codependence labeled as the cause of bad relationships, and then we have heard it labeled as the description of bad relationships. With so many people blaming so much on codependence, and with so much vagueness about what it is, we may make the mistake of thinking it is not real. Or we get impatient and choose to just ignore the whole topic.

But this is not like a kind of music that we do not like and which we can ignore with no significant effect. It's more like gravity, which keeps right on affecting us whether we ignore it or not.

Although the term *codependence* was devised to describe the behavior of people who were relating to alcoholics and addicts, it has evolved to refer to the patterns of behavior that undermine healthy relationships. These patterns begin early in life as a result of what goes on in the family (see the Figure 4 below).

An effective family is able to mobilize its resources and provide what a child needs.[38]

- Food, water, shelter, and safety
- Connecting, belonging, love
- Power that comes from learning, achievement, and feeling worthwhile
- Freedom that is independence, autonomy, one's own space
- Fun, pleasure, and enjoyment

A family is dysfunctional when it cannot provide a child's needs. Many factors can render a family unable to function properly, such as:

- alcoholism
- drug addiction
- workaholism
- extreme poverty
- frequent changes in dwelling places
- abuse, physical or emotional

- chronic illness in the family
- mental illness in the family
- unrelenting danger
- domestic violence
- repressive belief systems
- general family instability

However, it is not just obviously negative situations that lead to dysfunctional family patterns. Adults can be so immersed in successful enterprises that they have little energy to give a child what is needed for healthy development. Often community and national leaders are admired for their wisdom and maturity, but are so involved in their public obligations that they are distracted from children's needs in their own homes. The popular practice of hiring domestic servants and putting children in the care of people outside the family is not an adequate substitute for what the child seeks from parents. Children are surprisingly resourceful in trying to get what they need. If they cannot get their needs directly, as they would in a healthy family, they will adapt and seek other methods. It is the adaptations that are the origin of so-called codependence.

The figure below shows the adaptations that children use to compensate for needs that are not met directly.

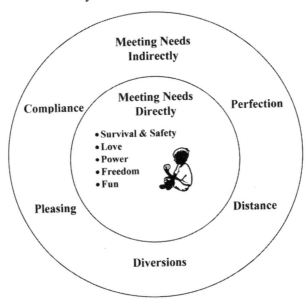

Figure 3 – Codependency

SAFETY OR COMPLIANCE

Even infants are aware of survival needs. Babies quickly become uneasy when the basic need for food, water, and physical comfort are not being met, and they let everyone within earshot know how unhappy they are.

As we get older, we realize that we need for the home to guarantee enough food and safety for us to live comfortably. If the basics are missing, or are on a hit-and-miss schedule, then anxiety becomes a part of daily existence.

In addition to our instinct for survival as individuals, we have an unconscious drive to survive as a species. Therefore, the need for sex is part of our human instinct for procreation. Of course, sexual activity is also used to address other needs in the same way that food is sometimes used for more than mere survival.

SAFETY

In a healthy home, the child learns very early that the adults have the will and ability to make us safe. The big people tell us clearly what is safe and what isn't.

"The stove is hot and will burn you and that will really hurt."

"If you put anything other than food in your mouth, you might swallow it and feel bad."

"If you play with sharp things, you might accidentally stick yourself so that it hurts really bad."

"If you walk around in the dark, you may hit your toe or bump into a table, and that can really hurt."

"Some dogs like to be petted, but some might bite. So, don't play with dogs until the owner tells you it's okay."

"If you run off on your own, you may forget where we are, and you will get scared. So, stay close when we are in new places."

Healthy homes tell the truth about what is safe and what is not. Children quite naturally check to see if the warnings were true, and if they were, we learn that big people can be trusted. We learn that life is not always pleasant and easy, but we can learn how to get by if we pay attention.

For some of us, safety was less certain. Adults are not always clear and honest about danger. Comedian Bill Cosby did a routine about how a child may hear the familiar bedtime prayer:

"Now I lay me down to sleep, I pray the Lord my soul to keep, And **if I DIE before I wake**..... Aw, no, I'm not never going' to sleep now!"

Adults often use threats to control children.

"If you don't stop crying, I'm going to leave you!"

"You should have known better (than to do something that caused great distress)!"

"When your daddy gets home, you'll be sorry."
"The boogie man will get you."
"If you don't behave (as I want), I will spank you!"
"If you're not good, God will punish you."

Fear seems like a handy tool when adults are looking for control. The error is in underestimating the effect of a threatening environment on a child. When children live in the midst of threats and irritation, they figure a way to cope. Some of us become rebellious. Some merely lay low and pretend to comply.

For example, an alcoholic parent is so focused on dealing with the chaos created by the substance abuse that he cannot pay consistent attention to a child's need for stability and safety. The child is often viewed as an irritating burden, an obstacle in the adult's pursuit of the relief sought in their diversions. So, the child becomes an expert in sensing the moods of the parent, and learns to either stay hidden, or do solicitous things that may make the parent feel grateful, or at least less angry.

In a home where the child is ignored because of adults' busyness, the child will either try very hard to obey the rules in order to get favorable attention, or may learn that doing something that is against the rules is the most dependable way to get attention. In either case, the goal is getting attention from the adults who can guarantee safety.

Children who had to adapt and find indirect ways to feel safe tend to grow into adults who are hypersensitive to their emotional environment. They may be keenly aware of potential threats to their well-being and have a stubborn pessimism about the future.

Adults with this history may find themselves preoccupied with safety and survival. In addition to physical safety, they may worry about their safety to express themselves honestly without fear of rejection or punishment. They may find themselves going to great lengths to avoid saying or doing anything that might cause people to reject them. An even more subtle pressure comes from believing that having loyal friends depends on what we do for them, which can be translated into anticipating their needs and responding before they ask.

The most effective way to gain a measure of serenity is to find what we needed from parents, namely, wise people who will give us reasonable assurance of hope. We need a network of people who can listen to our fears and respond with advice, reassurances, and most of all, sustained attention. A comforting truth is that we can choose people to do family things for us.

LOVE OR PLEASING

In a healthy home, the child is delighted in for his/her own sake. This love is based on appreciation of the child's unique self rather than comparison with siblings, other children, or an idealized image in the minds of the parents. The delight follows the child through each developmental stage and the appreciation changes with the child's maturing. With this love as the constant in the environment, the child is confident in his/her worth. It is possible to be truthful with adults because there is never doubt about their good will. The adults are perceived as guides who explain limits, and as allies who can be trusted to give practical advice in dealing with situations outside the home.

This love requires the adults in the home to be alert to the changes that occur as the child develops and to respect the child as a person separate from the adults. This love requires an investment of time to relate to the child, because only patient listening will uncover what a child is fearing, thinking, needing, and hoping. The capacity for personal intimacy is being developed as the child feels delighted in, listened to, related to, and appreciated as a person in his/her own right.

A dysfunctional family's resources are not up to this kind of focus. For a variety of reasons, the adults may be so focused on other aspects of life that the child does not get their best attention. For example, if the adults are concerned about their own image, then they may place great importance on the child's appearance, performance, and comparative standing with other children. Even if the child competes effectively, he/she learns that acceptance is related to the external factors, and the child learns that he/she is thought of as extensions of the adults, as an indictor of how wise or good the parents are. If adults are in this mindset, they will say things that indicate that embarrassment or pride is triggered by how well the child performs by the standards that matter most to the adults.

In families where love is not given freely, children learn to work for approval. They learn quickly what seems to please the adults, and they use this knowledge to adapt their behavior, hoping to gain signs of approval. The child becomes an expert on the subtleties of disapproval. The focus of attention is on what the adults want, and the child strives to do that in order to win the loving approval they need.

In some cases, the child is so frustrated in the effort that they rebel openly and break contact with the adults. Still, the need for the parental love has not vanished, as can be verified by countless testimonies of so-called "bad" people. The rebellion is merely a strategy for coping with the missing love.

Adults who grew up in dysfunctional homes may have difficulty noticing or understanding their emotions, and may have meager experience at pursuing what they want for themselves. Years of focusing on what others are doing or thinking can cause people to know others better than they know themselves.

People who try to win love by satisfying other people are often frustrated when they do not get the desired responses. The assumption is that a kindness done before a request is made will always result in effusive gratitude. When that does not happen, the helper is greatly disappointed, perhaps even angry. We are wise if we learn that trying to elicit desired emotional responses by what we do is a set up for frustration.

As mature adults, we have a lifetime of experiences that shape our expectations about love. I did not fully understand the power of knowing this until I gradually absorbed what a friend said to me: "We tend to think that we teach people how to love us by the way we treat them. That is not true. We teach people how to love us by the way we treat ourselves."

We have all seen this verified. We have seen people who lack confidence, who think themselves to be lowly and unworthy, and who are uneasy in the presence of those they consider their superiors. We have watched their awkward body language, their downcast eyes, their nervous expressions, and their jumbled speech. And we have seen how people tend to treat such people with varying degrees of disrespect. It seems that their feelings of unworthiness trigger uneasiness and perhaps even contempt in other people. They have conveyed what they think of themselves, and other people cooperate by treating them badly.

On the other hand, we see people who look at people eye to eye, who speak with confidence and listen with interest, who in their bearing convey self-respect. These people are likely to receive the kind of respect that they have for themselves.

When I visited New Delhi, India, street beggars helped me understand this. They approached with heads held high, smiles on their faces, and asked politely for alms. There was none of the shame-faced mumbling, or at the other extreme, the hostile demanding, that I had seen on the streets of New York City and would see later on the streets of San Francisco. When I commented on this to my friend who had spent a lot of time in India, he explained that each person thinks of this life as important in the soul's development. No matter what their station in life, they are resolved to do it with excellence and good will. In so doing, they believe that they prepare their souls for higher levels of maturity.

We can learn to value and respect ourselves regardless of whether we meet someone else's standard of beauty, intelligence, or achievement. As mature adults, we need a community of people who will affirm our self-esteem, or if we do not have it, help us experience the kind of love that every person deserves. It is not too late to be loved just for ourselves.

POWER OR PERFECTION

We notice that children begin at a very young age to enjoy success. They struggle to master new skills and then rush to have them applauded by the adults in their lives. It is ingrained to enjoy the power of achievement. In a healthy family, adults applaud the child's progress at each stage of development. The child is given opportunity to learn new skills without pressure of instant mastery. Adults help the child know that trial and error is necessary to master difficult skills, so the child moves forward without paying undue attention to the inevitable failures that accompany progress.

In a dysfunctional home, the pressure is on. The person who believes that words cannot hurt has never felt the sting of comparisons: "You'll never be as good an athlete as your brother," or "Why don't you get good grades like your sister?" or the unspoken challenge to measure up to the success of the parents. So, the child either gives up early, or takes on the contest that will never be won.

In other homes, the child who achieves may be resented for making the adults or other siblings look bad by comparison. In this case, the child feels cut off from full membership in the family, and often resorts to finding other people to serve as a surrogate family.

These kinds of experiences prepare a person for a lifetime of perfectionism. A person who believes that he/she is valued because of being smart, or good, or well behaved, or industrious, or organized can never relax. To let up is to risk failure, and failure is equated with rejection.

This mindset was clearly expressed by the highly successful television reporter, Tom Brokaw. In a television interview, he said he had always felt like the Great Pretender, and that he would someday be found out, and then everything would be gone. In spite of a lifetime of developing skills and wisdom, he still felt that his only hope was in being perfect.

The perfectionist's motto is the familiar adage: "If you can't do it right, don't do it at all." A wise teacher saw me living this way and challenged me with her own adage: "There are some things worth doing imperfectly." At first, it sounded like a nonsensical wisecrack. Then the profound truth dawned on me: some things are so important that we should do them even if we cannot do them perfectly. I gradually came to see that perfectionism is an insidious mindset that keeps us from enjoying life's routine pleasures, and even more, keeps us from exploring experiences that might surpass our familiar abilities.

Perfectionism can be especially destructive for mature adults. No matter how well we take care of ourselves, we cannot defy the reality of aging. Our strength, reflexes, and endurance will never be as good as they were. In fact, they will get worse if we live long enough. If we are bound to do everything perfectly, we are setting ourselves up for constant disappointment. We will have enough things that will become impossible without restricting life simply because of our unrealistic expectations. We will do better to remember that many things are so important that we are willing to do them imperfectly. A network of peers can help us see this tendency and make adjustments.

FREEDOM OR DISTANCE

In a healthy home, children are free to be and do what is good for normal development. An infant cries, coos, and makes funny noises to experiment with sounds. Adults accept this interruption of silence as a good thing in their lives. A toddler is constantly curious and in motion, and parents invest energy in keeping up. A three-year old is establishing an identity separate from adults and enjoys saying "No" to see what happens, and parents give as much leeway as safety and good sense allow. A second grader makes friends and builds relationships beyond the boundaries of home, and adults see socializing as something to celebrate. And so it goes. As the child grows, the adults adjust to the metamorphosis and affirm the emergence of a person they are eager to know.

One of the surest signs of a dysfunctional home is a high degree of control. Adults may be chaotic themselves, but they impose on children rigid boundaries at every step of their development. When small children cry, they are shushed and threatened if they do not comply. Growing up in this kind of environment can cause a person to be cautious, especially when dealing with authority figures or institutions. The most frequently used strategy to win some degree of freedom is to develop distance, either physical or emotional.

We need the freedom to develop as we choose. As we mature, we often learn to express ourselves more freely and act more spontaneously than we have in the past. Younger family and friends sometimes are distressed when our advancing maturity is characterized by growing independence. It is really quite natural. Having reached a stage of life when we have an abundance of experience, we begin to focus on things that are most important to us. The frequent impatience we see in mature adults in most cases is not due to some kind of dementia. Rather, we have become aware of the bigger picture and are less inclined to waste time on rituals, procedures, and people who are superficial or meaningless.

The renewed appreciation for freedom that many mature adults feel is also expressed as the desire to be creative. This drive usually takes one or more of the following forms:

- A desire to express creativity in arts, or crafts, or writing,
- A desire to give back to the community by helping people,
- A drive to go on a spiritual quest and find spirituality that is more satisfying and comprehensive.[39]

Morris Schwartz was a college professor at Brandeis University in Waltham, Massachusetts. In 1994, Morris learned that he had amyotrophic lateral sclerosis (ALS), Lou Gehrig's disease, an irreversible illness of the neurological system. The only prognosis was a depressing litany of incremental misery.

Many have arrived at this crossroads. Their choices are limited, but they do still have some freedom left. Morris's question to himself was, "How do I use the time left?"

He decided that he would not quietly wither away, as if he were ashamed of dying. Instead, he decided to make his own death a learning experience for his students. He would narrate his final journey to his former student, Mitch, telling the truth about what it was like and answering questions from those who had not yet reached this final stage.[40] The wide appeal of the book, *Tuesdays with Morrie*, is that even in the direst situations, we have ways to express our freedom.

FUN OR DIVERSIONS

Children are born with an instinct for having fun. As soon as we develop motor skills, we use them to do things that give pleasure: wiggling our fingers, swatting anything within reach, throwing things, bouncing and eventually running. As we age, the instinct to have fun is part of our makeup. Indeed, our brains have what has been called a "pleasure center," which is actually one of the functions regulated by the part of the brain called the hypothalamus. The importance of this is to know that no matter what our age, having fun is part of what is needed in order to function in a healthy, normal way.

In dysfunctional families, children are restricted from behaviors that interfere with what adults want, and childhood pleasure is not high on the priority list. Children are forced to suppress their natural exuberance lest they risk the wrath of the adults or older children who have been given special rights over the younger children.

Children in these homes learn to fit in. They learn to discern what will get some measure of approval from people in the family that has power over them. If they have to become pseudo adults in order to take care of themselves and other family members, they will. Their need for fun is redirected into the satisfaction they get from adapting to an environment that is unfriendly to children.

Granted, sometimes the reasons may seem legitimate. For example, when someone in the family is seriously ill, or when there are aged grandparents in the home, or when adults' jobs are so demanding. All these situations result in adults not having enough time or energy left over for caring for children. At other times, the inhibiting environment may be created by family members who are behaving in unhealthy ways.

This kind of background makes it difficult to enjoy the basic simple things in life: authentic loving relationships, playful activities, enjoyment of nature, community connections, and learning new things. A person who has difficulty in finding wholesome pleasure may turn to distractions and diversions. The tip-off will be that the diversions are done frantically, compulsively, and without gaining full satisfaction that true pleasure is supposed to give.

In a healthy home, children are permitted to have fun in many ways that fit their stage of development, so long as they are not being dangerous to themselves or others. This kind of freedom prepares us to enjoy life, and thus as we mature, we can savor pleasure in the many good aspects of life that are available to us.

We need to have fun on a regular basis. If we do not, life will lose its appeal and we will evolve into the kind of old folks who are caught in an endless recitation of physical ills and irritations with the world at large. Nobody enjoys that, including the complainer. There is a strain of Puritanism in our Western culture that makes us feel a bit guilty at wanting or needing pleasure. Yet, the enjoyment of small moments of routine pleasure is a necessary part of being happy. This means we must give careful attention to making sure we have fun.

Fun is a matter of individual taste. People even appear different from each other when observed having fun. Thus, we sometimes feel coerced into some activity because well-meaning people conclude that we are not having fun, or at least, not enough fun as they measure it.

FAMILY ROLES

A major interference in a child's needs being met is the use of family roles. Psychologist Alfred Adler, 1870-1937, was the first to suggest that some families cause children to fit into roles, rather than letting the children's inherent qualities determine the way they fit into the family. When families do not function effectively, the roles are used as shortcuts in order to make life simpler for the adults. The children are trained into the roles and use them as best they can to get the adult attention and approval they need. The roles are described here in general terms, but they may be modified within a given family. Also, the roles may change as children arrive or leave the family. An only child may adopt any of the roles at one time or another.

We increase our chances for happiness when we notice the lifelong patterns that may be interfering with current relationships.

Hero

The role of Hero is usually assigned to the firstborn. This child often assumes the mantle of responsible child, and is often perceived as six going on thirty because he or she is inclined to act much older than the chronological age. The Hero child gives the family self-worth by presenting an admirable image in the community. These children often excel at all sorts of endeavors because they are very focused on making good. They have internalized the belief that their place in the home and community depends on their continuing excellence, and they seek to prove themselves constantly.

Since this role is so much a part of our family culture, we should not be surprised to see it depicted in popular TV shows. A good example was in the comedy series Ozzie and Harriet, which was televised 1952-1966. The oldest son, David Nelson, played the perfect Hero child, giving the impression of maturity and patience as he dealt with his aggravating younger brother.

Another Hero child was depicted with more depth in the TV series, The Walton's, from 1972-1979. John Boy, played by Richard Thomas, was a pseudo-adult and accurately showed the privileges and liabilities of that place in the family.

In real life, the role of Hero child is not as smooth as it appears in TV shows. They get the applause of appreciative adults, but people in their own age group often find the Hero kids a bit too good for their own good. And Heroes know that they must keep up the appearance of perfection, so they feel internal pressure to conform and succeed. Many of them confess as adults that they have had a life-long feeling of being imposters, and that they would be disapproved of if their true nature were ever discovered.

Being a Hero child can cause a person to develop into an adult that is rigid and controlling. A Hero adult is often judgmental because of the life-long trust in perfectionism as the safe way to live. This attitude can be overt or subtle, and it is applied to the self as well as to others.

As we mature, the residue of being a Hero child can make us uncomfortable with the imperfections we see in others and ourselves. It can keep us from the intimacy and companionship that we need in order to succeed in this final stage of life. We do well to notice if we have a habit of being a Hero, because we can consciously give ourselves permission to be more honestly human. To echo my teacher: "Some things are worth doing imperfectly."

Scapegoat

The concept of a scapegoat was part of the religious rituals of early Judaism. The people symbolically put their sins on a goat and then sent it out into the wilderness or threw it off a cliff. Through this ritual cleansing the people could feel good about themselves.

In some families, the second child is given the role of scapegoat. This is the person who acts out, tends to be defiant, may get into delinquent behavior, and may achieve at levels below his or her potential. The term "scapegoat" is apt because this child's behavior diverts attention from the inadequacy of the adults and the home. Instead, attention is focused on the various ways that the acting out child's behavior creates uneasiness, and the child is blamed for the failure of the family to be completely satisfied and happy.

Even though the attention is negative, for the Scapegoat child it is better than being ignored. In fact, the Scapegoat child often gets in the habit of getting attention by doing things that will get negative feedback from family members, school teachers, and other authority figures. Whereas the Hero feels powerful by achieving according to the rules, the Scapegoat feels power by creating drama in the home or in school, and by their ability to keep authority figures off balance and disturbed. Being the center of attention is more important than being perfect.

The internal life of the Scapegoat is often characterized by feelings of being deprived, treated unfairly, out of step with everyone else, and a failure and disappointment to people. The overt defiance covers feelings of isolation and rejection.

When these patterns are carried over into adulthood, a person spends a lot of time in angry opposition and blaming. Being familiar with defiance can lead to behavior that is unhealthy or even self destructive. The habit of being persistently, aggressively critical of those who seem to be in the mainstream can result in being marginalized. The habit of being suspicious and oppositional to authority and institutions can cause unnecessary negative consequences.

If we continue habits of an early experience as Scapegoat, we will not be fully involved in a community of mutual support and encouragement. We will be happier if we learn to be involved in a community that will give us attention for positive behaviors and attitudes.

Lost Child

In some families, third born children often assume the role of Lost Child or forgotten child. The family invests a lot of energy in approving the Hero, who is frequently the first born, because that child gives the family esteem and status. The second born is often the Scapegoat, and the family's energy is invested in dealing with that child's negative drama. So, the third born often falls into the gap and becomes the Lost Child.

The message to these children is to be good, take care of themselves, and demand little of the family's emotional resources. They learn early in life to be as inconspicuous as possible. These children are the ones who are apt to drift off when no one is looking, and their not being missed verifies their perception that they are of minor importance to the family. Their power comes from their feeling of independence and freedom from the routines that bind everyone else. They can roam when and where they please.

The Lost Child may have a rich inner life, but it is not usually shared with many people. They have learned that being unnoticed is a good strategy for staying safe. They sometimes turn to diversions that can be pursued alone. Many who have this role report inner feelings of loneliness, neglect, and anger. Acting and writing are good outlets for people who have been the Lost Child in their families.

A 2009 movie, ***Up in the Air***, starring George Clooney, depicts some of the patterns that can derive from being the Lost Child. Clooney's character works for a company that provides short-term contractors to fire people in companies that are downsizing. He flies around the country and stands in for bosses who do not have the nerve to do the unpleasant task of giving people the bad news about their vanishing jobs.

The echoes of the Lost Child experience are best seen in the development of the character's mindset and emotional stances. One of the most telling is his polished presentations that he calls, "What's in Your Backpack?" He encourages people to see that whatever attachments they have to people or responsibilities are burdens and hindrances, and says that getting what you want is best achieved by being free and unencumbered.

Lingering habits of the Lost Child can increase the danger of becoming isolated at a time of life when we need a community of encouragement and acceptance.

Mascot

In some families, the Mascot function falls to the fourth born, or in smaller families, the baby of the family. This child is often treated as if they are too naïve or too fragile to understand the complex issues of the family, so they are protected. Their primary duty is to be entertaining and make the family feel good, so they often use humor to break the tension between other family members. They become the family clown or social director, taking the family's attention away from unpleasantness. They may appear immature for their age. Their power comes from being the center of positive attention and from knowing that the family will take care of them.

The habit of avoiding reality does not serve Mascots well as they grow into adulthood. Their focus on other people makes them kind and generous, but it also can cause them to get involved in relationships where people take advantage of them. Many Mascots report that they have feelings of embarrassment, low self-esteem, and anger.

Lingering habits of being a Mascot will be useful in social situations, but will not gain the kind of help that a person needs to continue into full mental, spiritual, and emotional maturity. The habit of thinking that someone else must take care of them can create insecurity as they age and the candidates for caretakers are fewer.

Mascots benefit from a community of people who will affirm their strengths and their capacity for taking care of themselves. They can learn from others who have taken on more responsibility as life situations change.

Summary of Roles

The relevance of family roles is that they may give some insight into why things were not perfect in our families. We want to see our habits clearly so that we do not blindly repeat patterns that did not get us what we need, and we want to avoid merely jettisoning behaviors that may reflect some of the best parts of ourselves. The goal is to look honestly at what went on, and then to see how we can make the most of life from this point forward.

GOOD BOUNDARIES

The greatest satisfaction comes when we have the skill and courage to live honestly with people. A significant contribution to authentic relationships comes from the work of Fritz and Lore Perls as they developed Gestalt therapy.[41] The German word *gestalt* refers to something which is experienced as a singularity although it is composed of distinct elements. Many insights that have been incorporated into current widespread understanding of relationships are based on their present-centered approach.

This means that the most important consideration is what is actual, not what is potential or what is past, but what is here and now. What is actual is always in the present time and right in front of us. Other schools of psychology invest vast amounts of time and energy on what happened in the past, what all that meant, and where it might lead. A present-centered approach raises questions such as: What am I doing? How am I doing this? What is my experience of this? Is this working well for me? How is this organized?

From this point of view, the details of the past are important only as they affect our feelings, behaviors, and relationships in the present. This approach says we get best results by looking at each experience and noticing whether each one is completed satisfactorily. If anything is interfering with completion of healthy interactions, then we devise practical ways to make life more workable.

This is a good approach because it is doable and does not require us to invest lots time and money in learning complicated psychological systems. With regard to living honestly with people, we can consider how to develop healthy boundaries, which Fritz and Lore Perls said were at the heart of good relationships.[4]

BE HONEST ABOUT YOURSELF

When we are not honest with ourselves, we may accuse other people of doing what we are doing. The psychological jargon term for it is *projection*. This means that we see in others what we do not wish to see in ourselves.[42]

We see this error easier when other people are doing it. For example, an aggressive world leader may accuse another world leader of being power-hungry, cruel and insensitive to the needs of his own people, motivated solely by greed and power. Or a pampered celebrity may accuse the people he has to deal with of being self-centered, immature, and unreasonable. Or an isolated person may say that his neighbors and family do not know or care about his needs. Or as an attention hungry person said, half-jokingly, "She's trying to get all my spotlight." We would rather see imperfections in other people than in ourselves.

The positive alternative to projection is being honest about ourselves. I can still remember the feeling of relief I had when I was able to admit to myself and others the truth about myself. To my surprise, I found myself being much more tolerant of other people. I am now certain that I had been doing a lot of projecting and blaming. Being honest about myself lessens my need to be hypercritical of other people. In the lists of characteristics below, compare corresponding numbered statements.

PROJECTION
1) Believe that my worst opinions are precisely true
2) See my evaluations as being objectively accurate
3) See no connection between my faults and their faults
4) Demand perfection
5) Hide my own faults and emphasize the faults of others

BEING HONEST WITH MYSELF
1) Aware when I am exaggerating other people's weakness
2) Aware that my dislike for a person is coloring my judgment
3) Aware that their faults coincide with faults that I feel bad about
4) Aware that no one is free of limitations
5) Willing to be known as a person with specific limitations and faults

KNOW WHERE YOU LEAVE OFF AND OTHERS BEGIN

Sometimes we really do not see the boundary between ourselves and other people. The psychological term for the merging of egos is *confluence*. Just as the body has rhythms, such as the heart's beating, so also healthy relationships have the alternation of connecting and separating. However, sometimes people are not willing to allow any kind of separation, and in the name of good will and unselfishness, some people lose themselves in the thoughts, feelings, and behaviors of other people.[43] The confluent relationship can take place in the home, at the workplace, in academic life, in community life, indeed, in any area of life.

As we mature, we gain enough perspective to tell whether we were overly fixated on our children. Children need loving care and attention in order to develop into healthy adults. However, the best parents will be alert to a child's growth and allow the child to gradually assume more independence and self determination. Schools have developed a term for parents who continue the kind of vigilance that was needed only in the earliest stages of childhood. They are called helicopter parents because they constantly hover over the children.

Did we hover? If we did, we did no favors for ourselves or the children. By now, we will be able to see if we neglected some personal needs and made life unnecessarily difficult for ourselves. And we will be able to see that many children resist helicopter parents one way or another, and we end up losing the very intimacy and respect we hoped for. The children who were not shrewd enough or strong enough to resist obsessive parents paid the price in their own delayed or stunted development.

Confluence can also occur when a person, because of romantic attraction, becomes enmeshed with the other person. At first this is highly desirable because it seems synonymous with intimacy. However, when the two people become so entangled that they lose their own identities, the relationship moves into something very different from the mutual attraction that brought them together originally. When one or both people fade into each other, the relationship loses its power to be mutually enriching. They eventually have nothing to give each other.

From our vantage point of years, we can see that some people made the mistake of taking literally the metaphor, "The two shall become one." The Biblical image that was quoted in so many wedding ceremonies is like all symbols: it has limits. The image is best used to picture a joining of resources and destinies. We would not expect people who marry to be surgically bound to each other, and would find such literalism insulting or silly. The same good sense should apply when people suggest that marriage involves merging their personalities and egos.

The importance of thinking about this kind of relationship is that we can learn what we need from here on. If we have had the habit of thinking that all good relationships must be personal mergers, then we will not find relationships with the kind of people who will support our search for serenity. We can consciously decide to learn where we leave off and others begin.

The alternative to confluence is intimacy. In the lists of characteristics below, compare corresponding numbered statements.

CONFLUENCE
1) Feeling other person's woes as my own
2) Losing sight of boundaries between self and the other person
3) Afraid of anything that is different
4) Not allowing enough separation to make new contact
5) Depending on the enmeshed relationship to take care of me
6) Feeling responsible for the other person's life
7) Feeling unable to do anything by myself
8) Escaping from self
9) Take other person's problems as my own, regardless of the other person's actions
10) Turning my will over to others

INTIMACY
1) Feeling sympathy for other person's woes
2) Connected to another person
3) Appreciation of sameness
4) Making contact between two different persons
5) Feeling responsible for my own life
6) Acknowledging that people have the right to make their own decisions
7) Able to be responsible for myself
8) Enjoyment of interpersonal intimacy
9) Offer support to the person's effort to deal with problems
10) Being supported by a person or group

WRITE YOUR OWN SCRIPT
A great benefit in aging is that we learn to be skeptical. The years have shown us that a lot of what is advertised as truth is actually varying proportions of substance and rubbish. Sometimes the error is intentional, sometimes not, but the fact is that people who believe everything they hear will be misled much of the time. The psychological term for swallowing whole the attitudes, behaviors, feelings, and judgments of others is *introjection*.[44] The common sense term is *gullible*.

Most of what we learn begins with someone else. The difference in being teachable and gullible is the degree to which we sift information and make it our own. Throughout our lives we have been bombarded by *should's* and *ought's* at home, church, school, work, etc. And now there is added a new level of celebrity experts who expound with unalloyed confidence about personal relationships, political consequences, military strategies, economic trends, and the mind of God. Some people give unquestioning credence to information if it comes from an authority they have decided to trust, such as a parent, or religious leader, or teacher, community leader, or celebrity wise person.

If we are wise, we gradually learn that even well-intentioned people can be wrong about all sorts of things. It is up to us to filter all the concepts and advice and discern what is dependable and worthwhile for us.

The healthy use of information from outside ourselves is to consider how it can be used to our best advantage. We can then write our own script, using the elements we choose, rather than numbly playing roles created by someone else.

There are always people who are ready to tell us what we should be doing and feeling. Some of them understand our situations, but some do not. Sometimes other family members design roles for us that benefit them, but we find their scenarios unnecessarily restrictive and out of touch with our abilities and needs. Sometimes other age groups seek to impose situations on us that they would not want to have for themselves, and often their plans have little to do with our actual abilities or needs. If we pay attention to our instincts, we will probably sense when we need to exercise more self determination.

In the lists of characteristics below, compare corresponding numbered statements.

INTROJECTION
1) Attitudes and behaviors are *should's* created by others
2) Outside wisdom is unexamined
3) Lose touch with my own preferences and adopt preferences created by others
4) Copying others without discrimination
5) Either accept all or reject all
6) Sources of wisdom are those who control us (e.g. parents, authorities)
7) All responses must conform to old scripts

ROLE PLAYING
1) Assume attitudes that benefit my own well being
2) Assume behaviors that get what I want and need
3) Aware of my own preferences

4) Aware of the limitations of the outsiders
5) Selecting what is useful, discarding what is not
6) Free to choose roles or aspects of roles
7) Respond to new situations appropriately

BE GOOD TO YOURSELF

We can sometimes be our own worst enemies. Language that can tip us off to this attitude are statements like, "I am ashamed of myself," or "I don't trust myself," or "I have to force myself to do this job," or "I don't like myself." Statements like these show that we can be divided against ourselves, and that we are trying to get satisfaction by reforming ourselves or even by trying to create a self that never was. **The underlying assumption is that we are the problem**, and if we could just get ourselves properly aligned, then we would be satisfied. The psychological term for this is retroflection.[45]

We can see this behavior in animals when one animal crouches or cowers in the presence of another in order to avoid attack and win acceptance. When animals or people sense that a fight for dominance will likely result in failure, then lowering one's own status seems a good strategy. When we are using retroflection, we take the adage "Beat 'em to the punch" and use it on ourselves. If we sense that harm is coming, we do it to ourselves.

For years, this was my focus. I was dissatisfied with certain aspects of my life, and I assumed that the solution lay in getting myself properly adjusted. My best energies were directed toward improving myself, rather than addressing actual conditions in relationships or career that were creating dissonance. This approach took me into a profusion of self improvement books, where I looked for *the answer*. I took courses on personal growth, hoping to sit under a genius that could show me a brand new healing process. I was constantly on alert to new approaches to spiritual development. I researched the religious traditions of my youth, delving into the various ways they had been applied in different eras and among different groups. I was hoping to find some magical core of secret knowledge that would change everything and bring a liveliness that I believed had somehow gone dormant.

Eventually my self improvement pilgrimage led me into meditation. I had seen personal testimonies from all kinds of people who reported good results. I met a university professor who had extensive personal experience with people who were experts in the realm of meditation.

Through him, I found a series of audio tapes that were created by the Monroe Institute in Charlottesville, Virginia. By playing cassette tapes and using earphones, I was able to experience a state of consciousness that was new to me. In this relaxed, peaceful state of mind, I gradually became convinced that I was not a flawed person. That was not the same as saying I was perfect. Rather, it was a new conviction that my life's dissonance could not be solved by self improvement projects. I began to consider whether the things and people outside of me might have something to do with my lack of serenity.

The opposite of blaming self for all that is wrong in life is self respect. In order to trust and respect ourselves, we may have to decide how to relate to some popular notions about our basic nature. One stream of tradition that casts humans as intrinsically bad is a widespread teaching of the largest Christian denominations. They call it original sin. In fact, the term never appears in the Bible. It is an interpretation of certain portions of the Bible that was formulated by Tertullian (160-220) and Cyprian (200-258) and was later popularized by Augustine (354-430) and John Calvin (1509-1564). This group of theologians said that humans being do not just make mistakes or create problems. They said that human beings **are** the problem, and that our flawed nature prevents even the best intentioned person from doing good. In effect, human beings are flawed at the core.

Jesus

The same Bible that contains the statements that were used to create the doctrine of original sin also contains statements about human potential for maturity. For example, Jesus said during the famous Sermon on the Mount: "You, therefore, must be perfect [growing into complete maturity of godliness in mind and character, having reached the proper height of virtue and integrity], as your heavenly Father is perfect." Matthew 5:48 (Amplified Bible)

This statement expresses faith in the human potential for goodness, and it was spoken not just to an inner circle of the elite, but to a general audience. In John 14, Jesus indicated that he was willing to entrust his mission to ordinary people. This indicates that whatever the state of a person's soul is at birth, Jesus believed that people had the option of choosing to be noble, unselfish, and loyal.

Freud & Plato

Another powerful influence in American life is the influence of Sigmund Freud. He pioneered in treating non-physical illnesses, but he also infected the national psyche with his pessimistic, negative view of human nature. He taught that the purpose of society is to restrain the universally destructive impulses of the individual.

Plato, writing around 360 B.C., in his ***Republic*** has one of his characters say: "...in all of us, even in good men, there is a lawless wild beast-nature which peers out in sleep."

In the rest of the story, Plato has the character say that noble and high-minded pursuits would make a person unlikely to be bothered by beastly impulses. Freud did not share the hope that noble thoughts, good intentions, and meditations would keep the evil impulses at bay. He believed in the literal and pervasive beastliness which he believed was revealed in dreams. He assumed that the hidden unconscious drives and instincts are primitive, and as a result of this formulation, people came to be viewed as dangerous instincts thinly covered by the controls of civilization.

Psychologists

Other psychologists such as Carl Jung, Abraham Maslow, Viktor Frankl, and Carl Rogers had much more optimistic views about human nature. While they acknowledged some human drives can be indulged in ways that can lead to destructive results, they also pointed to strong evidence that people also are affected by drives and instincts that lead to noble life. They pointed to the drive from early childhood for personal growth, the desire to fulfill innate potential, the widespread admiration that people hold for an ideal self, and the instinctive willingness to sacrifice one's self for some perceived higher good. They argued that there is real choice between the conflicting drives within human beings.

U.S.A Choice

The more positive views of human nature were never as influential in the United States as Freud's. It seems likely that a culture with a pessimistic religious view of humans' basic nature found Freud's theories a neat fit. Therefore, our culture has been profoundly influenced by two powerful streams of thought. On the one hand, our dominant institutional religion has taught that the intrinsic evil of human nature was located in the invisible spirit. On the other hand, Freudian dominated psychology theorized that evil was found in the labyrinths of the human mind. Even though neither had much respect for the other, in their own way institutional religion and secular psychology were cohorts in undermining our hopeful opinions of ourselves.

Self respect is honoring our instincts and our inner push to do what is good for ourselves, and to do it in ways that preserve our own best values. This mindset is vitally important as we mature. When we come to the stage of life when we have more time behind us than in front of us, we need to feel that we have made a good job of this life.

In the lists of characteristics below, compare corresponding numbered statements.

RETROFLECTION
1) Focus most energy upon controlling self instead of environment
2) Interacting without thinking about the environment & people
3) Immobilized by competing tensions
4) Blame ourselves for wrong actions of others

SELF RESPECT
1) Moderating impulses in order to control environment
2) Interacting with the environment & people
3) Maintaining creative balance between tensions
4) Realistic about other people's wrongful actions

FACE REALITY
I grew up in the quasi-Southern state of Kentucky, but I still was trained in the Southern rules of courteous social engagement. We were supposed to smile, speak graciously, and say things like, "You all come," which was really a friendly circumlocution for "Bye, now." I saw that this could be confusing to people of more direct speech when a non-Southerner responded by saying, "Okay, when?"

One of the benefits of aging is that we often become bolder about telling the truth. We often become more direct with people. But directness is much more than the courage to be honest and speak in clear terms. It is also staying focused enough in the present moment to see what people are really saying and what is really happening. This is the opposite of turning away from unpleasant truth because it might be upsetting to us or might create unsettling interactions with other people. In psychology, this pattern of avoidance is called *deflection*.

Being direct does not have to be so blunt that people feel they have been confronted or insulted. Sometimes we hear people who are rude and harsh, and then excuse it by saying, "I'm just being honest." The crucial difference lies in the mindset as we listen and interact. If we assume good will in the other person, direct speech can still be based on positive feelings, and can be appealing. There is something profound about having someone listen to you carefully and respond to you with warmth and honesty.

Perhaps even more difficult than speaking the truth clearly is hearing the truth fully. When I first entered the pastorate, I was dismayed to see how frequently doctors did not tell their patients the full story about their health. After becoming friends with a doctor, I asked him why doctors kept so many secrets from patients, especially those who were seriously ill. He smiled and said, "Because most people don't really want to hear bad news. And if someone is really curious, they will probably ask. Most doctors have learned that it's better to keep quiet and wait for questions."

Deflection is basically avoiding bad news. The hope is that by avoiding, we can escape. This is the probable meaning behind the visual maxim of the three wise monkeys, an ancient symbol. Side by side, they sit. One covers his ears – hear no evil. The next covers his eyes – see no evil. The third covers his mouth – speak no evil. The implied benefit is that this strategy would keep evil away.

This is an appropriate symbol for deflection. The problem is that the strategy simply does not work, at least in the long run. Bad news does not evaporate merely because we refuse to acknowledge it. In fact, in many instances, what we refuse to acknowledge worsens while we pretend it does not exist.

This is too easily illustrated in matters of physical health. With advancing years, health maintenance becomes more important than it has ever been before, and this means getting regular medical checkups and then getting the full story. Every one of us can name people who delayed getting information and suffered drastically as a result.

The folly of avoidance extends far beyond physical matters. Relationships often become unsatisfying because one or both of the people is not willing to acknowledge that changes are necessary. Often the excuse is, "There is nothing we can do about it, so why bring it out into the open." The answer is that by looking at something together, people can join in facing a common issue. They can establish a closer bond by dealing with something that is some kind of threat to their mutual happiness. Even if they cannot eliminate the problem, being together against the problem changes their situation.

With maturity, much of the reality that we pushed aside has now found us. We are living amid consequences of choices we made. Our best strategy is, from now on, to adopt the habit of facing the truth as quickly as we can. Thus we lessen the consequences of being blind-sided by negative consequences, and we increase our chances for happiness and fulfillment. We cannot improve on what we will not see.

In the lists of characteristics below, compare corresponding numbered statements.

DEFLECTION
1) Avoiding new information
2) Seeing change as destructive
3) Limiting access to information that would call for change
4) All outside wisdom is rejected
5) Trusting no one

DISCERNMENT
1) Examining new information
2) Seeing change as potentially good
3) Deciding what to accept
4) Awareness of the limitations of outsiders
5) Deciding whom to trust

RULE OF THIRDS

Another way of thinking about healthy boundaries in relationships was conceived by Jan Lowry, Director of The Gestalt of Memphis. It is a common-sense way of thinking about what we see in relationships.

The Rule of Thirds is that we all have people in our lives that fit into one of three categories. The term "thirds" does *not* mean that the categories are necessarily numerically equal.

For You

You have people in your life who are for you no matter what. They celebrate your victories without envy, and they are genuinely sorry for your defeats. They delight in you now, rather than waiting until you have corrected imperfections and achieved success. They smile reflexively when you enter the room. Your failures do not alienate them because they are attracted to your essence, not your superior performance. Merely being around these people makes you feel at your best, as if they are giving you energy.

The people who are for you are not all in your primary family and not all of your family is automatically for you. Some for-you people are pals, some are neighbors or teachers, and some are relatives. Being separated by distance or time does not diminish the positive effect these people have on you, and when you see them after a long absence, you feel that you pick up where you left off.

Neutral

The neutral people are casual acquaintances that may seem like close friends because of the amount of time you spend with them. They enjoy your company to the degree that you comply with their preferences. If you are having a good day, they enjoy being around you. If you are not, they will drift away, either mentally or physically. They do not wish you harm, but neither do they have intense desire for your success.

You can enjoy the company of neutral people at ball games, movies, playing cards, the coffee shop, or anywhere that interactions are kept at a casual level. They can make good neighbors who are willing to pick up your mail and feed the pets while you vacation. They can be pleasant to work with, as long as you do not expect them to go out their way to help you.

When neutral people are in your family, they seem to you more like boarders than relatives. Or, if you are the child, you may feel like you do not quite belong in their world, without knowing why.

Sometimes people can marry a neutral by abbreviating the getting acquainted time. The mistake is in assuming that physical attraction is the same as emotional intimacy. When the romantic urgency subsides, the emotional distance gradually becomes more evident. While neutrality is acceptable in casual relationships, it can cause considerable dissatisfaction to a person who is expecting intimacy.

Against You

In spite of the widespread belief that we can get along with anybody if we try hard enough, there are people in your life who are against you no matter what. These people take pleasure in your failures and react with envy or irritation when you succeed. They get annoyed at you for things that they tolerate easily in other people. They seem instinctively to compete with you in every situation, even when there is no apparent reason for it. If you observe them interacting with other people, they seem different than they do with you. When you are around these people, you may find yourself off balance and not at your best. After being with them, you may feel an energy deficit, and may feel as if a weight is lifted when you walk away.

Some who are against you are in your family, maybe even a parent or a sibling. We are reluctant to think this, but when we look objectively at the patterns of interactions, we realize it may explain a lot about why some families have so much turmoil.

IMPLICATIONS OF CATEGORIES

We spend a lot of time and effort trying to win over the people in the neutral and against-you categories. Sometimes getting better acquainted with strangers may cause them to move into our for-you category, but people that we have known for a reasonable amount of time do not change much in their way of relating to us. Therefore, our vain effort to create good will often leaves us feeling frustrated and insecure.

Spending a greater proportion of our time with people in our for-you category tends to make us feel affirmed and strengthened. We are more relaxed and confident because we are not contending with people who do not respect us and do not have our best interests at heart. As we age, we begin to be aware that we do ourselves a lot of good by being around positive people.

Test this in your own experience. Think of a time when you were in a crowd of people where you felt insecure. Someone conveyed to you, by subtle words or just the way they looked at you, that you were a lesser person within their ranks. Recall how inhibited you felt, how your mind seemed to work slowly and your speech was clumsy in your own ears. Remember how hard you tried to measure up, to fit in, and how awkward you felt.

Contrast that with a time when you were among real friends. Recall the way your mind worked, how your speech flowed effortlessly, and how much at ease you felt. When we are fully ourselves among people who are for us, we are at our best.

An important and humbling implication is that we are also fitting ourselves into other people's thirds. For some of the people in various aspects of our lives, we are for them. For others, we are neutral or casual. And for still others, we have a basic antipathy. We are against them.

Another surprising fact is that the third that I associate with you may not be the same one that you associate with me. You may be for me, no matter, what, but that will not automatically make me for you. Or you may be against me and yet I may consider you to be someone in my neutral third. And so the differences multiply.

Can people move from one third to another? It is possible, with mutual effort. The reality is that it does not happen often, usually because at least one of the people is not high motivated to change the familiar "dance" of their relationship.

STUDY QUESTIONS ON REAL OR ROLES
1) What are the healthiest relationships that you have had?
2) What is difficult about healthy relationships?
3) What is one thing you could do to get more out of your relationships?
4) How have your best relationships helped you?
5) How do you stay connected to important friends who do not live nearby?
6) What could you do to improve your current relationships?
7) In what mode of relating (Parent-Child-Adult) do you find yourself most often?
8) Tell about a recent time when you were in the Parent Mode. What did you like about it? What did you dislike about it?
9) Tell about a recent time when you were in the Adult Mode. What did you like about it? What did you dislike about it?
10) Tell about a recent time when you were in the Child Mode. What did you like about it? What did you dislike about it?

EXPERIMENTING WITH BEING REAL RATHER THAN PLAYING ROLES
Choose an action or write one of your own.
☐ I will seek ways to meet my needs directly rather than indirectly.
☐ I will refrain from playing whatever role I had as a child and relate to all people as an adult.
☐ I will seek ways to be open and honest in all relationships.
☐ I give myself permission to write my own life script.
☐ I will talk with at least one person in My Third each week.
☐ I will notice when I go into the Parent mode and question whether it is appropriate and beneficial.

OBSTACLES TO HAPPINESS
1) What makes it difficult for me to choose to be real rather than playing roles?
2) Is the obstacle a
   ☐ Thought or belief   ☐ Emotion   ☐ Attitude   ☐ Behavior
   ☐ Consequence/situation?
3) What would I have to do to make a different choice?

PEACEABLE OR CONTENTIOUS

Contented with Win/Win or Living in a Win/Lose World

LIVING CONTENTIOUSLY

Happiness is difficult to sustain if we live constantly with a win/lose attitude. Many in our society have been conditioned to believe that living with a certain amount of aggravation and irritability is the normal condition. After all, everyone has disagreements, misunderstandings, unfulfilled expectations, and hurt feelings. Added to that is a popular assumption that reaching certain status or age gives people the privilege of being rude and unkind. The contentious frame of mind is typically expressed through some form of anger, either of the fly-off-the-handle kind or the slow, simmering resentment that is nurtured over a span of years. Sometimes it is hidden behind cosmetic smiles. Sometimes it shows itself as a general crankiness.

Even though anger is one of the natural emotions that is part of healthy living, nurtured resentments are a different matter altogether. They damage relationships by keeping us in a contentious mode even with the people that we claim are intimates.

We have all seen spouses needle each other mercilessly over long standing irritations. We hear people complain about their mates while chatting with friends. We may laugh at the put-downs and sarcasm when we see them in movies or TV. In real life the excuse, "I was just kidding," does not fully convince us that affection was behind remarks that ridiculed, chastised, and belittled.

Many parents spend most of their time with children scolding, correcting, and giving stern instructions. If we have done that, we probably said, "It's for their own good," and meant it. From the kids' standpoint, though, it may feel more like unvarying irritation than warm affection. One of the most common issues that mental health counselors see in clients is the feeling that they were not loved by one or both of the parents. This most often happens when parents present a constant severity in their dealings with their children.

These are only a few of the indicators that we need to learn how to live peaceably. The significance of doing this is more than merely smoothing our personal relationships, as important as that is. For our own good, we need to get out of the habit of animosity and irritation, because this state of mind detracts from our mental, emotional, and spiritual welfare.

PEACE DISTURBERS

Living peaceably is not merely absence of open hostility. It is a constant choice of attitude and behavior. The culture around us does little to help us maintain peace, so we must take notice of the elements that tend to disturb our peace.

→ passive agressive
Parent mode

Control

A major peace disturber is the desire for control. Control is such a common way of thought that we may not be aware of it. We may think that we merely have definite ideas about the way things look, the way people behave, even the way traffic moves. We may say that we just have high standards and feel rather proud of our discriminating tastes. The truth begins to emerge when we listen to our conversations and see how much time is given to negative judgments about people and situations: the cut of their clothes, the length of their hair, the form of their relationships, the type and volume of their music. Our lives become organized around *should* and *ought*. All of this comes from our desire to make the external world match our picture of the ways things should be. The assumption, of course, is that we are consistently and precisely correct.

Striving for control creates inner stress because we seldom get as much compliance as we want. Constantly trying to impose our thinking and will on others is frustrating because, to paraphrase Abraham Lincoln, "You may control all the people some of the time, you can even control some people all of the time, but you cannot control all of the people all the time."

Trying to manage everyone else creates interpersonal tension because, in one way or another, most people resist being controlled. The controller must be on guard to outmaneuver the rebels' best defenses, whether subtle or obstinate. The controller is stuck in the attitude of a critical parent (see discussion in **Adaptable** in this book). People on the receiving end of controlling behavior feel that they are being treated with disrespect, and they find ways to fight back.

A familiar example is the scene of getting a young child to bed. The parent is bigger, stronger, and smarter than the little kid. But watch their "dance," the predictable movements and reactions.

Parent: "Okay, it's time for bed."

Child: "I can't find my teddy bear. I can't go to sleep without Teddy."

To the parent, it seems like a good deal: investing a few more minutes in order to get a docile sleeper. And the tyke is not defying authority; just asking for a sleep aid. If after a quick search, Teddy is still missing, the negotiation for an acceptable substitute begins. Of course, at any time the parent can simply say, "Because I say so," but avoiding the inevitable uproar seems worth the extra energy.

Parent: "Okay, now you're ready for bed."

Child: "I need a drink of water. I can't sleep when I'm thirsty."

Again, the child is not in open rebellion; she is just asking for something to making sleep easier.

Who is in control? We might say that the parent has the strength and authority to end the game at any point. But the child's instinctive wielding of underdog tactics makes it a difficult call to make. When this kind of scenario is repeated often in a variety of situations, we begin to see that being in charge is getting one's way. It is not the size of the combatants or the power of available weapons; it is whose agenda is followed.

So go the days of a controller. No matter how good we are at manipulating and controlling, we will run into people and situations that will not bend to our wills. It only takes a few of those to ruin our day and make us feel tense and unsettled.

As we mature, we begin to realize that constant competing takes its toll. We can see that it wears us down to be constantly at odds with people. The major losses are not just energy, though. We lose more important things, such as warmth in relationships, affection from people who get regular doses of our harshness, and trust from people who fear that truth will trigger weighty disapproval.

The reverse of controlling is to be adaptive to people and situations. In relationships, adaptability is experienced as cooperation. We no longer have to be in charge, and therefore we receive insights and strength from others, rather than feeling that we can depend only on ourselves. With regard to self, adaptability is full awareness of our imperfection. We can stop trying to twist ourselves into an acceptable facsimile of that image we have in our minds.

As we mature, we learn that even the illusion of control is increasingly difficult to maintain. Society limits us. In prior years, our opinions and actions may have been trusted, but the mere fact of age automatically brings our competence into question. Our bodies betray us. Decreased agility conveys to younger generations that we are declining, and they often assume that our minds and judgment are no more nimble than our limbs. Loss of youthful reflexes and vision makes younger people think that we do not have enough vitality to carry through on projects, even those which do not require perfect strength and coordination. If we are hoping that control will give us serenity, the passage of time will bring increasing frustration.

Competition

Another disturber of peace is seeing life as a contest. In our culture, competition is woven into the fabric of everyday life. It begins before we can remember. How soon a child says the first words or takes the first steps becomes a chance for parental pride. Every aspect of growing up is an occasion for succeeding or failing: learning to read, making good grades, making friends easily and with the right people, excelling at physical play and games. And make no mistake; the kids know whether they are a source of pride or an embarrassment to their families.

Al Capp, the creator of the comic strip, Li'l Abner, was a clever guest on talk shows. On one such occasion he talked about a trip to Mexico. He launched into a satirical monologue on why Americans visit third world countries, which he said was basically in order to feel like royalty. He said most Americans can go to a third world country and on one month's salary, live like a king. He said being royalty is all about having lots of people who are suffering and groveling all around you. It's all a matter of contrast. The attitude of entitlement is that we are most satisfied when we have benefits that others do not have.

Side Effects of Competition

For the most part, our culture honors those who come out on top. And then we seem genuinely surprised when people become obsessed with winning. Students have been told repeatedly that their entire futures depend on how they score on tests. Then they are caught cheating. Sports heroes and coaches see that winning can result in life-long financial security and a place in so-called halls of fame. So they break the rules to give themselves an advantage. Politicians see that telling the simple truth guarantees that they will have no chance of getting elected to an important position. So they lie a little about a lot of things and become artists at never giving a straight answer to the simplest questions. Scientists must compete with each other in a race for money to make good ideas workable. So, some fudge on experiments in order to show better results. Religionists see that power and influence get more acclaim than simple goodness. So they nurture whatever image that gets the most approval and adherents.

The High Cost of Winning

These familiar disappointments reveal an important truth about the nature of competition. This truth slipped up on me while I was working as a therapist in an addiction treatment program. For each client, the healing process involved working on the traditional twelve steps of Alcoholics Anonymous, and that includes being part of an ongoing group. Occasionally a client would be so adept at the treatment regimens that he would be labeled by staff and the other residents as "a role model." After a while I noticed something else the role models had in common: they all relapsed very quickly after finishing the program. Many of them returned to start at ground zero in their recovery.

At first this pattern merely suggested that even the professionals could not predict with any accuracy who would be successful in the recovery effort. I gradually realized that the star pupil status itself was the problem. Achieving the image of a role model requires a person to hide anything that is not perfect, and then devote considerable attention to maintaining the good image. With that kind of diversion, they pay scant attention to the actual growth they need in order to be healthy. The role models left the program with the honor of being stars, but without the skills they needed to stay clean and sober. Competing, even if unconsciously, interfered with getting the most important benefits.

As we seek peace and serenity, competition as a habitual mindset tends to interfere with our getting them. Notice the signs in common situations. You meet a friend for a friendly card game or a set of tennis or a round of golf. It's a beautiful day and you are grateful for the health and energy to be active. You begin to play. The game progresses and you are not doing well, that is, you are not getting the best of the score. A common pattern is to then focus more and more on the bad run of luck, or the stroke that is not working as well as it has in other times, or even on the partner's ineptness or lack of enthusiasm. The day is ruined, or at the very least, diminished.

Competitiveness is not limited to games, of course. Notice that no matter which way the conversation veers, there are some who must outdo the others, even if the contest is about who saw the worst accident, or who had the most painful surgery, or who has the worst situation in life.

Two Human Needs

Competition tends to increase productivity and result in higher levels of performance, and this is accomplished by calling on our desire to establish our individual uniqueness. This is one of two major human needs. The other is to bond with people; to form strong, permanent, intimate relationships. We need to feel personally unique and we need to be connected with people. As with so many virtues, the trick is to keep them in balance, so that the pursuit of one does not make us ignore the other.

To achieve peaceable living, we must drop the patterns that interfere with developing the supportive community that we need at this stage of life. The term "community" is used here in a more limited way than the broad use, which typically refers to a grouping of people who share a place or even external similarities.

Here, community is a network of people who are joined voluntarily for common purposes. A community based on peaceable living is one that provides a network of mutual helping and caring. This kind of community waits on our willingness to discover and embrace peaceable living.

It's not as easy as saying, "Why can't we all just get along." Our own impulses and the actions of others create discord, so we must learn how to deal with them in ways that move us toward peaceable living. Our task in this step is to find peaceful patterns and use them.

CONTINUUM OF CONFLICT AND PEACE

In order to see this more clearly, we look at a set of ideas put together by sociologist Elise Boulding. She formulated what she called a continuum of conflict.[1] She showed that the manner in which we deal with conflict can be charted according to how much or how little peacefulness is used. Reading from left to right, we start with the most extreme/violent reaction and move toward more peaceful reactions.

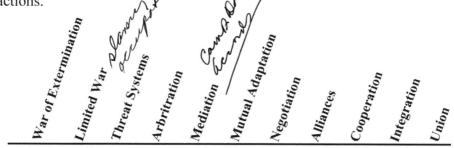

Figure 4 – National Continuum of Conflict

When we first look at this continuum, we may think that the terms apply more to countries rather than individuals. However, we can restate the terms so that are more descriptive of personal responses.

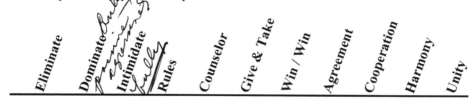

Figure 5 – Personal Continuum of Conflict

It may be that we find ourselves more often at some of these points, but it's likely we are familiar with several of them as ways we use in different situations. It is also likely that we tend to vary our response according to the people we are dealing with. The goal is to make progress, moving gradually from animosity toward peaceable living.

History is full of examples of nations or groups that were so focused on their own needs that outsiders had no substantial value. They set about to eliminate those outside their group because they believed that it was purely self-defense in one way or another. Even if the outsiders were not engaged in overt hostilities at the moment, their mere existence made it possible that they would be a future threat. The ultimate solution was justified by the presumption of extreme threat, the conviction that no other solution was available, and the fear that continued existence of the competitors would result in future danger. This option is still popular in world affairs.

Personal War

On the personal level, attitudes at this end of the continuum usually do not lead to actually killing another person. Rather, we simply do things that are designed to remove people from our lives. With aging, it is natural for the number of relationships to decrease to some extent. However, if we have the habit of getting rid of people simply because they interfere with getting our way, then at the very stage of life when we need a support network, we find ourselves becoming increasingly isolated.

To move to a more peaceable mindset, we need ways to raise our level of appreciation for people. We do that by shifting our attention from characteristics that confuse, or irritate, or frighten us. This is not always easy, because we tend to measure everyone by how close they are to us. Psychologist Gordon Allport said that bias against outsiders is a result of over-estimating insiders.[46] That means that we idealize our own view of the world, exaggerating the good and minimizing the bad. With this picture of reality, we judge the outsiders as not measuring up.

That is why, on the national or group level, people come up with de-humanizing names for people they want to eliminate: jap, kraut, gook, redskin, nigger, wetback. On the personal level, we do the same thing. To get rid of people, we reduce them to characteristics and behaviors that are only a small part of them: overly emotional or aloof, sloppy or compulsive, fat or skinny, cynical or gullible, talkative or taciturn, judgmental or permissive, disloyal or clinging, mean or simpering. By equating the whole person with aspects that we do not like, we justify getting rid of them.

Coping with Our Enemies

How can we learn to value people more highly? One strategy is to figure how to defend against the negative feelings they trigger in us. Perhaps a personal example will help. I was in a church that included a woman who seemed to have

Continuum of Conflict
← Hostile → Peaceful

an unusual ability to be irritating. If I had been the only one who reacted to her in that way, I could have thought it was merely my personal dislike. However, I knew that she created discomfort in most of the people she interacted with, and many of us had developed the habit of simply avoiding her whenever possible. To make matters worse, she seemed oblivious to her effect on people, and she aggressively inserted herself into most of the groups and activities within the congregation.

I confided in a member who had professional training in dealing with difficult people. To my surprise, his counsel had nothing to do with clever tricks to control the woman's behavior. Instead, he recommended constructing what he called inner defenses against the intrusion of negative influences. He shared his own. He said that he envisioned a stone castle, surrounded by a wide moat filled with water. When he felt the approach of influences that would unsettle him, he merely envisioned going into the castle, raising the drawbridge, and then he feel safe and secure. He said the best defenses used one or more elements in nature, so he used stone and water.

I thought it was an interesting approach, but also a bit weird coming from a trained psychologist. I did not think about it again until the evening that we were sitting together during a pot-luck meal, and the woman we had discussed came in and sat down beside me. I could feel myself getting tense as she started her usual ranting about an endless list of things that bothered her. The muscles in my back were so tight they were almost cramping, and I could feel the beginnings of a tension headache. I looked across the table at my friend. He was calmly eating, with a relaxed expression on his face. When the woman tried to draw him into her game of uproar, he smiled easily and said with a friendly tone, "Oh, my dear, you are so silly." I could almost hear his drawbridge locking into place. He was then free to be guided by his own will rather than being controlled by a negative response to someone.

Need for Support

Another lesson to learn is that friends do important things for us. A young doctor had recently moved to a small town in Kentucky and was invited to join the largest church in town, where many of the community leaders attended. Part of the pitch to him was that it would be a good place to make friends. He said, "I already have all the friends I need."

This is possible when we are young, healthy, and affluent. As we age, our situation changes. Having a support system is no longer a luxury; it becomes a necessity. Few of us can thrive without having other people who value us highly and give us support, sometimes emotional, sometimes physical, and sometimes financial. Loners who have lived with a leave-me-alone attitude find that the habit is difficult to break when we get older. We find it hard to shift into unfamiliar friendliness and inclusiveness, and we discover that people have taken our unmistakable cues. They leave us alone. So, making a habit of getting rid of people is one that works against our own well-being. Being aware of that can motivate us to move toward peaceable living.

DOMINATION

For nations or groups, limited war is conflict that stops short of exterminating the opponent. The limit may come from a desire to get some benefit from the other side that would be lost if they were destroyed. History is filled with examples of armies that conquered people and then used them as resources to make their own lives easier. In some instances, the limits of force may have reflected the conquering nation's own standards of justice and decency.

Personal Conquest

On the personal level, domination is behavior that conquers a person, and probably causes discomfort of various kinds, but without the intention of getting rid of the person or even ending the relationship. Indeed, staying connected to the person is useful to the one in control. In addition to whatever benefits come from overwhelming the opponent, the feeling of being in control is enjoyable in itself.

The realm of politics is an example of limited war on a non-military level. The goal is dominance, and having the conquered available after victory is an important part of the ongoing satisfaction. The vanquished provide resources that the victors want to enjoy, and the opportunity to rule over opponents is an important part of the victory.

Another example is athletics, either as participants or loyal rooters. Even if we are no longer involved in direct competition, or have never been, attaching ourselves emotionally to teams is a way of feeling good when they overcome their opponents. Being on the winning side, even when we are merely on the sideline, is an emotional high. And here again, part of the appeal is having bragging rights over opponents who live to fight another day.

Many successful business people say that the ultimate satisfaction is not in the amount of money they make but rather the elation at winning over competitors. That is why some people who have accumulated more wealth than they could ever spend continue their aggressive business dealings. "It's all about the game," some have said.. This fact is important as we watch the maneuvering that appears to be only about money.

Good Intentions

For others, the primary objective, at least so far as they can tell, is the good of the other person. For example, parents who spank their children usually say it is "for their own good." They see it as an acceptable strategy, perhaps a last resort, for keeping the children within the boundaries of good behavior.

In fact, some people may object to seeing this illustration as being so far on the non-peaceable continuum of conflict. But consider: during the phase of life when physical force is used to control children, peace is not usually the primary aim. At this stage, the parent assumes that we know best, and whatever it takes to impose our will is in the best interest of the child. In most families, physical punishment is discontinued by the time a child is considered old enough to respond to other types of discipline.

The usefulness of mentioning spanking as an example of a way of dealing with conflict is that most of us probably have experienced it, both as children and as parents. We know the dynamic between punished and punisher is typically not, at that point, one of peaceful feelings. We understand that it is all about control and dominance.

The major difficulty of dealing with conflict by using raw power is that we tend to have less of it as we get older, at least the kind that enables us to forcibly control others. If we are not bigger, stronger, or have the resources to have someone act for us, we eventually reach the limits of our power. If our habit in dealing with conflict is to compel compliance, we will find ourselves increasingly on the losing end of the contest.

INTIMIDATION

Nations that develop elaborate threat systems want to gain control without having to use force. This is done by alluding to the past or by promising severe actions that have not yet been used.

The so-called Cold War between the United States and the Soviet Union from 1945 to 1991 was a prime example of this strategy on a national level. Both sides in the conflict, and all the nations that aligned with each of them, were constantly reacting to real or imagined threats from the other side. Each side invested in weapons and protection systems, each side fashioned internal policies that affected their citizens. It was all driven by mutual intimidation.

Personal Intimidation

On the interpersonal level, intimidation is used to exercise control without having to resort to overt action. Most of us understand what it feels like to be threatened. We can remember being pushed around by someone that was bigger, stronger, and made us believe that we would suffer if we did not submit. Many of us have vivid pictorial memories of such times, even if they were in childhood, and we can still feel the fear and shame at being controlled by mere threats.

Unfortunately, not all threats are in the past. Throughout our lives we encounter people at work, in the community, even in our own families that seek to control us by threats, either to do something to us or withhold something we hold dear. Some make no apologies for their aggression; indeed, they see it as a sign of strength. Others may not even be aware that is what they do, and would be surprised if someone told them.

When we have been intimidated, we may adapt the style without even being aware of it. When we try it and it works, it can become so much a habit that we do not recognize how often we do it.

I did not know this until I looked back on how I controlled my children. During my own childhood, physical punishment was the orthodox way of disciplining children. By the time I had children, I had learned a lot about more positive ways of getting them to do what was best. However, I had a habit that I was not fully aware of: I used intimidation to get the behavior I wanted. Sometimes I conveyed, either by facial expressions or tone of voice, the possibility that I would get angry. Often that was enough to get them to do what I wanted. I didn't realize until later that intimidation may work in getting one's way, but it does not create peace. It merely imposes order for the time being, so long as the threat is believed.

Intimidation is such a habit for some people that it is used in most relationships. At work, with friends, with strangers – in every situation, putting pressure on people to do what we want is such a habit that we may not know we are doing it. Sometimes it is by talking louder and longer than others. Sometimes it is using whatever place of authority we have to impose our will in areas where we have no particular expertise.

As we get older, intimidation becomes increasingly ineffective, primarily because more people are willing to call our bluff. Perhaps they get stronger, or what we threaten doesn't seem so bad, or even more likely, we get weaker. But even if that does not happen, intimidation as a way of dealing with conflict costs us long-term benefits. We win small battles, but in the longer view, we lose the support of people who refuse to be bullied.

Desperation

There is another factor that makes the first three stations on the continuum of conflict risky, whether for nations, groups, or individuals. That factor is desperation. An ancient and widespread warning is to beware of the cornered rat. While it is literally true that rats that have no escape route are dangerous, the allusion is to the human tendency to eventually use violent means to deal with whatever threatens us. When people become desperate, they are willing to defy forces that would ordinarily control or intimidate them into submission. When all hope of a peaceful solution is removed, people quite often choose to do things that do not seem reasonable to those who are trying to control them. Desperation often begets bold action.

My first awareness of this truth came in the fourth grade. There were no school buses in the small town, and anyway, the walk home was only a mile through the downtown and into the residential outskirts. It was a comfortable routine until another fourth grader and his buddy discovered entertainment in walking along with my sister and me, teasing and taunting and generally making us feel threatened. I was not surprised at Hubert (his real name would be instantly recognized by all my old classmates), because he was habitually mean, sneaky, and foul-mouthed. His buddy, though, had seemed friendly up until the stalking began. Each day it got a bit worse, until finally one day, Hubert tripped me and pushed me down onto the grass of a lawn. He didn't hit me; he only sat on me for a few minutes. His buddy stood by and laughed, and held my sister so she couldn't help me. After a few minutes, they tired of the sport and moved on. The rest of the way home, the shame and rage seemed like twin anvils slung around my shoulders.

The next day they fell in behind us as we walked through town. As we made our daily stop at the Post Office to pick up the mail, Hubert and his buddy crowded in behind us, brushing up against me and grinning. They were letting me know that it was going to be another fun day for them, only this time maybe more so. At that moment, something shifted within me. I had no hope for escape. I could outrun them, but by sister could not. I knew they would not respond to reasoning; they had already shown that. I had no hope of anyone rescuing me; we were headed for a long, isolated walk through quiet territory. As they stood leering at me, I took off my watch and handed it to my sister.

"Here, hold this. When I get down the street, I'm going to have the awfulest fight you ever saw." I went to the mailbox. When we came out of the Post Office, they were gone. They never stalked us again. Somehow they sensed that for me, all was lost, and that a cornered rat cannot be dealt with casually. The power of desperation.

Powerful nations and armies have frequently underestimated the effects of desperation. And people who are accustomed to imposing their will on others fail to understand how likely it is that someday the best of controls might no longer work.

People who use force and control in dealing with conflict are at risk. The people we bully physically, financially, or emotionally may one day turn on us. And since we are more likely to need the good will of people as we get older, intimidation is not smart for us in the long run. We do better to spend time with peers learning different skills for dealing with people and situations that disrupt our serenity.

USING RULES

In national or group matters, arbitration is the process of two sides agreeing to abide by the decision of a third party, usually one that seems to be unbiased against either of the sides, or at least shows evidence of being able to make a fair decision. It is a step away from might-makes-right. In arbitration, both sides are still interested in winning, but they agree to let the matter be determined by someone else.

The courts are a formal example of arbitration. When we resort to this way of resolving conflict, we make our best case and then agree to abide by the decision. People often complain that we have become a very litigious society, suing each other over everything from spilled hot coffee to falling on a slick floor. While this is still contentious, it is more peaceable than using force or intimidation. At this point on the conflict continuum, we trust in rules to give us advantage over those who are between us and getting our way.

On the personal level, we look for lists of rules to help us pressure people into doing what we want. The should's and should-not's of our society, or our small sub-group of the larger society, are often used to control people. The rules may be religious tenets gathered from scriptures, or more recently developed traditions that can be even more binding than scripture.

I grew up under the control of one such tradition. In the small town of my early years, the Southern Baptist church exerted strong influence over its own members and the population of the entire town. Specifically, the Baptist view was that social dancing was not something that good people did. Therefore, such events as proms and after-game sock hops simply never happened in the community. Dancing was not part of the general social scene of the town.

The orthodox reason for the taboo was that dancing would be sexually arousing, and therefore inappropriate. Teenagers saw the irony of the tradition. Dances would have involved a large group of teenagers in a well-lighted place, vigorously expending energy in rhythm to music, and in clear sight of sponsoring adults. Instead, the regular alternative was teenagers pairing off in cars, going to dark places in the country and parking for hours, where their natural sexual impulses had no external controls whatsoever. The rule actually increased the danger it claimed to eliminate.

This often happens when people deal with conflict by establishing rules. The assumption is that everything is a win/lose situation. One of my friends has very different ideas from mine in many areas: religion, politics, interpersonal relationships, etc. When we are in a group and she mentions a topic about which we have differing views, she immediately cuts off any response from me, and she says it is because she doesn't want to "fight about it." I had no intention of fighting; I just wanted to be heard. But that is not possible if life tends to be win/lose.

Rules and rule-makers have a narrow focus. Rather than engaging people, rule-makers address situations. They hope by establishing rules to encompass behavior and thereby control people. Interactions are then about orientation on the rules, enforcement of the rules, and punishment of rule-breakers. And the goal is still to achieve victory over the other person.

It may be that two sides alternate about who is applying rules, but the result is the same: temporary control. For example, a husband and wife may duel each other by pointing out each time the other fails to live up to a standard of rightness that they both agree on. The duel is about trying to exert control, not about establishing peace between the two. It is intriguing to notice how many so-called situation comedies on television are based on this kind of ongoing struggle between spouses: Ralph and Alice Kramden on the *Jackie Gleason Show*, Archie & Edith Bunker in *All in the Family*, Ray and Debra Barone in *Everybody Loves Raymond*, to name a few.

As we mature, we see many proofs in personal relationships that rules may inhibit the timid or provoke the bold, but in neither case do they create peace. There is no rule that clever people cannot figure a way to get around. The very fact that one person is trying to impose control by using rules makes the relationship less than equal and even less than personal. If one side appeals for mercy, the rule-makers shrug and say, "There's nothing I can do. Those are the rules."

Ongoing groups, such as twelve-step groups, are built around the clear structure of strategies that have been proven to work. And yet the groups promote flexibility in thought and action. Each person is encouraged to develop their own understanding of the insights and to apply them in ways that fit them most effectively. Written guidelines are not put forth as rules, but rather as principles that are worthwhile simply because people have reported them to be useful.

This kind of group can be helpful in seeing how we may have been using rules to manipulate people. It helps us find a style that is more respectful of the uniqueness of each person and each person's pilgrimage toward maturity and serenity.

LISTENING TO GUIDANCE

The mediator/counselor is someone whose presence, experience, and non-binding advice can shift the two sides out of their adversarial mindset. An example on a national level was the talks between Menachem Begin of Israel and Anwar Sadat of Egypt in 1978. They represented nations that had long been in contention over issues that seemed to have no easy solution. In addition, they expressed personal dislike for each other, which made negotiation very difficult, if not impossible. Nevertheless, they agreed to meet at Camp David with President Jimmy Carter to discuss ways they might achieve more peaceable relations between their two nations.

They kept at it for twelve days, in spite of the fact that at times they would not even speak to one another. In the worst times, they relied on Carter's private conversations with each of them. He had no formal authority to impose his will, so he used his skills at persuasion to get both men to see things in new ways. Having the United States give financial incentives to each side helped, but in the end, he could only encourage, advise, and exert personal influence. They had to find a way that both sides could win if they were to avoid moving toward certain destruction. They finally emerged with the Camp David Accords.

Personal Counsel

On the personal level, finding peace often depends on connecting with someone who can help us. Sometimes it will be one person, such as a counselor or wise friend. Author Eckhart Tolle recalls a good example in his book *A New Earth*.[47] Late one evening, a neighbor rang his doorbell and frantically requested to talk with him. She was middle-aged, intelligent, and well educated. He knew that she carried many bad childhood memories of the Nazi days in Germany, when many of her family members died in the concentration camps and she had barely escaped with her life. Upon entering, she began a panicky story of a disagreement she had been having with her property managers about service fees and repairs to her home. It was obvious that in her mind she had elevated the routine matter to the level of a major life crisis. Rather than immediately taking her side in the disagreement, or trying to convince her that the situation was not a huge crisis, Tolle chose merely to listen to her with his full, sympathetic attention. He said, "There was nothing to do other than remain open, alert, and intensely present with every cell of the body. I looked at her with no thought and no judgment and listened in stillness without any mental commentary."[48]

The woman talked compulsively for about ten minutes, and Tolle simply maintained his silent, calm, empathetic presence. Suddenly she stopped talking and looked around at all the documents she had spread out to help tell her terrible story. As if awakening from a bad dream, she became calm and settled. Then she said, "This isn't important at all, is it?" He answered, "No, it isn't." She went home and slept peacefully.[49]

While sometimes we need specific advice and new options for action, at other times, what we need most is for someone to be fully present. This is the truth behind the familiar testimony that people give about the importance of someone "being there" for us. It is an uncommon gift to have someone give us their full attention when we need something, rather than listening briefly and then trying to impose quick solutions on us.

Mediators

Sometimes what we need comes best from a group of people whose combined wisdom is greater than any one member's. Whether the mediators deal with us one-to-one or as a group, they do important things for us.

- Mediators help us hear each other differently.
  Do you remember the first time you ever heard your recorded voice played back to you? We are often surprised at the way we sound to others. A counselor often lets us hear for the first time what we sound like, not in the literal sense, but in the sense of what our messages sound like to someone else. When we are caught in an ongoing contentious relationship, we cannot hear ourselves with objectivity. Mediators reflect to us what our messages sound like from the outside. And since we do not consider them as enemies or competitors, we can see whether what we are saying matches our perception that we are making sense and have good intentions. Having someone to reflect to us is a glimpse of ourselves that we cannot get by ourselves.

- Mediators help us identify the most important issues.
  An interesting, frustrating experience is listening to what is advertised as a political debate. It is not really a debate, of course, because the opponents do not engage the issue in depth. Each one eagerly waits for a chance to talk over the other, and they exaggerate each other's views in order to make them seem absurd. They are so interested in making their own points that they are not paying attention to the more basic issues.
  We have heard the same thing on a personal level. When I was a staff counselor at a family counseling center, parents often came to consult me about problems they were having with their teenagers. Most of the irritated parents covered similar complaints about their teenagers: choice of clothes, messy rooms, music that was unpleasant and too loud, unsavory friends,

disrespectful attitudes toward other family members, poor academic performance. When I talked with the teenagers in private, I heard complaints about
parents that imposed unreasonable curfews, criticized them for everything,
and wouldn't let them use the family car. When I was able to help, it was with
people who were willing to look past the surface peeves and address the more
important issues, such as how to develop mutual respect, and how to build
mutual trust, how to develop caring for the person who is dealing with the
pressures of being a parent or a teenager.

The same dynamic applied to couples who came for help with marital problems. Husbands pester wives about shopping habits. Wives nag husbands
about neglected chores. They both complain about how the other deals with
the kids. Petty annoyances often get so much attention that they seldom talk
about more basic issues, such as how they feel when they are together, what
they need that they are not getting, and whether life in general is satisfying. When I was not able to help, it was with people who were unwilling to
quit worrying about minor irritations long enough to address more important
matters.

- Mediators help us see common values that we can build on. Our values are
  our deeply held beliefs. If we live by them consistently, they give our lives
  form and substance that fit who we are. If we let anything distract us from
  living them, they are like a piece of grit in our shoes, making us unable to go
  on with comfort. Betrayed values create a sense of life unlived and unfulfilled.
  Whether we live by them or not, our values are the filters through which we
  view the world. They are the language we use to interpret what happens.

  In conflict situations, a mediator is sometimes needed to identify common
  values, because values are directly connected to our emotions. When we
  respond emotionally, we are often not being open-minded about those who
  seem to be at odds with our values. An unbiased person or group can sometimes help us find common ground that neither side can see.

  Shared values are the glue that holds together nations, organizations, communities, or informal groups. If we cannot find common ground, we are likely
  to have dissension that leads to various levels of animosity.

- Mediators may help us see the limits of dealing with specific situations. For
  example, in a marriage counseling situation, a skilled mediator may help
  people see that developing mutually satisfying solutions is not possible. It
  may be that one person is not willing to bring an equal amount of good will
  to the process. It may be that harm has been done that cannot be forgiven.
  It may be that one person is more committed to gaining an advantage than

making peace. In such situations, the mediator can help people see reality. In such instances, the conflict is moved toward formal arbitration rather than toward informal peacemaking.

A man in one of the pilot groups, whom I will call Joe, reminded me that some conflict cannot be resolved by anything less than formal means. Joe had entered into an agreement with someone he had known for twenty-five years, and whom he thought he could trust. The man said one thing, but put different terms in the written contract, and Joe did not discover the discrepancy until after the man was bringing legal pressure on Joe. When Joe tried to talk to him on the basis of past trust, he found that the man's financial advantage was more important than sustaining the friendship.

We may not need mediators to know when we are being mistreated, but a skilled mediator may help us see it before an unethical person can do us serious harm. And the mediator may help us use formal legal means rather than jumping to the use of intimidation or outright force in order to stand up for ourselves. A mediator/counselor person can help us find the best possible way to get through emotional reactions that naturally come with being treated unfairly. Peaceable living is finding the least extreme way of dealing with unpleasant situations and unfair people.

FINDING MEDIATORS

Where do we find people who can give us the kind of perspective that bridges gaps between us and people we dislike and mistrust? If we are lucky, we may have some of them already in our lives, masquerading as ordinary friends.

My good buddy and I were having breakfast in the student center in graduate school. A guy whom we both knew approached us and struck up a conversation. Ron chatted with him amiably and I simply remained quiet and continued eating. After a few minutes, the guy moved on without sitting down.

Ron began to laugh. "Boy, you really gave it to him."

I was surprised. "What do you mean? I didn't say much of anything."

"Precisely. You have a way of getting it across without ever saying a word."

There followed a conversation in which he gave me some information about myself that I have remembered through the years. I have the capacity for conveying disapproval without ever speaking, simply by expression, body language, and overall attitude.

Everyone has things that we do that are so much a part of our routine behavior that we are unconscious of the effect on people around us. And often these habits of attitude and communication are obstacles to peaceable living. People who will tell us about ourselves in ways that we will listen can help us see ourselves and other people in a different light.

Wise Friends

Another person who did this for me was a friend from childhood. Elizabeth Jo and I were in the same class through elementary and high school. After graduation, the thirty-five of us scattered onto different life paths. She appointed herself the connector and convener of our group. She remained in the little town where we grew up, but she extended herself from California to Alaska to Virginia and everywhere else the class members moved. She had our numbers, both literally and figuratively. When something happened to one of us that she thought the rest of us should know, she started calling. All across the country, spouses who had not grown up with Elizabeth Jo gradually came to know her as the voice on the line who was bringing news about one of our old friends, and giving us persuasive reminders to come back home for the annual reunion. She sent us regular updates of addresses, phone numbers, and email addresses, and encouraged us to stay in touch with each other.

A few years ago, Elizabeth Jo died. Most of us who were still living gathered for her funeral. And as we talked about her role in our lives, a theme emerged: she was a friend who treated us all with respect and honesty. She had a way of teasing and laughing and telling us the unvarnished truth about the stuff that others would not say to us. To our faces. And she did not gossip about us to the others. She was the mediator that promoted peace among us.

Group Wisdom

Sometimes the wisdom we need comes from groups of people who have learned how to deal peaceably with difficult people and situations. Ongoing groups are often the place where we are surprised by commonality, and out of our common experiences, we can distill some tried-and-true methods. When we first gather to share our common pilgrimage, we initially view each other as strangers. We see only the facades of first impressions. Up till now, we have revealed just enough personal information to encourage chit-chat, but not enough self-disclosure to risk personal rejection. As time goes on, and the meetings allow for honest sharing about the zigzag path of progress, we begin to hear echoes of our own stories. The specifics are different, but the pressures and the pain are the same. We begin to learn from each other. We find common ground and stand on it with a sense of togetherness. We are ready to let the group help us find new ways to deal with the problems that we have not been able to solve by ourselves.

GIVE AND TAKE

Mutual adaptation is when two sides change tactics without changing their basic goals. They alter behavior because there is a balance of power and the tactics previously tried have not worked well. Both sides reach the point where the pain of the conflict is greater than the pain of going through a change. The use of raw power has not worked because they are evenly matched. Threats have not worked because they have called each other's bluffs. Mediators have not shown them common values that they can build on. So, finally they decide that they must simply agree to some trade-offs. They each agree to give up some things in order to get some other benefits.

In tribes or nations, mutual adaptation happens when the warring factions decide that they cannot overcome the opponents, and they reach an agreement to divide up whatever it is they are fighting over. It may be territory, or natural resources, and they make arrangements to divide up what they have been unable to dominate.

Personal Give and Take

On an individual level, the adaptations will be about things that are more personal. One example is the growing trend for spouses to take separate vacations. Two people have differences about what would provide a re-creative experience, and they do not see a way to bridge their differences. So, they agree to go their separate ways.

More frequently, however, spouses in conflict simply agree to live much of their lives in a parallel pattern. They may not enjoy the same hobbies, so they agree to pursue their favored habits rather than look for something new they might do together. They may not like the same people, so they develop a different set of intimate friends. They may not be able to agree on religious practices, so they agree to follow different paths of spiritual development.

Another strategy used in many families is to delegate areas of life to one person, and then everyone else disconnects. For example, the husband may be in charge of the finances, and the wife and children have no information about the family's financial situation. Not only does the designated person carry the burden alone, but the others may unwittingly increase the pressure because they do not know when their actions affect the overall situation.

Or the wife may be given responsibility for the children's primary care, which may include some or all of the children's education, discipline, and religious training. In this scenario, the husband is not involved in the daily routines of the rest of the family. The benefit is that the adults are not in conflict about differing views of situations. That makes life simpler. The liability is that valuable shared insight and influence are not used, and the uninvolved person is viewed as emotionally absent. And again, the responsible person's job may be made more difficult by the unwitting interference of other family members.

What does this have to do with us? We often have patterns of coping with potential conflict that are old habits, and so deeply engrained that we do not even notice them. As we move along, the effects become more important to our serenity. Mutual adaptation seems to be an effective way of dealing with conflict. However, one of the results is distance between people. In our earlier years, this may not have been a problem, indeed, may even have been something we liked. But as we age, we begin to feel the disadvantages of emotional distance.

For one thing, we gradually lose our access to unlimited new people and situations. In earlier years, we assumed that there would be plenty of time to make up financial shortfalls, lots of new people to fill the gap left by unsatisfying family relationships, and generally good health to take care of ourselves independently. As we age, it is to our great advantage to make peace in ways that keep us personally connected to important people in our lives.

FINDING WAYS FOR EVERYONE TO WIN

This is the point on the continuum where people in conflict try to make peace by finding a win/win situation. This works well only when both sides are assertive enough to take care of their own interests. We can see why this is important when we look at the makeup of assertiveness. Assertiveness, at its most basic level, is asking for what you need and want. It includes the following patterns:

- Taking time to make up my own mind
- Willing to change my mind
- Freedom from having to justify my feelings — *never explain / no defense needed*
- Deciding how to lead my own life
- Setting my own priorities and following them
- Setting my own level of engagement in worthwhile activities
- Respecting myself even if some people express negative opinions of me
- Freedom from having to justify my actions
- Deciding how I want to be treated
- Willing to say, "No," when I truly object
- Willing to acknowledge when I do not know or do not understand
- Willing to say that I do not care about some things
- Asking for information or help
- Admitting mistakes
- Acting on my own instincts

- Maintaining positive relationships
 Curtailing relationships that are harmful to me

If there is an imbalance in power or confidence, then negotiation will not work well. The person with more power will tend to claim unequal benefits and the person with less power will give in. Sometimes these behaviors are conscious, sometimes not. The fact that this method calls for a balance of power is the main reason why people who are experiencing relationship difficulties often find that using a counselor is the most effective way to start problem solving. It may be the only way to learn how to take care of ourselves. We have the option of working with a wise counselor or a well-directed group.

This was the starting point for me. One of the requirements for certification as a Gestalt therapist was to participate in a therapy group for two years. When I saw this on the curriculum list, I was not concerned. I had taken graduate level courses in psychology and counseling, and had functioned as a counselor with individuals and groups for twenty-five years. I was sure that I would be quite comfortable as a member of a long-term group led by a professional Gestalt therapist.

When I entered the twelve-person group as a new member, I found that the group was in the midst of discussing how assertiveness, or lack of it, had affected their lives. As the list of assertive behaviors (see the preceding list) became evident, I began to feel uneasy. I realized that I could not honestly claim most of them as habits, and in fact, several of them were either rare or non-existent in my behavior. So I kept silent.

Rather than point out my lack of participation, the therapist simply started one day's session with an exercise that would require an answer from each person. She asked us to answer the question, "What do you want most out of life?"

"No problem," I thought. Then she elaborated, "Your must answer what you want for yourself. Your answer cannot be about some benefit to anyone else."

It sounds simple enough. However, I felt myself becoming more anxious as the topic moved around the group. I could not find in my mind what I wanted most for myself. I realized that my habits of thought were so geared for looking at what other people wanted or needed that I could not shift and look inward.

Lack of assertiveness affects our ability to live peaceably. We might think that if one side is habitually thinking about giving in, then peace would seem the natural result. Not necessarily. A peace too easily made is mere compliance, and resentment goes underground. Unless we bring out the things we need and want, then win-or-lose is what we have, whether we know it consciously or not.

Another surprising thing about non-assertive people is that since we only know about winning or losing, when we do win, we tend to do it aggressively. That is, we overdo it. This usually only happens when we have a big advantage, such as a parent/child or employer/employee or rich/poor. Without the tools for taking care of ourselves in the face of strong competitors, we think that we must either be victor or victim. We either give in or overwhelm.

Assertive Role Models

There are many role models for either aggressive or passive behavior, but not many for assertiveness. I met one as I attended graduate school in 1980. Bill had the rare ability to take care of himself without being belligerent or insensitive to others. He was finishing his graduate degree and would soon be available for fulltime employment. A prosperous, sizable local church was impressed with his skills and maturity, and they expressed interest in hiring him to direct all their educational programs. They had reached the point when they were ready to make him a salary offer. When Bill heard their offer, he realized that they were doing what a lot of churches did in the city where the seminary was located: they were looking for a bargain. The senior minister knew that many graduating students had established family connections that made them look for local employment. This created a buyer's market as local churches looked for qualified staff members.

Many young men in this situation were either aggressive in their pushing for more money, or accepted the low salary with unexpressed resentment. Bill did neither. Instead, he said, "I see that this is the amount of money you have to invest in your educational programs. How much of my time would you like to buy with this salary?"

They said, with surprise, "All of it!"

Bill said, "Oh, I see. Well, this will not be enough to buy all of my time, but I will be glad to talk with you about how much time I can give you for this amount of salary. And then you can decide if that will be enough time to accomplish what you want done."

They decided this young man was far too sophisticated in his thinking, and they moved on to someone else. And he found a place that valued his intelligence and assertiveness.

One of the key lessons we can learn is the difference in assertive and aggressive. It is essentially making sure we get what we deserve without taking what rightfully belongs to someone else. In the company of other people who are trying to grow, we all help each other while helping ourselves.

FINDING COMMON GOALS

Another way of dealing with conflict is to form alliances. Instead of competing against each other, nations or other groups look for common goals that they can pursue as partners. The benefit of the alliance is that it frees up the resources that were being used to compete with each other, and in addition, gains the combined strength in the partnership. In this method, basic principles remain the same and the partners agree to focus on what they have in common.

On a tribal or national scale, alliances help us confront a danger that is threatening to one or both of us. It may be a shortage of resources or it may be another tribe or nation that is threatening us. The new partnership sends a message: "What happens to one of us happens to both of us," and we are mutually strengthened. There is a conscious effort to alleviate pressure by sharing benefits, such as technology and other resources.

Personal Agreement

On a personal level, this is a choice to look for common goals rather than being separated by differences. For example, in the world of work we can focus on the things we do not like. The boss didn't appreciate my effort, or favors someone else, or didn't pay me as much as I'm worth, or watches over me as if I cannot be trusted. We can stay in the drama of the boss versus me, and seek to draw other people into the same mindset. Or we can choose to focus on the work that needs both boss and employee to get done, and we can see ourselves as part of a team.

In the neighborhood, we can be hyper-vigilant about anything neighbors do that irritates us: letting their dogs soil our territory, playing music too loudly, not caring for their yards in a way that suits us, and having opinions that we find offensive. Or we can choose to forge a network that creates a safe neighborhood and enjoyable social events.

In church we can be smug about our style of goodness and contemptuous of all others, spend the majority of our time defending and dispensing doctrines that are seldom put to any benevolent use, and treat the institution as a stockade to hide from unpleasant situations and unruly people. Or we can choose to make it a community of people humble enough to help each other toward maturity and generous enough to extend helping hands beyond our comfort zones.

In the family, we can stay locked in the unsatisfying patterns of childhood, constantly replaying old scripts and reliving old disasters. Or we can choose to grow up and out of childishness, and become a support for each other in the battle with life's rude surprises.

Benefits of Shared Goals

A powerful benefit of agreement is feeling a connection with people who share some of our goals. Even if we are able to accomplish many of our goals by ourselves, we do well to find ways to link with people in shared ventures, because there are aspects of our personalities that emerge only in relation to people and human needs that cannot be met except in a community with people we know and trust.

Support groups are a school for learning how to go beyond differences and find common goals. To the newcomer, the group seems like a jumble of people who are so dissimilar that the only thing that they could possibly do is get on each other's nerves. The basis for common understanding is the problem they share, and the basis for common effort is the need to find ways to untangle their lives. The meetings become occasions for sharing information about what has worked and what hasn't worked. The encouraging environment encourages people to try new solutions because we see that failure will not cause banishment, but rather will garner renewed encouragement to try again.

Habitat for humanity →
Sharing of strength

WORKING TOGETHER

The primary difference between agreement and cooperation is the degree of common effort. In an agreement or alliance, we have common goals, but much of the work may be done separately. In cooperation, the work is done together.

A neighborhood alliance might agree that they want a community that aesthetically pleasing to all, and might agree that they will work toward this common goal. And so each family is responsible for making their property an asset to the overall beauty.

Cooperation is often seen in rural areas when farmers help each other sequentially to do some task they cannot do by themselves. So, neighbors will gather and flood the problem with their combined effort, whether it is putting up a barn in one day, or getting in the harvest to help a sick farmer, or pitching in financial resources for someone who has fallen on hard times.

The value of this level of peaceable living is clear. There will be a lengthening list of things we cannot do by ourselves. One of them is building our self-esteem in the face the realities of aging.

The Red Hat Society was established for this very reason. The founder of the group, Sue Ellen Cooper, writes on their website:

The Red Hat Society began as a result of a few women deciding to greet middle age with verve, humor and élan. We believe silliness is the comedy relief of life, and since we are all in it together, we might as well join red-gloved hands and go for the gusto together. Underneath the frivolity, we share a bond of affection, forged by common life experiences and a genuine enthusiasm for wherever life takes us next. (www.redhatsociety.com)

The Red Hat Society is a good model for helping ourselves. After years of people talking about how our culture devalues the elderly, mature adults are getting more attention, at least as a group. We get modest discounts on entertainment tickets, travel fares, and some restaurants. But if you talk with us as individuals, the token benefits do not come close to addressing the issues that diminish day-to-day dissatisfaction. They are the equivalent of feeding a homeless person a really nice meal every Christmas…with nothing in between. Appreciated, but not nearly enough.

We need to help ourselves rather than depending on the government, or social agencies, or random sympathetic citizens. One reason is that we know better than anyone else the shape of our needs and what truly helps. The other reason is that in helping each other, we benefit in ways that we do not when we are being passive. As we work together, we learn and teach about lessons that come only with the passage of time. The infinite variables in experiences make us all unique. **We evolve and grow until the day we die.** Nobody can do for us what we accomplish when we work together for ourselves.

"Integration" — handwritten annotation

our "presence" most important thing absolutely — handwritten annotation

WORKING IN HARMONY

The first thing that comes to mind for most people in our culture when we hear the word "integration" is racial mixing. However, integration is also a way of dealing with conflict that is beyond race relations. The defining characteristic of integration is the stability that comes from both sides getting something important that they really want. It is not merely settling or trading off; it is achieving something important as a result of working together in harmony.

An example of this in racial integration was explained by Martin Luther King, Jr. He said that black people needed white people in order to move beyond their fears, for only by achieving a trusting relationship can we live without fear. He also said that white people needed black people in order to lay aside our guilt, for only by making amends and building mutual respect can we live without shame. In this example we see that each side needed something that they could get only by working together.

The same is true in many conflict situations. For example, as we age we often find ourselves at odds with various family members. The conflict may be about living arrangements, or sharing resources, or time spent together, or other issues that come as family members move through different stages of life. Often families deal with these issues by making power plays or trying to manipulate each other. Even when we get our way through trickery, it is never fully satisfying because we lose something in the transaction. We do better when we look for ways that each side gets something important.

I am now at the age my mother was when she was beseeching us to travel from New York to visit with her at Christmas. She was blatantly playing the pity-and-guilt theme, giving an account of how many more times other siblings had visited and how long it had been since she had seen her two elementary school age granddaughters. The long car trip gave me lots of time for feeling manipulated. Some time into the visit, the mutual resentfulness subsided enough to let normal enjoyment emerge. It happened as she was showing her granddaughters old pictures. She was savoring the telling of old stories and they were entranced by the faces of family history. She was giving them something no one else could, and they were giving her something that was only theirs to give. And the transaction extended to me as well, because by making the effort I was giving and receiving a family blessing that I could get in no other way. The harmony was sweet.

Some of the conflict that we face comes from dealing with health problems. The people we have lived with for years may develop conditions that require increased care, and we may feel overwhelmed by the sheer weight of physical and emotional demands. The stress comes as each person is trying to get what they need, and at the same time, knowing that the other person is not getting enough.

I listened to a radio account of one family that faced this situation. Roger suffered from Alzheimer's disease and his wife, Mary, was his primary caregiver. She had been referred to a respite care program by a physician, and getting help was the occasion for having her story recorded for broadcast. Joe was a senior-aged volunteer who wanted something useful to fill his time. He joined a respite care program and was sent to Mary and Roger's home to stay with Roger while Mary did chores on her own. In the recorded conversations, we heard them working out the plan. Mary introduced Joe to her husband and told Roger that she needed to run some errands. Joe made small talk with Roger and assured Mary they would get by just fine. Mary talked about how she was getting so exhausted trying to take care of Roger, and at the same time, look after herself and the routine needs of their home. Joe talked to her about how he was happy to help and that it made him feel good to do something that was important. He said that he would read to Roger while she was gone.

In this poignant story, Mary and Joe were each facing situations that were disturbing to their peace of mind. They helped each other get something important in their mature years. They each needed something different, and as they worked together, they felt relief and satisfaction.

Becoming part of an ongoing group is a good way to learn from each other about ways to deal with situations that diminish our satisfaction in living. Some problems do not respond to aggressiveness and coercion, but they can be mitigated by working together in harmony.

This is good to remember. We never outgrow our need to belong, and we never outlive our ability to be helped by being in the company of kindred minds and spirits.

SHARING HEARTS' DESIRES

The most peaceable situation is when we are so unified that we share the same goals and therefore our efforts are harmonious at deeper levels. Before we assert that we should pursue complete union in relationships, we must first acknowledge that absolute singleness of purpose seldom exists even within one person. Each of us is confounded by feelings and urges that are not orderly, but come in a hodge-podge of conflicting drives that would take us in divergent directions.

For example, each of us has a basic need for bonding, for closeness to and acceptance by other human beings. At the same time, we have a basic need for space, separateness from others, room to be one's own self, to be autonomous. These two human needs co-exist and compete in each person, and few can honestly say we keep them in perfect balance. Our lives are a never-ending dance in which one leads for a while and then the other. That is, if we are fairly healthy-minded. If we are not, one takes permanent control and life takes on the character of the imbalance.

In everyday matters, we have the same lack of unity. We want to save money, but we also want to enjoy the thrill of new stuff. We want to be healthy and svelte, but we also love the pleasure of indulging our appetites. We want to be responsible and trustworthy, but we also like the feeling of letting down and letting go. We want to be generous, but we also feel scared to share what might be in short supply. We want to be kind, but we also feel rage about some kinds of misdeeds. We want to be strong, and yet we feel the pull toward being so helpless that someone will take care of us. So, we must deal with the daily contest between competing desires.

If that is true, how can we hope to get in step with other people? What are the true desires, the ultimate purposes of other people? A psychologist friend distilled the answer to this: "Trust the behavior." After all the elaborations and justifications are offered, watch what is done. This method is based on the belief that we all follow our most powerful motivators. We may do some things every now and then that do not reflect our deepest aims, but on the average we follow through on what we think is most important.

So we look for people whose path is one that we affirm and want to follow. We look at ourselves with enough honesty to discern our pathway and we fall into step with those who will lend their strength and trust us to do the same.

FORGIVENESS

We will never find peace unless we have learned how to move on past our bad emotional experiences. After watching two ducks that got into a brief fight and then separated, flapped their wings vigorously and floated on peacefully, an observer imagined the difference it would have made if the ducks had human minds.[50] Humans tend to keep the effects of conflict alive by telling ourselves stories. If ducks were like us, each might have said to himself,

> I can't believe what he just did. He came within five inches of me. He thinks he owns this pond. He has no consideration of my private space. I'll never trust him again. Next time he'll try something else just to annoy me. I'm sure he's plotting something already. But I'm not going to stand for this. I'll teach him a lesson he won't forget.[51]

The human penchant for making up stories for ourselves causes us to live with the pain of old hurts. No matter how skilled we are at dealing with conflict, there will be people and events that wound us. Our own inner peace and our ability to live at peace with others depends on our willingness to let go of the past. If we do not, then the past captures both present and future.

STUDY QUESTIONS ON PEACEABLE OR CONTENTIOUS

1) On the continuum of conflict, where do you find yourself *most often*?
2) What is your most frequent source of irritation?
3) What would it take for you to be at peace?
4) What does it mean to you when you say that you are peaceful?
5) What is something that regularly interferes with your peacefulness?
6) What is one wish about other people that would make your life more peaceful?
7) What is one wish about yourself that would make your life more peaceful?
8) Is there someone whose mere presence makes you feel more peaceful?

EXPERIMENTING WITH PEACEABLE LIVING

Choose an action or write one of your own.

☐ I will notice each day the occasions when I feel in contention, strife, competition, or conflict with someone.

☑ I will make a list of the effects (physical, emotional, spiritual, etc.) that I feel when I am in situations where I am not at peace.

☐ I will choose a situation in which I am usually contentious and experiment with a more peaceable way of dealing with it.

☐ I will talk with someone whom I view as peaceable.

☐ I will choose to forgive someone for an old hurt.

OBSTACLES TO HAPPINESS

1) What makes it difficult for me to choose to live peaceably rather than contentiously?
2) Is the obstacle a
   ☐ Thought or belief ☐ Emotion ☐ Attitude ☐ Behavior
   ☐ Consequence/situation?
3) What would I have to do to make a different choice?

Cultures of Peace — Elise Boulding Boulding

SPIRITUAL OR PHYSICAL

Attending to Intangible Influences or
Heeding Only Physical Reality

Eventually every person feels the need for help from beyond the self. We reach some point where we know that we cannot make it on our own. Here are some indicators that we may be unwittingly trying to live strictly on our own power.

- Failure of any kind makes me feel very uneasy.
- I try to hide my failures from other people.
- I have been able to keep many of my mistakes secret from most people.
- I live by the rule that the best way to get something done right is to do it yourself.
- I am uneasy when I turn over important tasks to someone else.
- When people see me fail, I try to explain it away or blame someone else.
- I feel most comfortable with people who do not see me fail or make mistakes.
- I have not met many of my goals.
- I believe that the best way to have people like and respect me is to perform well.
- It is difficult for me to enjoy an activity unless I am winning.
- Meeting standards set by others is very important to me.
- I believe that many people succeed more easily than I do.
- I have been delaying several projects because I am not sure I can do them well enough.
- I live by the rule if you cannot do something right, do not do it at all.

When I was fifty, I figured I could do most things I could do when I was twenty, even if I could not do them quite as well or as quickly. When I reached sixty-three, aging intervened forcefully to change my life. Since then I live with limitations that require a change of my behavior and force me to revise the ways

I define myself. I live with indisputable proof that my power alone cannot do everything I need. The important question is: where can I find help?

HIGHER POWER

Many of us have experiences that convince us that there is reality beyond mere individual human beings. The hints are in events such as musical concerts, or live theater, or worship, or a walk along the seashore, or a celebration among intimate friends, or an honest conversation. We are going along, doing things that are natural and familiar. Then there is a shift of some kind, and we feel that we have reached a different plane of human experience. It does not matter what name we give it. The important thing is to acknowledge that in these moments we are profoundly affected by something beyond ourselves.

Where is the power that is other than and higher than us? Twelve step programs purposely make few statements about the exact nature of the higher power. That vagueness helps people avoid the inevitable squabbling over details of individual belief systems. Rather, we point to a general direction where many have found transforming power.

RELIGIOUS DISCIPLINES

Many people instinctively equate higher power with their view of God. Those who believe in God can find in sacred writings, traditions, and rituals a rich source of instruction about a wide range of practical matters. By using the tools provided by our traditions, by making an honest effort to make professed beliefs part of everyday life, we can be strengthened in difficult situations.

I saw this proved when I was a member of the clergy. In the churches where I was pastor, the basic tenets included regular Bible study, prayer and meditation, meeting with fellow Christians, sacrificial giving, and compassionate helpfulness. However, it was common knowledge that many church members did not regularly practice what they claimed were their basic beliefs. In fact, ignoring the basic disciplines was so widespread that it was often referred to in a joking manner.

In every church where I was pastor, I offered a program called "Ten Brave Christians."[52] Church members were invited to voluntarily join a small group whose members would follow basic disciplines absolutely for a period of thirty days.

1) Each morning devote the first thirty minutes to devotional time. In that session, study a prescribed Bible passage and write down what its meaning is for you (rather than what you think a scholar might say about it).

2) During the daily morning session, pray specifically for each member of the group.
3) Each day give at least one hour to doing a kind deed. If possible, do it anonymously. If not, then do it with as little fanfare as possible. In the next morning's devotional session, write down what it was and how it affected you.
4) Give one-tenth of your income to the church.
5) Meet with the group each week to talk about the effects of the disciplines on your life.

The program seems simple and not all that challenging. I learned several things from the experiment in walking the talk for thirty days.

• It had to be voluntary. I made one attempt to alter the process by recruiting people whom I thought should be in a group. It did not work. People who required persuasion did not show the commitment that made the experiment meaningful to them. They took shortcuts or ignored elements when they felt pressured by competing interests.
• For the most part, the organizational leaders of the churches did not choose to participate. I gradually realized that they had several reasons for not being part of the group. Many of them sought benefits from their chosen roles that had little to do with the kind of benefits from being in the group. Also, in a small intimate group, organizational status was not operative. Over the course of 25 years and multiple groups in four churches, I saw less than a dozen organizational leaders become part of the experiment.
• The unpredictable mix of people made the groups unique and lively. I can still see in my mind that first group that assembled in 1967. My first thought was, "Oh, no! This isn't going to work." In the ten people, there were three in their 60's, three teenagers, two in their 20's, and two in their late 30's. One of the teens was shy and diffident, one was generally viewed as being a bit of a know-it-all, and the other was a very popular cheerleader for the high school basketball team. One adult was a very bright schoolteacher, another was the local barber, one was an intelligent elderly unmarried woman, and two had little formal education. The group members seemed to have little connection with each other in either the church or community. Yet, their diversity became one of the greatest benefits. Over the course of years and multiple groups, I learned to trust people to make their differences part of their gift to each other.
• Though the groups usually stopped meeting regularly after the 30-day experiment, their relationships with each other remained profoundly different

from what they were prior to the group experience, and different from other relationships.

- Those who did not choose to participate, i.e. the vast majority of members, tended to view the experiment with something akin to suspicion. It seemed that the very existence of a group that was adhering to disciplines that the majority had agreed to label as dispensable was a bit threatening. I noticed that the organizational leaders especially tended either to offer excuses about their non-participation or to disparage the groups as being "radical."

- The people who completed the experiment tended to be more devoted to their church than before, though on a different level. They seemed to have a different level of knowingness as they participated in the traditional functions of the congregation. They seemed to know how to enrich without drawing credit to themselves.

- The experiment often triggered profound awareness. For example, a woman in her seventies had been a church leader all her adult life. As she aged, her leadership was sought less and less. She said, "I didn't realize until this group what Christianity was all about. I am so sorry I've wasted so many years." She was expressing what many others had, namely, that the benefits of congregational involvement are not the same as the benefits of following the basic disciplines of one's faith.

The basic practices in most religions provide ample opportunity for accessing power beyond ourselves. The only hurdle is willingness to walk the talk.

BASIC ASSUMPTION

The basic assumption of all religions is that we are more than our physical bodies. This truth is easily observed but difficult to explain. About the best that the brightest have been able to do is to describe the indicators of the something-more and the effects it has on a person's life. In spite of scientific ability to ana-lyze the physical body with microscopic precision, we are not much closer than ancient philosophers and theologians to understanding the something-more.

The Hebrew and Greek words that were later translated *spirit* referred to wind and breath. The mystery of the intangible forcefulness has not been eclipsed by modern understanding of how the brain operates. Empirically, we see that some-thing is at work that we can neither describe fully nor manipulate with certainty. Intuitively we know it is the most important part of us.

Religions have sought to define this aspect of our being. Each has its own terms and stories to explain this part of the self. They have all devised guide-lines that propose to get maximum benefits for the spirit part of us. For our purpose, we will let the readers decide which tradition seems to fit best with their own experience. We will look at some general patterns that have shown positive results when people applied them.

Furthermore, we will not get distracted by people who are casual adherents to their chosen tradition. Honesty compels us to admit that in all religions the majority of the adherents select the guidelines they follow according to their own convenience and the approval rating of the people whose opinions they value most. For casual disciples, the result is a community experience that may be quite positive in many ways. However, it is not necessarily an experience that involves the deeper aspects of the self.

We give our attention to that aspect in the individual that is something more than the world of our physical bodies. We will look for the effects of the intangible force that is felt and seen in all our lives, whether we have noticed or not.

PEAK EXPERIENCES

If we strip away all religious language and ask people about moments that are unique and powerful, every person can think of them. They are filled with wonder, awe, and excitement. In those moments, we feel different from the way we do most of the time. In those moments, we often have insights that cause us to reinterpret all that went before and rearrange everything that comes afterward.

A peak experience has some (but not necessarily all) of the following characteristics:

- Very strong or deep positive emotions akin to ecstasy
- A deep sense of peacefulness or tranquility
- Feeling in tune, in harmony, or at one with the universe
- Feeling a sense of unity and harmony with all people
- A feeling of deeper knowing or profound understanding
- A sense that it is a very special experience that would be difficult or impossible to describe adequately in words (i.e., ineffability)
- A resulting sense of purpose in life

These benefits are available when we cultivate this part of our lives until it becomes a habit. We can do things that will increase the frequency of the powerful moments. And even when we realize we cannot schedule them with anything approaching precision, we can preserve the positive effects of the break-through incidents.

Now for a more careful look at the experiences that nurture that part of us that we call spirit. In the course of our lives, we may have only a few times when we feel an experience so powerful that it affects the rest of life, but when those times occur, we usually remember them forever. Though the specifics differ greatly, peak experiences have a great deal in common.[53]

1.   They have a unifying effect, causing us to feel that all the conflicts of the inner self have been dispelled, and giving a feeling of complete harmony with the entire universe. Here is a personal testimony:

> I stood alone with Him who had made me, and all the beauty of the world, and love, and sorrow, and even temptation. I did not seek Him, but felt the perfect unison of my spirit with His....It was like the effect of some great orchestra when all the separate notes have melted into one swelling harmony that leaves the listener conscious of nothing save that his soul is being wafted upwards, and almost bursting with its own emotion.[54]

The eloquence of this description may surpass the way we have described our experiences, but the core of the unifying feeling is the same. This is the peacefulness that sometimes comes to us when we are immersed in the sounds of chants or music, or when we float on a quiet stream, or gaze at a colorful sky, or watch the face of a sleeping child, or when we are part of a group of people who are all focused on the same kind of thoughts and feelings. Sometimes the ordinary is suddenly expanded until we know things by feeling them rather than by learning them. At such times, the self feels integrated, whole, at peace. And the self feels at one with the world and its people. In these moments it is easy to love and forgive because the boundaries between people seem to merge.

This kind of experience has special advantages for mature adults. The older we get, the more experience we have in being marginalized. It's a bit like the experience we had as children playing on a school yard merry-go-round. The bigger kids would push the merry-go-round faster and faster, and the little kids would spin off onto the ground.

Being forcibly moved to the margins of others' agendas is no game. So, any experience that gives us a feeling of being at the center of significance, of being an integral part of the whole is a healing experience. It counteracts the feeling that we are sliding to the edges of everything that is important.

2. Peak experiences cause us to perceive knowledge, insight, awareness, revelation, and illumination that are beyond the grasp of the intellect. First-person accounts:

Clarifying →

The more I seek words to express this experience, the more I feel the impossibility of describing the thing by any of our usual images.[55]

…..

There came upon me a sense of exultation, of immense joyousness accompanied or immediately followed by an intellectual illumination impossible to describe.[56]

The older we get, the more often we are viewed as having out-lived our intellectual competence. Many of the technologies and gadgets that younger generations consider mainstream are only recent footnotes in our lives. If we are smart, we avoid reminding everyone just how long we lived without all the things they consider routine necessities. But even then, we can begin to question our own ability to keep up mentally.

Spiritual experiences can reaffirm our capacity to see life aright and live it with good judgment. In the center of peak experiences we are reminded to trust the values that have been refined through decades of experiences. If a spiritual experience does not fit neatly into a comprehensive system, the power of the experience trumps logic. A person is likely to modify a belief system rather than discount the reality of the experience. However, we should ***not*** expect other people to necessarily accept our epiphanies as solid evidence. Rather, we accept them as gifts and count ourselves fortunate.

3. Peak experiences can be turning points for us. Another first-person account:

The vision lasted a few seconds and was gone; but the memory of it and the sense of the reality of what it taught has remained during the quarter of a century which as since elapsed.[57]

We know that life has profound meaning because of the new understanding. When the mundane washes over us, we call on the memory of that original experience to sustain us.

We see life not just as a succession of days, but as a pilgrimage that has meaning. We feel the need for answers to crucial issues about life and existence. And so we return to the profound insight of those moments that revealed truth that we have verified with our experiences.

Often the most profound spiritual growth occurs in our mature years. The turning points may not be visible to anyone watching us, but we know the difference it makes when we have a shift in the inner terrain. The shift may come when something happens in the outside world to change the flow of our daily lives. Or it may come because of a sudden awareness that seems to have no significant triggering event. It is as if all the pieces finally fit together in a way that we can see the full picture. What we know for sure is that everything is different from that point onward.

4. Peak experiences tend to be fairly brief, though they often feel as if they are lasting much longer than the actual time. Most last a few seconds, some perhaps up to ten minutes. It is rare to sustain a mystical state for more than a half-hour, or perhaps one to two hours at the longest.

> Then, slowly, the ecstasy left my heart; that is, I felt that God had withdrawn the communion which he had granted, and I was able to walk on, but very slowly, so strongly was I still possessed by the interior emotion. Besides, I had wept uninterruptedly for several minutes, my eyes were swollen, and I did not wish my companions to see me. The state of ecstasy may have lasted four or five minutes, although it seemed at the time to last much longer.[58]

When these moments come in the midst of public worship, they seem fitting. They may also come as unexpected interruptions of ordinary activities, such as when we are walking through a wooded area, or sitting beside a stream, or listening to the surf. Then their importance may be difficult to sustain when we go back to daily routines.

Quick significance adds to life's excitement. We sometimes feel intimidated by projects that require sustained, intense effort. Knowing that enlivening experiences can be brief is good news.

5. When people have mystical experiences, they usually say that they cannot put into words what has happened. That means that every experience is beyond even the most eloquent description.

> I feel that in writing of it I have overlaid it with words rather than put it clearly to your thought. But as it is, I have described it as carefully as I am now able to do.[59]

Trying to explain a religious experience is like trying to convey what music sounds like to someone who has never heard it. The mystical experience is a subjective state, and all efforts to define and describe will be only faint representations of the real thing. And because the experience is so different from the everyday states of consciousness, our efforts to come up with the eloquence to do them justice may illicit disbelief in the uninitiated.

One of the more aggravating effects of aging is loss of speech fluency. As we age, we are at higher risk for medical problems that may affect speech, such as stroke or early onset Alzheimer's disease. Even if we do not have a specific disease, the aging process tends to decrease the speed at which we find the words we want to use to express our thoughts.[60] Being aware of our decreased fluency can be frustrating if not downright embarrassing.

It is comforting to know that our spiritual experiences are not limited to verbal descriptions. We can find reassurance in knowing that inner awareness will always exceed our expressive abilities, no matter what our age or intelligence. So, we can relax in knowing fluency is not an issue in spiritual growth.

6. In the most powerful experiences, we feel as if something is acting that is beyond our own wills.

> I stood alone with Him who had made me, and all the beauty of the world, and love, and sorrow, and even temptation. I did not seek Him, but felt the perfect unison of my spirit with His. The ordinary sense of things around me faded. For the moment nothing but an ineffable joy and exaltation remained.[61]

We may do the things that have been advised as preparation for mystical experiences, but when they occur, we do not feel as if it is self-generated. A part of the authority of the experience is the conviction that we are acted upon.

This brief summary of the most profound religious experiences is a reminder that there is a spiritual dimension to every person, and this aspect can be a powerful source of joy. As we reach the stage of life when our bodies begin to betray us, it is important to have access to that which is beyond the physical realm. The spiritual realm is an unmatched source of joy.

INSTITUTIONALIZED RELIGION

Although all religion begins with experience, it continues on the reported memory of that initial experience. And here is where the path always gets confusing. Those who heard from the people who first had the experience were one step away from the joy. They were being coached on how they could find the joy for themselves. Understandably, some of them thought that the secret was in the details, so they took great care to follow the patterns they saw in the reporters of ecstasy. They hoped that thinking and doing the right things would guarantee the joyful experience. Thus, the birth of religion.

At some point most of us learn that orthodoxy (believing and doing the correct things) is not synonymous with joy. Some people who have been perfect in belief and conscientious in behavior also find experiences that give a genuine sense of joy. Others have believed and done right, but still feel a pervasive sense of uneasiness and turmoil. Still others who have been just as tidy in the externals turn out to be mean, persnickety, and just plain unpleasant to be around. We may feel sympathy for these folks, but we should not view them as good examples of religion, anymore than we would consider spam to exemplify fine dining.

The danger inherent in any organized religion is that it can become the goal in itself rather than being a means to a higher goal. All great spiritual leaders have addressed this human tendency, but it remains. All religion begins as a way of achieving joy. In our eagerness to have it ourselves, we copy the events we know about, hoping the ecstasy is in the details. But what worked once may not work exactly the same way for every person. Nevertheless, the events are forged into rituals. The rituals become familiar and routine, and they give a certain kind of satisfaction in being dutiful. But this is not the same as joy. Beware of joyless religionists. In their frustration, they thresh about and do great harm to themselves and many around them.

The most subtle danger in organized religion is that it suggests that by our behavior we can control the Higher Power. We are taught to pray, and for many people prayer is making a list of our concerns, making these known to God, telling God what we want done, and then focusing our intention so strongly that God will respond to our wishes.

For many religious people, the same controlling desire is the motivating factor behind righteous living. The idea is that doing good somehow obligates God to do what we want and to treat us better than the people who are bad. In the final analysis, we can say that organized religion sometimes works to bring joy, but often disappoints.

BEYOND RELIGION

All of my life I have heard people say, "If you have your health, you have everything." Even as a child, as I listened to the chorus of agreement, it seemed to me that there was a note in the midst that was slightly off key. I remember standing very still and listening with my mind, but the faint message was always just beyond my conscious understanding. Now I realize that the faint discordant note was about the difference in body and spirit, about external freedom and internal freedom. The popular adage is wrong.

We can gain external freedom and still not be free internally. We all know people who have many external reasons to be contented, and yet they are bored, or lonely, or irritable, or restless, or discontented. In fact, we may have noticed this dissonance even in ourselves. And when we do, we can be sure it is a spiritual issue. In spite of fair weather on the outside, we feel unsettling sensations from the depths of ourselves, so subtle that we may be able to deny their existence much of the time.

Furthermore, we can gain internal freedom in spite of external limitations, and that includes the burden of bad health or unpleasant circumstances. I have known people who were conscripted into life-long struggle against terrible disease or disability, and some of them say that the battle has given them some qualities and wisdom that they would not want to do without, even if it meant having an easier time. It is frequently surprising at where the human spirit thrives and where it languishes.

There is a reason why twelve step groups use the term "Higher Power" rather than more specific names: each person's spiritual pilgrimage is unique. We should expect to find one person with our exact same fingerprints, voice print, and DNA before we find someone whose spiritual path has been exactly the same. We crave community with people who have similar appreciations, and that is fitting. This is the foundation of the power in twelve step groups that are organized around common experiences. However, as uplifting as the group experience can be, there are aspects of our journey that must be faced alone.

In the Bible, the private aspect of spirituality was often connected to locations that suggested isolation. The oldest stories point toward the mountains as places where one would make a solitary pilgrimage to have experiences that would change the person forever. The desert, away from routine living, was often the setting for experiences where people found new spiritual insight and new direction. And the Biblical location that was picked up and carried over into intensely emotional songs of ordinary people was the valley. All of these images made people think about the necessary isolation that is part of any authentic spiritual pilgrimage.

> And He said, Go out and stand on the mount before the Lord. And behold, the Lord passed by, and a great and strong wind rent the mountains and broke in pieces the rocks before the Lord, but the Lord was not in the wind; and after the wind an earthquake, but the Lord was not in the earthquake; and after the earthquake a fire, but the Lord was not in the fire; and after the fire [a sound of gentle stillness and] a still, small voice. *(1 Kings 19:11-12, Amplified Bible)*

The metaphor of a "still, small voice," or perhaps even better, "a voice in the stillness," refers to those moments when we feel that we have been visited by something beyond ourselves. This kind of revelation happens only when we draw aside from the constant stimulation of the environment and the cacophony of human voices. We step out of the busy parade in order to pray and meditate.

PRAYER

Prayer is calling forth our best thoughts and feelings, and in expressing them, silently or verbally, we are invigorated and soothed. Prayer is much like playing familiar inspirational music, but with the more profound effect of engaging the whole mind as well as the emotions.

Some prayers are simple to say, and yet gather up myriad connotations and applications. One example is the so-called serenity prayer that is used in many twelve step meetings.

> God, grant me the serenity
> To accept the things I cannot change,
> The courage to change the things I can,
> And wisdom to know the difference.

The elegance of the prayer is that it speaks with equal power to all levels of experience and intelligence. Each recitation of the prayer can mean something different, so that we are captured my different words or phrases according to what is happening to us right now. The prayer flows into us and takes on the form of our unique existence. It means something to everyone, but never exactly the same to any two people.

I have had people tell me about being in the most desperate situations imaginable – buffeted by the consequences of their own foolishness, feeling their will to survive slipping away, fearing that they would not be able to endure the hardships of a future that appeared as a bottomless abyss – and they said they kept going by reciting the serenity prayer. In those moments, the self is open to a Power that is beyond. And that contact, however unprovable and inexpressible, is necessary to finding our way.

Prayer is the moment when we gather all that we are and invite the Higher Power to participate in our existence. Therefore, we do well to make it a private matter. Otherwise, the verbalizations become bits of role-play for the benefit of spectators. In that case, we not only miss making real contact with the Higher Power, but we also drift into the silliness of informing the Higher Power about current events and advocating for projects that the gathered audience values most highly, which suggests that the Higher Power is unable to set priorities without human intervention.

Jesus, as many spiritual leaders before and after him, advised that public prayer created a temptation to show off, and that authentic prayer is a transaction between a humble person and the Higher Power. In the same conversation, he gave an outline for prayer that generations have used to great benefit. Here again, notice the simplicity that can apply to all kinds of people.

> Our Father who art in heaven,
> Hallowed be Thy name.
> Thy kingdom come.
> Thy will be done
> On earth as it is in heaven.
> Give us this day our daily bread.
> And forgive us our debts,
> As we forgive our debtors.
> And lead us not into temptation,
> But deliver us from evil.
> For thine is the kingdom and the power and the glory forever. Amen.
>
> *Matthew 6:9-13, King James Version*

If recited as mere thoughtless verbal ritual, the words have little power to connect us with anything more than nostalgic feelings about simpler times. However, when spoken with the full focus of our best attention, the words become a prayer that connects us to Power beyond ourselves. **Prayer is the mindful focus of our best attention on the important issues of life.**

One of the benefits of aging is that we learn to sift through what is unnecessary and get down to what is worthwhile. This applies to people, activities, and even spiritual matters. The act of simple prayer makes sense to us because we are facing ultimate issues. We tend to feel that empty, showy wordiness is a waste. It is time to be genuine.

"Communication w/ Higher power — Gathering best thoughts & lifting them to a power beyond myself."

MEDITATION

Meditation is the second tool recommended for gaining direction from the Higher Power. In many ways, it is the flip side of prayer. Where prayer requires concerted thoughtfulness, meditation is the skill of settling into **a state of mind where our coherent thoughts are not the main focus of attention**. It can be compared to those times when we are in the midst of a crowd and get sleepy. We can still hear everything, but the voices and the words fade into the background as we slide into a state of relaxation.

Entering the Stillness

So it is in meditation. We can never completely still the flow of our internal dialogue, and as long as we are conscious we are aware to some degree of what is going on around us. Yet, we can purposely let our minds drift into a kind of consciousness that is different from the one we use to deal with the daily business of living, or even that of considering what we want to say in prayer.

I am somewhat embarrassed to admit that I did not know about meditation until I was middle-aged. Like many sincere Christians in mainstream denominations, I thought that meditation was a quieter form of prayer in which I would concentrate steadily on a thought or situation for an extended period of time. I equated mediation with contemplation. It is quite different. Contemplation calls for focused, intense concentration. Meditation is welcoming stillness of the mind.

Finding a New Way

The person who opened my understanding was Bill Rodenhiser, who was at the time I knew him a respected teacher in the religion department at the University of Richmond. He had spent extended times in India studying the beliefs and practices of various groups that followed highly esteemed teachers called gurus. As we discussed the vital place of meditation in their spiritual growth, I realized I could not identify with what he was telling me. He suggested that I might be interested in exploring the altered state of consciousness in mediation, and he told me that the Monroe Institute, near Charlottesville, Virginia, had produced cassette tapes that some had found helpful in learning about meditation. I bought a set of the audio cassette tapes and tried them.

I soon discovered that the sounds and vocal guidance on the tapes moved me into a different state of consciousness. It reminded me of the way I felt when I was between sleep and wakefulness, either just before going to sleep or just before coming fully awake. Yet, it was not a fleeting state of mind, and once I discovered it, I learned that I could sustain it for extended periods of time. I compared it to learning to ride a bicycle; once the feeling of balance is learned, we know it from then on. Once the meditative state was discovered, I found that I could return to it quickly and easily.

Each of the Monroe Institute tapes lasted about twenty-five minutes, so I began to allot time for this experiment. The instructions included finding a thirty-minute period of time when I would not be interrupted, in a place quiet enough that sounds from the environment would not trigger distractions in thought. Obviously, I had to be out of ear-shot of telephones, car horns, and loud music.

I soon came to view these intervals as very important. I found myself settling into the altered state of consciousness more quickly and easily, and it seemed that with practice I felt more stable in that external noises did not jolt me out of the meditative state. My balance was improving.

Surprising Benefits

To some this may sound like mere relaxation. Indeed, it is a very relaxed state mentally and physically, and that by itself was worth the effort and time. However, I began to notice other effects. I became convinced that the meditative sessions were improving the way my mind worked. I felt as if my brain had more power, though I could not say why or how that would be true. Also, it seemed that my brain was less cluttered, and this helped as I was trying to solve problems or just express myself.

I also noticed a positive effect on my emotions. It took more to get me into an irritable mood, and I seemed more able to step back from situations and view them from a distance. I later learned that the concept of detachment is actually about the skill of letting go of a desired outcome long enough to see things in a different light. In this context, detachment does not mean lack of caring or concern; it means not being restricted by a specific expectation.

For example, parents may be so desirous of comfortable happiness for our children that we find it impossible to consent to their doing anything that we think is unwise. In this case, detachment would help us step back far enough to see our maturing children as people who will shape their lives, either with us or against us. Rather than being in tense opposition to them because they are not following our vision of their lives, we can learn to see them as unfolding dramas that they are writing themselves.

Just as my meditative state seemed more stable with practice, my emotions seemed more stable and less at the mercy of surrounding events and people. It was as if my visits to a deeper part of myself were having permanent effect even when I was in my ordinary state of mind.

One final effect: I noticed changes in my thinking. I give one example of a profoundly personal nature. During the course of my years in the ministry, I gradually came to realize that I had spent a major portion of my life trying to fix myself. As I sought newer methods and improved skills in being a minister, there was always a sense of not having found my place. I was quick to absorb any evidence that suggested I was deficient in my overall development, either as a minister or as a person. It was hard for me to celebrate others' achievements because I tended to see their success as a judgment on my lack of performance. I was on a restless journey without a known destination. However, I did not know this until something happened.

New Perspective

After I had been meditating for several months, a thought surged into my consciousness: "You do not need to be fixed. There is nothing wrong with you." If it had been only once, I might have discounted it, but it came to me repeatedly in the exact same form. Each time, the thought was addressing me, rather than my having the thought and saying, "*I* don't need to be fixed." Any other time, given my trust in psychological dynamics, I would have tried to analyze a new thought, asking, "Where did *that* come from." Not so in this case. The thought was as authoritative as it was surprising. The new thought began to take root. It was not that I started thinking of myself as perfect, but rather that I began to doubt that there was some serious flaw that needed to be repaired.

This may not sound like a big deal. To me, it was. In fact, I realized it was the central issue of my existence. Though I had not been conscious of it until the thought came into my mind full-formed, I then realized this had been a basis assumption for my entire life. I had been on a pilgrimage to find out what was wrong and correct it. But now I came to consider a new viewpoint: I did not need to be fixed; there was nothing wrong with me.

Meditation is frequently the avenue for new understanding about self, the world, people, in fact, everything. As we plan for a state of mind that is relaxed and open, we often become aware of perspectives that are quite different from what we work out on our own. Small wonder, then, that meditation is part of the advice for finding contact with the Higher Power.

Unlikely mystics

My confidence in meditation grew when I worked in addiction treatment centers in Northern California. As a new counselor in a residential treatment center, I was interested to see that the program agenda listed "Meditation" as a session that was scheduled on weekends for all the forty-five residents. When I asked about it, I was told that whoever was on duty usually read a copy of a relaxation exercise that someone had found somewhere, but that it didn't seem to have much effect that anyone could see. No one seemed to know how it got started.

I attended one of the sessions to see what was happening. The forty-five residents were sprawled around on the floor, some of them leaning up against the walls and others lying flat. The counselor assigned to lead the class read the exercise in a gruff voice, often interrupting himself to growl at various residents who were either not paying attention or dozing off to sleep. Everyone, including the counselor, seemed relieved with the twenty-minute session was over.

I asked if I could lead next week's session, and I was immediately given the assignment that no one else really wanted. I decided to replicate as much of the Monroe Institute experience as I could. I recorded sounds of a surf on a cassette tape and found a player that had stereo speakers that could be placed at opposite sides of the room. I already knew the verbal guidance into a relaxed state, having listened to it countless times in my own meditation. I arranged with other staff members that the session would not be interrupted once we started the session.

It is useful to mention that this group of forty-five men was quite diverse. At least half of them had done time in prison, many of them for violent crimes such as armed robbery and aggravated assault. Several of the men had been in gangs and admitted that they had killed more than once. Some of them had come to our facility near death, either from exposure from homelessness or because of AIDS. Many of them looked skeletal upon arrival. Most of them had been referred by a court or they would never have come.

When the men gathered, they did not suspect that this session would be different from the previous ones. I first told them that meditation is an altered state of consciousness, and some of them wanted to know if it was anything like a drug high. After the laughter died down, I told them that some of the same things are happening in the brain, but there are no bad effects from meditating, they are never out of control of the experience, and it doesn't cost anything. I had their attention.

I then told them some benefits of learning how to meditate. For example, for those who were having trouble sleeping, this would be an effective way of getting relaxed enough to drift off to sleep. That applied to several of them, and they were immediately interested, because some of them paced the halls all night long, exhausted but unable to sleep. I told them this is something they could learn to do on their own.

I also said that it was an effective way of reducing the physical tension that came with the stress of multiple life changes they were going through. I emphasized that we would be using these sessions as training, and then they could use this approach any time they wanted. So, with the idea that it might help them with everyday life, they were ready to give it a try.

They sat straight up in chairs with their hands lying palms down on their thighs. The straight posture is important in relaxation and it also makes sleeping less likely. With the lights out, the late afternoon shadows made the room dimly lit. I turned on the cassette player and let the sounds of the surf fill the room. One of Robert Monroe's theories was that ocean surf somehow correlates with the internal rhythms of all humans, and that is why we are soothed and calmed by it.

One Format for Meditation

Here is a close representation of the exercise I used in that first session and all the ones that followed. I spoke in a quiet, relaxed voice. After each complete statement, represented in the following paragraphs, I paused for two or three seconds.

Feel your eyes close as you listen to the sounds of the ocean waves. Let your body feel the sound washing through you.

Feel your body be straight and tall as you sit in your chair. Imagine that your head is held up by a cord attached to a giant balloon floating over you.

Let your hands lie on your legs, hands down. Let your feet be flat on the floor. Listen to the soothing sound of the ocean waves.

Feel the relaxation begin with the soles of your feet. Feel your feet sink into the floor. Feel the bones and muscles grow soft in your feet, as if they are turning to water.

Feel the relaxation move up into your ankles. Feel your ankles become loose and relaxed.

Feel the relaxation move up into your legs. Feel your calf muscles loosen and droop.

Feel the relaxation move up into your knees. Feel the muscles all around your knees loosen and relax.

Feel the relaxation move up into your thighs. Feel your thighs sink into chair.

Feel the relaxation move up into your pelvis. Feel your entire pelvis relax and sink into the chair.

Feel the relaxation move up into the large muscles of your back. Feel those muscles turn loose.

Feel the relaxation move into your abdomen. Feel all your internal organs lying comfortably and easily inside you.

Feel the relaxation move up into your chest. Feel your breathing become easy and relaxed.

Feel the relaxation move up into your shoulders. Feel your shoulders droop and sink.

Feel the relaxation move up into your neck. Feel your throat open and relaxed.

Feel the relaxation move up into your jaw. Feel your jaw drop and relax. Feel your tongue lying heavy inside your mouth.

Feel the relaxation move up around your eyes. Feel your eyes sink into your head. Feel your eyelids become heavy.

Feel the relaxation move up your forehead. Feel the tension leave as your brow smoothes and relaxes.

Feel the relaxation move onto your scalp. Feel the tingle as your scalp relaxes. Relax and listen to the sound of the waves.

If at any point someone showed signs of being asleep, I quietly moved to him, without interrupting my guidance, and touched him gently on the shoulder. If someone had his eyes open, I quietly moved to him, without interrupting my guidance, and moved my hand down over my own eyes, closing my own eyes. If when I opened my eyes he was still looking at me, I smiled, nodded, and repeated the movement over my own eyes.

Imagine that you can see your breath. See your breath as it comes in your right nostril and goes out your left nostril.

As you watch your breath coming in your right nostril, count "one." As it goes out your left nostril, count "two." Watch your breath and count.

Listen to the waves, watch your breath, and count.

See in your mind a safe place. This can be anywhere that your mind chooses: at the seashore, in the mountains, on the plains, in the forest, in a town or city, high in the air....anywhere that your mind chooses. See this place in your mind.

See yourself in this safe place that your mind has chosen. See yourself relaxed and safe.

See yourself walking, looking all about you. Feel the joy of being in your safe place.

As you walk, begin to go faster, until you feel yourself lifting off the ground. As you lift off the ground, look down and see yourself rising higher and higher. Feel the joy of soaring and feeling safe.

As you fly through the air, you are moving ahead in time.

You are now in your own future, soaring above where you will someday be.

Look down and see where you live. See how safe it is, how beautiful to the eye.

See yourself moving among people who love you. See them smile when you come near them.

See yourself strong and happy. See yourself doing things that give you joy. (long pause)

Watch yourself and feel the joy of being safe, of being loved, of being happy. (long pause)

Now I want you to prepare to leave this place and return to the present. As you do, know that you will return, so there is no pain of leaving and no fear of never seeing this place again. It is your place.

You are now flying again, soaring back toward the present. Look down and see the earth passing beneath you.

You are getting nearer the ground and you can see the place that was your entry point, the safe place that was chosen by your mind.

As you touch down, look around you and feel the joy of being safe.

Before you leave, I want you to find a place where you can write a word that you can see in your mind. It can be on a stone, or in the sand, or on a tree...anywhere that you can write a word than only you will know and only you can see.

Let your mind give you a word that will be your signal to come back to this place, where you will see the word written clear every time. It is a word that you will speak in your mind when you are relaxed, and it will bring you back to your safe place.

Let the word appear before you. See it clearly. Write it in a place that you choose.

We will now return to the state of mind that we use to deal with everyday life in the present. As I count backward from ten, you will feel your body gradually become more alert. When I reach the number "one," you will open your eyes and feel rested and alert.

Ten.....Nine.....Eight...You feel your body getting more alert .... Seven.... Six.... Five.... Your body is even more alert... Four .... Three ... Your body is almost fully alert ... Two .... One

You are now fully alert. Open your eyes.

Initially I was surprised that most could enter a meditative state during their first session. Even though they all had chaotic pasts, it was actually rare to find someone who could not achieve the relaxed state and envision what was suggested in the guidance. I came to view meditation as something quite natural for all people, somewhat like floating in water. In both cases, prior inexperience was quickly overcome with a bit of guidance.

Some used meditation to overcome sleeplessness; others, to reduce tension; others, as an aide to prayer. People found benefits even if they only used meditation occasionally, though regularity seemed to offer the best effects. Also, it did not require a lot of time; even 10-15 minutes at a time provided noticeable good effects.

JOY

Through the exploration of our own spiritual journeys, we find our own joy. We may be tempted to think that joy comes mostly as an uncontrollable surprise. For example, you meet a person that makes love seem natural and easy, and feel that your paths crossed by sheer good luck. Or you gaze at a child that is born healthy, and you realize that good fortune is not linked to anything that we can control.

While it is certainly true that joy often comes as an unearned blessing, it is also true that the collective human experience shows that we have the best chance of finding joy when we make a habit of living as spiritual beings.

DEVELOPING THE HABIT OF SPIRITUAL LIVING

The first step is identifying the experiences that trigger awareness that we are spiritual beings. The following list is not exhaustive and the order of strength would vary with individuals.

1) Inspirational writings

   When we read, we are being creative. Our minds create images that are unique to us. For example, have a conversation with friends who have read the same novel, and ask them to describe in detail the physical appearance of the characters. The difference in the way we see the characters is one of the reasons why movies about favorite novels are nearly always disappointing. Other peoples' images are not as good as ours, or so we usually think.

   Thus, it is important that we make a habit of letting inspirational words enliven our imaginations. Talking about the belief that the Bible is the Word of God does not have the same effect as sitting quietly and absorbing the impact that chosen passages have on us. Asserting that we value a chosen book as holy is merely a way of proclaiming our membership in some group. But reading the book with concentration opens the mind to insight that can revise attitudes and behavior.

New Sources

Inspiration is not limited to ancient books. While we may claim that certain books have a higher level of authority, there are still many other books that engage us in ways that are uniquely powerful. Sometimes it is because the author shares common experience. Sometimes it is because the author opens a line of thought that we had not previously considered. The important thing is to develop the habit of letting our minds be bombarded by the power of profound and wise thoughts.

I can still remember how, as an adult, I began to read some of the writings of the patriots who helped create our nation. First I was struck by the eloquence, and then by the depth of thought given to issues that I had scarcely considered. We may have grown beyond those early Americans in some ways, but their writings still have the power to quicken and expand the mind.

Inspirational writings stir the part of us that is beyond the routine concerns of everyday life. They remind us that we are more than mere physical bodies that are involved in economics, politics, and family matters. As we read, we commune with aspects of ourselves and others that transcend the physical world. And in those moments we know that we are spiritual beings.

2) Music

When we go to movies, the musical background often influences the way we experience the visual scenes. Wouldn't it be helpful to have appropriate music to accompany everyday life? In fact, that is up to us. The music we choose sets the tone of our experiences. That's why special holidays are so powerful to us: the music. Music does things to our brains that cause us to relive portions of our lives that we want to retain.

I recently received an email that contained a link to a website that plays whatever music we want to hear. www.theradio.com As I typed in my requests, the sounds of the past reactivated memories and feelings. I felt more fully alive.

Music is an important tool in staying in touch with the spiritual side of ourselves. Music that we associate with spiritual experiences can move us into remembrances that have new power. The words in hymns and songs carry extra meaning because they are enclosed by music that touches us in ways we cannot explain. Sometimes the music transcends the words, and other times it is the words themselves that move us into a mood of reverence.

3) People

Some of the people who inspire us are widely known; others are not. When we are in their audience, either in person, on film or television, we feel a special connection to the truths toward which they point. We want to believe that inspirational people have a higher level of goodness, but that may or may not be true. It is enough to say that something about them triggers the spiritual aspect in us. The important thing is not their virtue, but rather that somehow they are catalysts for heightened awareness of our own spiritual being.

Twice I saw Mahalia Jackson in person; in Owensboro in 1958 and in Louisville in 1962. At the Owensboro concert, I made sure I was there early enough to get a seat near the stage. As she sang, her voice was like a mighty force that no radio or television of that era could capture. Even more gripping was her personal presence. With each song, she seemed to enter some special realm that only she could perceive, and at times it seemed that she was scarcely aware that we were even there. Between the songs, and she sang for two hours, she looked at us shyly, and spoke to us quietly. And then she would start another song and again enter what was clearly to her a spiritual dimension.

By the time she came to Louisville, she had become much more famous. Again I made sure I got there early enough to find a seat near the stage. I wanted to see up close any sign that her growing popularity has affected her attitude or behavior. It had not. She was still the humble person whose singing was not really a performance so much as an immediate spiritual experience for her and anyone who was willing to go with her. She moved from rollicking joyfulness in "Keep A'Movin'" to intervals when she merely hummed liked a mother's lullaby in "God is So Good."

I was not the only one captivated by the experience. As I looked around me during the performance, and afterward as people tried to speak a word of gratitude to her for her gift, I saw all kinds and ages of people whose faces were wet with tears. One of my seminary classmates, a young Southern white woman, managed to get close enough to speak to Mahalia. With an air of respectful admiration, she said, "You do us so much good. Thank you. Keep on doing what you do."

Mahalia smiled ruefully and shook her head, "Oh, honey, I'm so tired I can't hardly turn around." She continued to inspire people for eight more years, until she died at age 61 of heart failure.

Quiet Greatness

A very un-famous person who left an indelible mark on my life was Butch Smith. He was a deacon in a modest-sized church in a small town on the Green River in western Kentucky. On weekdays during the school year, he drove a school bus in the mornings and afternoons. On Sunday mornings, he was often one of the ushers who walked down the aisle to pick up the offering plates and distribute them to the congregation.

As the new pastor, it was my function to ask one of the ushers, lined up shoulder-to-shoulder with their backs to the congregation, to say a prayer before the offering was taken. I had called on the men whom I had seen doing leadership actions in the church and community, and they performed the ritual prayer with confidence.

One Sunday, on an impulse, I called on the slender middle-aged man whom I had not heard say anything in public, who usually stood inconspicuously at the end of the row. He exhibited friendliness of the quiet kind, relaxed and pleasant in expression, but not saying much.

"Butch, would you lead our prayer?" Everyone closed their eyes. A few seconds passed; no words spoken. I thought perhaps he hadn't heard me, so

I repeated my request in a low tone. He nodded, and I closed my eyes again. Still no sound. I then worried that I had made mistake in calling on someone who was uncomfortable with the public ritual, and I looked at him and was ready to call on someone else.

Butch began to speak, as if he had been gathering himself. He sounded different from what I was expecting. He did not speak loudly, and my first thought was that people in the back of the church would not be able to hear him. His voice did not have the usual tone of most public prayers. He spoke in a subdued, intense manner that reminded me of the way we speak with a revered teacher or favored elder relative.

The room grew quieter, with none of the rustling that is the background noise of most worship activities. It seemed that everyone paused at the same moment. Or, as I have wondered since, was it only my own perceptions that had narrowed and shut out everything else?

He spoke with a simple eloquence that conveyed a concentration I had never seen in this context. He did not speak long, and there was none of the triteness that typifies so much ritual public prayer. When he concluded and the ushers scattered to distribute the offering plates, it was as if the normal level of awareness and action resumed.

I made a habit of dropping by to chat with Butch. We sat on his porch and talked about various topics. When I departed, I always felt as if I had been given something that I needed. I had the distinct impression that I was somehow strengthened by his gentle wisdom and benevolent spirit. He was not known as a leader in the community, and I do not know if others were as affected by him as I was. I only know that there was in him the capacity to trigger my best spiritual instincts and awareness.

Even as I write these two accounts more than forty years later, I can still feel the emotional impact that came from being near these two people. And when I pause to think of their presence and their actions, I am newly strengthened.

4) Actions

It is no accident that we see more acts of kindness during periods of religious significance. We have learned that doing kindness not only benefits the recipients, but also the givers. We feel a more intense connection with the spiritual aspects in us when we are acting nobly. So, if we want to move into spiritual awareness, one strategy is to act with kindness.

If kindness is indeed a catalyst as well as a side effect of spirituality, then we may rightly suppose that some familiar passages in scriptures have layered meanings. For example, when Jesus of Nazareth was teaching his disciples, he told a parable in which the standard for God's favor was kindness to powerless people. If we consider our own experience, we might well suppose that the acts of kindness may have caused spiritual awakening as well as being a result of spiritual maturity. (See Matthew 25)

5) Places

Most primitive groups have some kind of belief about holy places. They define them quite differently, but they have in common the belief that being in certain places increases the frequency and intensity of spiritual experiences.

For some, it is may be a mountain. For some, it may be near the sight and sound of the sea. For others, it may be inside buildings of rare architectural character and beauty. In many of these sacred places, there is a sense of connection with people who have preceded us there, and that adds to the sense of awe.

STUDY QUESTIONS ON SPIRITUAL OR PHYSICAL

1) What makes you believe that you are more than just your physical body?
2) When do you feel that you are more than and greater than your physical body?
3) What benefits come as a result of this belief?
4) What behaviors tend to move you toward spiritual awareness?
5) What can you do to keep this part of yourself strong and active?

EXPERIMENTING WITH SPIRITUAL LIVING

Choose an action or write one of your own.

☐ I will make a list of experiences that I consider important spiritual moments in my life.

☐ I will make a list of the spiritual practices that I consider important.

☐ I will faithfully observe all my list of spiritual practices for 30 days.

☒ I will talk at least once a week with people whom I consider to be spiritually mature.

☐ I will sit alone in silence for 30 minutes in the morning and 30 minutes in the evening for a period of two weeks.

☐ I will learn to meditate.

☐ I will meditate for 15 minutes in the morning and 15 minutes in the evening for 30 days.

OBSTACLES TO HAPPINESS

1) What makes it difficult for me to choose to live spiritually and not just physically?
2) Is the obstacle a
   ☐ Thought or belief   ☐ Emotion   ☐ Attitude   ☐ Behavior
   ☐ Consequence/situation?
3) What would I have to do to make a different choice?

HELPFUL OR SELF-ABSORBED

Helping Others or Obsessed by Own Needs

We know instinctively that there is something noble about being helpful. We speak of the military as "the Armed Service" because we revere the bravery and self-sacrifice embodied in people who "serve our country."

We listen as would-be leaders seek to convince us that they are not seeking power for its accompanying personal benefits, but rather in order to serve. And if we discern that personal ambition is primary over authentic willingness to serve, we are usually less inclined to support the candidate. It's not that we do not understand or even admire ambition. It is that we hope for a good and noble leader, and we know that genuine helpfulness is one of most important traits in the kind of leader we need.

Being helpful is also a necessary component of consistent happiness. It has many forms. It is giving food and clothing to people who need them. It is giving opportunity to a child whose environment cannot provide chances for optimum development. It is giving affirming words to someone for true skills and effective actions, and in so doing, helping them see themselves as we see them. It is giving respect. It is bestowing caring. It is interacting with people with an attitude of persistent positive regard.

What are we doing when we are helping others? Helpfulness is putting into practice what we have learned.[62] The thrust differs with people. For some, helpfulness comes from a sense of fairness. In this mindset, we are aware that we have enjoyed benefits not available to everyone else, and we feel that it is only fair that we do something for those who are less fortunate. It feels like giving back. For some, helpfulness grows out of a feeling of responsibility as defined by our religious or philosophical heritage. It is doing our duty.

What makes helpfulness important?

UNIVERSALITY

Some people think of God as being active in the world in a direct, personal way. For them, helpfulness is like being the hands and feet of their God. And "helping God out" is their way of supporting the good that they believe is divinely sought.

For others, the common good may not be attached directly to a Supreme Being, but instead they may think of themselves as responding to basic standards of civility and justice that are due all people. Either way, the impulse to be helpful rises out of the values that determine our view of ourselves and how we are related to our world.

When I worked as a counselor in addiction treatment centers, many of the participants viewed helpfulness as an expression of their basic humanity. Being helpful was a way of connecting with the parts of themselves they respected most and a bridge that took them out of their isolation.

In my career with United Way on opposite coasts, I have seen people of all economic levels step aside from pursuit of career enhancement to help people they may never meet. Some probably view their community involvement as a part of doing business, a necessary fee for maintaining a good reputation. But many go far beyond self aggrandizement. The degree of their investment of time and money shows an impulse to support the movement toward a common good.

COMMONALITY

When we help others, we are made keenly aware of how connected we are to the people we are helping. This means that we are not merely giving time or effort that we can easily spare, like tossing a beggar some loose change, or giving away a piece of worn-out or out-dated clothing. The true helping mode is when we extend ourselves enough to feel the situation of the other person. And when we do this, we are aware that it not only might have been us, but that it could be us in the future. Avoiding this feeling of vulnerability is what keeps us from helping more often and more extravagantly.

I remember the first time I saw someone reach beyond his comfort zone. I was a small town teenager, hanging out at the barbershop on a rainy Saturday, enjoying the conversational virtuosity that the barber displayed with everyone from a rough-talking 'coon hunter to a dignified educator. On this Saturday, a clergyman from a downtown mainstream church dropped in for a haircut. As he usually did, the barber managed to move the conversation beyond weather and basketball scores, and perhaps because there were only the three of us, the clergyman began to talk more about who he was beneath his role. He revealed that he hosted weekly meetings of alcoholics in the basement of the church, and then told how the fellowship worked. He said that a key factor was readiness to respond to calls for help from anyone who was on the verge of giving in to the impulse to drink, even if it meant getting up in the middle of the night or having someone come to his own home and stay until the urges subsided. He admitted that he was getting pressure from some prominent church leaders who thought that he was spending too much time with people of low character and not enough time building the kind reputation they wanted for their minister. He explained his behavior in simple terms: "That used to be me, and if I took one drink, it would be me again. I won't turn them away."

Part of what keeps us from getting involved is fear where it might lead. If we can give a word of advice, or write a check, or spend a couple of carefully scheduled hours dispensing food to the homeless, or drop in on people and then resume our comfortable lifestyle – then we are willing to show kindness. Real helpfulness is going further.

Hero or Human

It was New York City cold on January 4, 2007. Wesley Autrey was taking his daughters, ages four and six, home before going to his construction job. As they stood on the subway platform waiting for the next train, Wesley noticed a young man suddenly fall down, obviously having some kind of seizure. It was a moment of decision. Wesley is a middle-aged African-American and the young man is white. He might have said to himself, "Let someone else help him." Wesley might have worried that his daughters would be frightened by the man's strange behavior and said to himself, "I have to watch after my own." Instead, he stooped and put something between the young man's teeth, doing the best he knew to help until the seizure passed.

Cameron Hollopeter, a student at the New York Film Academy, stood up, still obviously unsteady on his feet, but seeming to recover. Suddenly, he lurched backward and fell off the edge of the subway platform onto the train tracks. The startled onlookers could hear a train coming. Wesley had another moment of decision. Hadn't he done enough already? What could anyone do in the face of such extreme circumstances? Whose life was more important in this situation?

While everyone else stayed frozen in place, Wesley jumped down onto the tracks and tried to tug Cameron back up onto the platform. But the young man was either stunned by the fall or having another seizure and Wesley could not move him. Knowing the train was nearly upon them, he pulled Cameron between the rails, a space of one or two feet deep, and lay on top of him to keep him from flinching into the path of the deadly wheels. When the train stopped, Wesley's cap had grease on it from the train's undercarriage, so close it had come to them.

Afterward, the other commuters applauded and told the news media that Wesley was a hero. He got a $5,000 reward, a day off from work and universal acclaim in a city where you supposedly do not talk to people you do not know, let alone rescue them. Wesley Autrey said, "I just tried to do the right thing. It ain't about being a hero; it was just being there and helping the next person. That's all I did."

Labeling him a superman is a good excuse for not doing the kind of thing he did. If we are not superhuman, we cannot be expected to do anything special. Then staying safe is okay, maybe even virtuous.

But Wesley's insistence that what he did was the normal human reaction puts us all on the spot. Somewhere in our core we know that he is right. Being willing to help a person in great need is the essence of doing the right thing. And it is not reserved for supermen.

That is one of the reasons why helpfulness is so important to long-time members of mutual help groups. Our connectedness becomes more rewarding than our separateness. In putting ourselves out for people who need it, we find experiences that verify our humanity. Quite literally, as we give ourselves we find ourselves.

Empowerment

Edna entered a drug treatment program because her life had become too painful to endure. Keeping herself numbed out had ruined her health and taken her into a decrepit apartment in a dangerous neighborhood. Her teenage son linked up with a gang out of loneliness and self-preservation. Her live-in boyfriend regularly beat her up and stole what little money she scraped together by selling sexual favors. The turning point came when she realized that the boyfriend had started making sexual advances toward her twelve year old daughter.

After a year, Edna was still clean and sober and was working in the office of the agency that provided the drug treatment program. She had found a new place to live and her kids were in after school programs that had given them stability. One day the staff was collecting money to make some needed repairs to the agency building, and Edna came to me with twenty dollars worth of bills crumpled in her hand. I started telling her all the reasons why she needed the money more than we did. She grabbed my hand, folded it around the bills, and said with a quivering voice, "You don't understand. Being able to give means my life is back in my control. This means I'm strong again." I took the money and learned the lesson.

As we mature, we may begin to feel that we are losing aspects of ourselves, sort of fading away until we feel like partial people. By exercising our ability to serve, we can make a difference in other people's lives. In doing that, we feel creative and powerful. So, what we get from serving may be far more valuable that what we give.

BENEFICIAL

Helping has powerful positive effects on mental well-being and physical health. Studies of volunteers show that the act of helping people often causes feelings of pronounced happiness, followed by an extended period of calmness. This feeling has been called "helper's high" because its effects resemble the renowned runner's high. Both mental/physical states are characterized by initial exhilaration that is followed by feelings of emotional well-being. Engaging in helping raises the level of endorphins in the brain and reduces stress. Studies also show that helping behaviors tend to reduce feelings of hostility and isolation. The resulting decrease in stress gives relief for a variety of health disorders, such as overeating, ulcers, and asthma attacks.

The movie ***Blind Side*** is based on the lives of a well-to-do family in Memphis, the Tuohys, and Michael Oher, then a homeless African American teenager, now a professional football player with the Baltimore Ravens. The story is compelling because it is about real people. In one scene, Mrs. Tuohy and three friends were having coffee in a posh restaurant. The friends had expressed their misgivings about taking in a person of such obvious socio-economic inferiority, but one tried to be complimentary: "You have certainly changed that young man's life."

Immediately Mrs. Tuohy said with intensity: "No. He has changed ***my*** life."

People who help others report increases in feelings of joyfulness, hopefulness, emotional resilience, and vigor. They also report increased sense of self-worth and greater happiness. These are the kinds of positive emotions that have been shown in medical studies to strengthen the body's immune system.[63]

This means that helpfulness may be as important to our overall health as regular exercise and proper nutrition. This is a cheap and easy way to deal with many of the negative aspects of aging. If our doctors told us that we could take a pill that would have all the aforementioned benefits, we would be checking to see if our insurance would pay for it. The fact is that we can get all these benefits for little or no cost.

SIMPLICITY

What can we do? Just asking the question reminds me of childhood days, usually during school vacations at Christmas when the weather was bad, when we complained about being bored. The usual adult response was, "Oh, you don't have anything to do? Well, I have plenty of things to do." Realizing that we were about to be assigned chores, we scattered and found something to do.

Our issue is similar. When we are self-absorbed, we see so little that can be done. When we tune in to what is going on all around us, there is always something at hand that can be done to ease someone else's burden. A woman with her hands full is having difficulty, so you open the door and hold it. A stranger's car is stuck, and we pause, put out our hands and push. A neighbor's relative dies and we go by to tell how we know how they feel because we had the same thing happen to us. Kindly responses to everyday situations. It all seems natural and fitting.

When we get into this spirit, action seems to flow effortlessly and everyone benefits, helper and helped alike. Helping each other dig out after the storm, organizing a community meeting, preparing for a funeral, finding a chair for the person who is getting wobbly, offering to baby-sit or keep the pet, inviting someone to a movie to provide a break from pressure, organizing friends to make sure that someone's long recovery will not isolate them, sounding the alarm on behalf of someone who is being overwhelmed....we seem to know what our part is in making it better.

The outlets for helpfulness are as varied as our preferences. Here are some examples that can stimulate your own imagination.

Personal Helpfulness

A mature woman maintains her place in a church group that has a list of members to look after. In spite of several bothersome ailments of her own, Mary keeps track of her little flock. For some of the older people, social outings that include a bit of shopping and some entertainment keep them involved in the community. One of them is a woman in her late eighties. Dorothy has outlived the family members that care most about her happiness. She is now being circled by family members that are intent on curtailing her expenditures and getting control of her resources as quickly as possible. They are intent on constricting her world for their own benefit. Dorothy told Mary, and Mary talked to another mutual friend. Together they offered to do whatever Dorothy needed. As it turned out, she needed more than a listening ear. She needed someone to go to court with her and offer to be an alternative care team appointed by the court to look after her best interests. Mary and the other friend agreed. So, Dorothy no longer had to worry about being financially cannibalized, because she is being looked after by two friends whose only interest is in making sure she lives with dignity and as much enjoyment as possible.

Some mature adults show true bravery in serving other older adults, because it is often scary to see what could happen to us. One such woman summers in a historic New England city famous as a resort for presidents, yacht owners, and golfers. She looked for a place to connect with people who needed her personal attention, and she found a nursing home. She goes to spend time with the residents and gives special attention to those with Alzheimer's. She discovered that she has an instinct for working with these patients and she can see that they respond to her gentle tenacity. She is not part of any organized program; she found them on her own and goes and comes on her own initiative.

This may not, at first glance, seem as heroic as what Wesley Autrey did when he pulled a man from the path of a subway train. Yet, the mental and emotional tenacity to stand up for someone is that same instinct to give help when someone needs it.

Helpfulness comes from a mindset, and there are ample outlets for our energy. Clean house for a person who needs a break. Buy a stylish hat for a friend who has lost her hair to cancer treatments. Spend some time with someone who is frightened by uncontrollable circumstances. Go see an old friend whose health has failed. Listen attentively to the stories that contain a person's self-identity.

In many support groups, the role of personal mentor has been used to great advantage. Some groups call them sponsors, some call them buddies, and some call them life coaches. The mentoring role has long been recognized as a vitally important way to help people in becoming successful in business, education, sports, and personal development. A mentor is a trusted friend, counselor or teacher, usually a more experienced person.

The mentor feels a sense of purpose in giving advice that can enhance a less experienced person's life. It is also a chance for the mentor to draw together the threads of experience and see how even their failures can become useful tools for helping someone else.

Community Programs

In Jacksonville, Florida, the city has developed a program that depends on mature adults. Child care providers have found that many abused children seem to feel safer with people older than their parents. This awareness gave rise to a program for matching up mature adults as surrogate grandparents with pre-school children. The substitute grandparents provide a gentle, loving person to an emotionally wounded child. In return, the children give the adults an emotionally rewarding mission in life.

Also in Jacksonville, a non-profit organization called Community Connections has a program that cares for children of homeless people. In the daycare program for the homeless infants, volunteers come to the center to assist the professional staff. The volunteers rock the babies and read to the preschoolers. They are making sure that in their earliest days, the children get the loving kindness that is so vital to their healthy development.

Many communities have programs for providing meals to people who need help. All these programs depend on the help of volunteers to serve the meals. Most of us can stand in a serving line and show friendly helpfulness to people who are down on their luck.

Most communities have a United Way nearby. These local organizations can provide information about programs that are doing much needed work in a highly responsible manner. With this information, you can find people who are already doing something that relates to your own passion. You do not have to spend time in creating a structure for helping. You can simply get on board.

There are many organizations that make helpfulness easier. A new one was established in 1995 as a 501I(3) nonprofit organization, The Random Acts of Kindness Foundation. It is a resource for people who are willing to spread kindness. On an internet website, they provide a wide variety of materials including activity ideas, lesson plans, project plans, teacher's guides, and project planning guides, publicity guides, and workplace resources. All these can be found and used free of charge at www.actsofkindness.org. The Foundation is privately held and funded. They accept no donations, grants, or membership dues. They do not provide financial assistance to individuals or organizations. The Foundation has no religious or organizational affiliations. They simply encourage the practice of kindness in all sectors of society.

HISTORY

The power of helpfulness is not new. In the writings of world religions, the theme of kindness and helpfulness reaches across all boundaries of culture and doctrine. Some examples:

Jainism: *Have benevolence towards all living beings, joy at the sight of the virtuous, compassion and sympathy for the afflicted, and tolerance towards the indolent and ill-behaved.* Tattvarthasutra 7.11

Islam: *A man once asked the Prophet what was the best thing in Islam, and the latter replied, "It is to feed the hungry and to give the greeting of peace both to those one knows and to those one does not know."* Hadith of Bukhari

Anas and 'Abdullah reported God's Messenger as saying, "All [human] creatures are God's children, and those dearest to God are those who treat His children kindly." Hadith of Baihaqi

Judaism: *The world stands upon three things: upon the Law, upon worship, and upon showing kindness.* Mishnah, Abot 1.2

Hinduism: *What sort of religion can it be without compassion? You need to show compassion to all living beings. Compassion is the root of all religious faiths.* Basavanna, Vachana 247

Christianity: In one of Jesus' parables, he painted a verbal scene of God's identifying those who were good: *"I was hungry and you gave me something to eat, I was thirsty and you gave me something to drink, I was a stranger and you invited me in, I needed clothes and you clothed me, I was sick and you looked after me, I was in prison and you came to visit me."* And when they were confused about being credited for giving direct help to God, they were told, *"Whatever you did for one of the least of these brothers of mine, you did for me."* (Matthew 25:35-40)

Implicit in all the ancient teachings is the idea that responding to people's needs affects and defines the person who is giving the help. Helpfulness is a strategy for gaining the maturity of mind and spirit that we respect in great people.

CULTURAL ROLE OF MATURE ADULTS

Ours is a culture that values youthfulness. Even when a mature adult is being complimented, it is typical to say, "But you seem so young for your age!" The implication is that it is best to be as young as possible.

As we age, a variety of conditions interfere with our ability to work as hard or long as we once did. Even if we can still do more than many people, most industries tend to opt for younger workers. Few are able to compete in athletics at the top levels. In the mating market mature adults are generally at a distinct disadvantage, in spite of increasingly ingenious restorative surgical procedures. Politics seems to be one of the few fields where mature adults can be seen and heard and still respected. For the most part, mature adults who continue to excel must stay out of sight of the general public: authors, designers, architects, e.g. Even educators, whose accumulation of wisdom would presumably make them increasingly valuable, must depend on tenure to avoid being replaced by the younger and more sprightly, with whom students identify more easily. So, what is the natural role of mature adults?

One of the obvious roles is that which is valued in business settings: keepers of the vision. Businesses that forget or underestimate this function are likely to repeat the decline of such giants as Readers Digest and IBM. These are but two of the highly successful companies that lost much of their power when their founding visionaries were no longer guiding the enterprise. In more cultural terms, this function is reminding new generations of the lore of our society. All people need someone to give them a view of life seen from a broad perspective. Only age can do that. The mature adults in any society are needed to the pass on values, wisdom, tales, and life understanding.

It is difficult to identify the story-telling aspect of our society. Where would we look? The movies? Best-selling books? School curriculums? Some organizations do this for their members: scouts, Free Masons, religious groups. For the culture in general, most stories are for short-term entertainment or for topical instruction in marketable skills.

In older cultures, there is an oral tradition as well as a written history, and the stories teach each generation how to identify heroes and heroines. Sometimes the stories are tales or parables that are for interpretative teaching. In such stories, it is irrelevant whether or not the people ever actually lived. Sometimes the stories are about real people who showed the kind of character the culture admires most, and these people become role models for the generations that follow.

In many cultures, the mature adults are entrusted with this vital role because they have lived long enough to see beyond short-term trends. A professor once challenged his religion class to write down the sayings or adages they remembered from growing up. He said, "These are your true values, rather than what you would like to think your values are."

Do people care about stories? Apparently so, as shown by the interest in StoryCorps, An Oral History of America http://storycorps.org/about/our-story. Two permanent recording booths were set up in New York City, and one in Milwaukee, In 2005-2006, two mobile units, one in the East and one in the West set up for limited times in twenty-six American cities each year. In 2007, the StoryCorps Griot Initiative launched a third MobileBooth to collect the stories of thousands of African Americans, the largest oral history project of its kind since the WPA Slave Narratives of the 1930s. In 2008, the flagship StoryBooth in Grand Central Terminal closed, and the new flagship StoryBooth opened in Lower Manhattan's Foley Square. Also in 2008, a new StoryBooth opened in San Francisco, California, in partnership with the Contemporary Jewish Museum. The book, *Listening Is an Act of Love*, is released in paperback. Also in 2008, the launch of StoryCorps Alaska six month initiative to record and preserve the stories of Alaskans. As of this writing, StoryCorps is setting up new locations all over the country.

For $10, participants could bring relatives, friends or acquaintances to a booth and talk to each other about their lives. Trained facilitators helped record 40-minute sessions. Participants kept a CD, and copies are preserved at the American Folk Life Center at the Library of Congress. David Isay, who instituted the project said, "It's a very moving experience for people. A lot of times we see people just break down crying at the beginning of an interview, just because they feel so honored that this relative really wants to listen to what they have to say."

That is the fitting role for mature adults in our culture at large. Mature adults are uniquely suited for telling the stories of real people who dared, succeeded, failed, survived, regretted, learned, loved, died, and showed us how life works. And seeing that, we have some good information about the best ways to behave, and what will likely happen if we choose to go it on our own.

Of course, we certainly have ample history books to tell us what happened. But having written historical records does not have the same impact as having people who relate their personal memories. History books do not have the same kind of authority as elders who are passing on important wisdom to their own communities. We need the so-called objective history, but we also need the memories of people who lived through the important times.

We often hear people lament the lack of respect that our culture has for mature adults. If we look at the cultures who revere their elderly, we will likely see that their mature adults have the role as keepers of the vision of what life and character is at its best. Mature adults have personal knowledge, based on first-hand observation and trial and error in their own lives. It is a vital service to everyone that follows.

STUDY QUESTIONS ON HELPFUL OR SELF-ABSORBED
1) When was the last time you did something unselfish?
2) How did it make you feel?
3) List the various feelings you have when you do something that helps someone.
4) What have you done for someone that gave you great satisfaction?
5) Given your present situation, what can you do that is important to help others?
6) Is there something that you know how to do that is greatly needed?
7) Who is someone whose kindness you admire?

EXPERIMENTING WITH HELPFULNESS
Choose an action or write one of your own.
- ☐ I will do a kind deed each day and write down how it affects me.
- ☐ I will make a list of ways that I can be generous and helpful that do not involve money.
- ☐ I will make a list of people who helped me with no apparent agenda for personal payback or benefit.
- ☐ I will choose to do a volunteer helpfulness activity in a non-profit organization and write down how it affects me.

OBSTACLES TO HAPPINESS
1) What makes it difficult for me to choose to be helpful rather than self-absorbed?
2) Is the obstacle a
   ☐ Thought or belief   ☐ Emotion   ☐ Attitude   ☐ Behavior
   ☐ Consequence/situation?
3) What would I have to do to make a different choice?

TOGETHER OR SOLITARY

Genuine Community or Emotional Separation

TRANSFORMING POWER OF COMMUNITY

For twenty-five years, in various kinds of groups, I saw people make changes that they could never make on their own. One such place was in an addiction treatment center. In the treatment approach called therapeutic community, there are two major emphases. The clients are encouraged to become aware of a higher power and to use that power in their recovery efforts. They are encouraged to use whatever tradition they feel most comfortable with and to let the writings and practices of that tradition develop an awareness of a power greater than themselves.

The second emphasis is on the community of fellow clients. Typically, clients meet at least once a day for a group session in which they talk about their progress. In the sessions, clients learn how to be honest without being cruel, and how to be supportive without glossing over destructive behavior. In addition to the group session itself, the group members are taught to be aware of each other throughout the day, and to give support when it is needed and honest feedback when a person is violating their treatment regimens.

About once every two months, enough time to have a new crop of residents, I led the group in a teaching exercise. The group divided into two equal subgroups that gathered at opposite ends of a large meeting room. To one group I said quietly enough that the others could not hear, "List all the benefits you received from your Higher Power."

Then I went to the other end of the room and quietly said to the other group, "List all the benefits you received from your group." I gave them ten minutes to work independently, and then asked them to give me their completed lists. I covered them and taped them on the wall. When everyone settled, I uncovered the lists. They contained the same benefits....always. Some of the items were forgiveness, support, inspiration, wisdom, understanding, presence, motivation, confrontation.

At first, the clients seemed confused. Then they saw the surprising truth. The higher power is available either directly or through the group. The benefits are the same. And they realized that seeking the higher power in both dimensions helped them have a clearer view of the higher power.

The adage "It takes a village to raise a child" is true. The fact is that at all stages of life we need a benevolent support system in order to have life at its best. This truth undiminished as we mature. The flow of life in our society generally separates us from people who have been crucial to our development. We scatter as we follow our individual families and dreams. We are affected by the endless mobility patterns that are seldom questioned.

We lose more very important people to death. We feel the loss of people whose knowledge of us is irreplaceable. Their affection and esteem helped make us who we are, and their presence made us hopeful about whatever lay ahead. With each change of seasons, we feel ourselves diminished by each new loss of someone for whom there is no substitute. A part of us that only they knew is now dormant.

And it is not only the departures that are shrinking our "village." We ourselves feel less able to do the work of sustaining friendships and social contact. We are tapering off and slowing down. At the very time when we need practical help and emotional support, we find ourselves becoming less connected with fewer people.

This bleak picture leaves us asking, "Is there no hope, then, for happiness as I reach and go past middle age?" Yes, there is. We must rebuild our village. In the same way that a town that has been decimated by natural or human-caused disasters must rebuild itself and go on, we must also rebuild the community that we need.

Fortunately, there are proven ways to do it.

ALCOHOLICS ANONYMOUS

In 1935, a Wall Street stock broker and a medical doctor from Akron, Ohio, formed a friendship based on helping each other overcome their alcoholism. They developed a program of tasks, or steps, which would help a person achieve sobriety. An essential part of their plan was that a person would become part of an ongoing group of people who were working on the same issue. They believed that the effect of the mutual-help group would enable individuals to do what they could never alone. Today it is known throughout the world as Alcoholics Anonymous and has been the single most successful method of helping addicts achieve long-term health.

Although it steadfastly claims to be unaffiliated to any religious body or tradition, AA exemplifies some of the core traits of the early Christian churches.

- They employ no professional staff. The groups depend on the local participating members for leadership. The group meetings are guided by rotating assignments. More intensive training and nurture is provided by having long-time, stable members provide one-to-one guidance. The pairings are strictly voluntary.

- They own no property. They typically meet in church basements, empty meeting rooms, or rotate meeting in people's homes.

- Entry is gained on the basis of a felt need rather than demonstration of goodness or status.

- The sole purpose is transformation of people, and the process is never completed.

- They do not recruit members. Groups are populated by word-of-mouth referrals. The phone book and internet may provide succinct information about meetings, but no commercials or come-ons are published.

MASTER MIND

An effective program that is not so widely known was developed by Napoleon Hill, a successful attorney and journalist. In 1937 he published a book that was based on concepts he formulated as he interviewed such people as Andrew Carnegie, Thomas Edison, Alexander Graham Bell, Henry Ford, Elmer Gates, Charles M. Schwab, Theodore Roosevelt, William Wrigley Jr., John Wanamaker, William Jennings Bryan, George Eastman, Woodrow Wilson, William H. Taft, John D. Rockefeller, F. W. Woolworth, and Jennings Randolph, among others.

One portion of the book *Think and Grow Rich* dealt with what Hill called the Master Mind. Hill said: "No two minds ever come together without, thereby, creating a third, invisible, intangible force which may be likened to a third mind." [64]

He also wrote that, "Men take on the nature and the habits and the power of thought of those with whom they associate in a spirit of sympathy and harmony."

In order to apply the principles he observed in successful people, he organized a Master Mind group. They met regularly over a period of several years to stay in touch with the energy that seemed to them more than the sum of their collective wisdom. He attributed his considerable success to the shared power of the group.

The Master Mind model is still being used widely by people who are seeking success in a broad range of occupations and professions. In much the same way as Alcoholics Anonymous, participants report results that they believe would be impossible without the power they get from being part of the ongoing group.

FOUNDATION FOR COMMUNITY ENCOURAGEMENT

In 1984, psychiatrist M. Scott Peck and ten other people established The Foundation for Community Encouragement. Because of his best selling books, Peck was a popular lecturer in educational and business circles. His interactions with audiences made him aware of a widespread need for genuine community. He responded by developing a process for building a sense of community within organizations or groups. He reported his concepts and his work in the book *The Different Drum: Community Making and Peace.*

FCE developed curriculum and certified trainers to facilitate in the community building process. Hundreds of workshops, conferences, seminars, and speaking engagements have been conducted for thousands of participants in the USA, Canada, the UK, Asia and Australia. The focus of these events has been to teach groups how to achieve a sense of community or collective spirit and how to identify a common purpose and accomplish agreed upon goals.

STAGES OF COMMUNITY

Although each group is unique, they all go through predictable stages in order to reach genuine community.[65]

> **Pseudo-Community** – civility and pretense of good will
> **Chaos** – fixing, solving, converting, contending
> **Emptiness** – suspend certainty of beliefs
> **Community** – mutuality and reciprocity

Pseudo-community

We have all been in groups where people were faking friendliness. We are familiar with the social smiles, the eyes that glance in ours briefly and then scan for someone else they would rather be talking to, the forced energy that makes small talk sound like important conversation, the glib exchange of code words that signify we are insiders, and the avoidance of topics that would lead to serious disagreement. The rules of pseudo-community are well known:

- Don't do or say anything that might offend somebody;
- If someone does or says something that offends, annoys, or irritates you, act as if nothing has happened and pretend you are not bothered in the least;
- If a disagreement seems to be emerging, change the subject as quickly and smoothly as possible.[66]

These are time honored rules for making life go smoothly. But they also discourage individuality. They undermine honesty and turn conversations into dull rituals.

In most settings, the people who promote pseudo-community are not bad people lying for some evil purpose. Rather, they are people withholding opinions or information that might lead to conflict or tension. In fact, the intention is to be kind, even loving. Even so, it is still pretense.[67]

With maturity, we encounter more and more people who are reluctant to tell us the truth. It may start with medical professionals who do not give us full information about our own health. Often they want to avoid the unpleasantness of dealing with us if we get upset. Instead, they may give the full story to other family members, who are then drawn into the protective deception. The family members may tell our friends, with the admonition to keep the secrets. They may even believe that it is all for our own good. We usually catch on to what is happening and may feel isolated from the secret-keepers. Then we are further isolated by keeping secret that we know the secret.

People in organizations and corporations decide that they need an increased emphasis on youth, so they manufacture reasons why they want to replace us with someone else. They usually do not tell us the truth, so their disengagement makes us wonder how we may have failed at what we have been doing efficiently for years. We feel cut off from parts of life where we have found satisfaction.

Younger family members notice that aging has brought various changes in us. They begin to interact with us as if we have become different people, rather than merely having undergone some natural changes. They imply that we cannot make good decisions about matters that we have successfully managed all our lives. They talk with us as if we cannot discern the signs of their dishonesty, and we feel the emotional distance created by their "harmless" deceptions.

Pseudo-community is that phony cheerfulness and good will that seeks to gloss over facts that create any level of uneasiness. Agreement and compliance are the tools for seeking perfect harmony. In actuality, the result is superficiality and dullness.

As we age, we need truthfulness. We are not so emotionally fragile or weak-minded that we cannot cope with life's realities. Much more troublesome is the isolation imposed on us by family and close friends who think they are helping us. We need to have freedom to form our own reactions based on accurate information. We do not need to be treated as if we are children.

Chaos

Moving toward community that can do us any good requires that we stop pretending that all is well. In this stage, we face differences openly. We move beyond the placidness of superficiality. We engage with people on real issues, and as we do, we try to fix those who do not see life as we do. Our interactions are much more likely to be charged with energy and emotion. We are trying to convince and persuade. We listen only long enough to think up effective rebuttals to what the other person is saying. We are not seeking common ground; we are seeking converts to our way. And others are trying to do the same to us. So we are struggling over whose way will prevail.

Some people enjoy the excitement of argument and relish the chance to win battles. But even the most happy warriors are aware that the contests do not create friendliness. Even so, they are more interesting and genuine than the phoniness of pseudo community.

As we impose our views on others, we feel validated and important. Winning the struggle makes us glad that we made the choices and invested our efforts the way we did. It is freedom from confusion or regret.

My first memory of this stage was when I was fourteen years old. I spent a lot of time in the home of one of my friends, and was invited to attend their church on Sunday evenings. Even though I was an active member of another denomination, I went readily because it was an opportunity to have more fun time together, and because I felt flattered that his parents wanted to include me in an important family activity.

After a few services, the father invited me to sit with him in the living room and to discuss changing my beliefs from what my church taught to what their church taught. This happened several times. I had felt comfortable in my church, but the intellectual pressure of an educated and respected adult was causing me to doubt my belief system. And because I had affection and respect for the parents, I wondered if the adults who had taught me in my church had given me flawed information. I felt confused, unsettled, and worried.

Many of the chaotic situations we encounter are much more stressful. In my example, the people genuinely cared about me and eventually ceased to pressure me to adopt their viewpoints. In many situations, however, the conflict does not subside so easily. In fact, in many cases the adoption of the other's viewpoint becomes the test of whether we are personally acceptable or not. And when the issue is this vital, the situations are charged with high emotion. Reasonableness and civility are often forgotten in the interest of fixing and converting the people who are in the wrong.

For some of us, this stage creates so much stress that we avoid revealing enough truth about ourselves to risk serious disagreements. We may feel that the payoffs of excitement and fuller awareness of others' viewpoints are not worth what it costs in discomfort. We may also be afraid that the chaos will not be temporary, but may cause permanent rifts between us and people that we do not want to alienate.

If we do not feel confident about our emotional support system, we are less likely to risk anything that might result in losing important connections. This makes it all the more important for us to expand the group of people who know us well and have shown that their esteem does not depend on our compliance with all their viewpoints.

The fact is that we must risk some chaos to build the best kind of community. We need enough hope to believe we can survive the uneasiness of honest dialogue about important issues. Otherwise, we remain polite strangers with the people around us. We need enough common sense to know that we need more wisdom and resources than we can generate on our own. Otherwise, we eventually find ourselves in one of the many personal crises that become more likely as we age, and then we find that we need a cadre of kindred spirits to stand beside us.

Emptiness

The next stage toward community is difficult to do and difficult to explain. It involves inner adjustments to attitudes. It is letting go of mindsets that stand between us and other people. What do we have to let go of?

Assumptions and Impressions

We all have mental shortcuts that we use to put people into categories for quick understanding. Sometimes the categories are complimentary, such as expert, leader, hero, celebrity, star, scholar, and highly respected. When we insert people into these mental file folders, we tend to treat them with deference. We mentally award them exemptions and privileges that are consistent with our notion that they are superior to most people. We also put a barrier between them and ourselves.

The first time I realized this was shortly after I graduated from seminary. One of our most highly respected professors, author of scores of books on psychology and theology, had a close friend who committed suicide. In class lectures, the professor had told us that he believed having even one trusting relationship was enough to help people avoid the despair and isolation that lead to suicide. I imagined that the professor's grief for his friend might be intensified by his own inability to give the kind of help that would have averted disaster.

I knew that the professor had innumerable people of his own station to give him comfort. I was a mere student who had sat in his classes and on one occasion asked for his personal counsel, which he gave graciously. Finally, I overcame my reluctance and wrote him a letter of condolence, mentioning the lecture on friendship and suicide, and conveying my deepest sympathy that he had not been able to prevent his friend's isolation. I wanted him to know that I understood that he might be carrying a heavier load of sadness than others.

To my surprise, I soon received a handwritten letter from my revered professor. He said that no one else had mentioned that connection between his theory and his friend's death. Indeed, he had thought a lot about it, and my words of sympathy had helped him. He thanked me for taking time to offer a message at just the right time.

I have not forgotten the importance of not putting barriers between myself and the people whom I respect. They may need real connection more than they need to be admired from a distance.

Sometimes our categories are not complimentary, and we quickly insert people who create negative impressions into handy mental slots. We think of them as shallow, or stingy, or complaining, or pretentious, or uncouth, or misinformed, or argumentative, or bad-tempered, or selfish, or mean, or insensitive, or brash or any of the other qualities that put people outside our good will. We may never revisit our impression to see if the real person matches our mental snapshot.

Casual social contacts usually do little to change negative first impressions. We need chances to hear what is behind the public image before we can get more accurate understanding about values, motives, and character. We need to know something of a person's story, the parts that only he can tell. To get to his level, we must convince him that we are both trustworthy and willing to listen. Otherwise, we are stuck with the assumptions that we make up about people. And they may have slight resemblance to the truth.

Ideology, Creeds, Philosophy

Letting go of these is so difficult that many people cannot do it. Thus, community often waits for us to find people who already agree on beliefs that we are so busy defending that we cannot listen to a person who has different perspectives.

If our beliefs about the big things (such as religion and politics) prevent us from interacting with anyone who disagrees with us, then a strategy for making connections beyond fellow believers is to make contact at the points where we meet as ordinary human beings. This is what happens when we develop intimacy and trust by going through similar crises.

In the chapter on Spiritual or Physical, I referred to the bond that developed between people who shared the experience of walking the talk for thirty days. Their relationships were no longer based on agreement about doctrines or church politics. It was all about unusual experiences they had been through together.

In wartime, people establish powerful connections with each other as they endure horrendous events that threaten normality and health, maybe even life itself. Survivors may have very different views about many things, but the common experience of traumatic upheaval trumps everything else.

We have seen the same phenomenon among the families who lost loved ones in the 9/11 disaster in New York City. Before the terrorists struck, the families of the victims were people of diverse political and religious viewpoints. It is likely that many of them might not have liked each other much, maybe not even treated each other with kindness. The horrible events of that day put them in a new and completely human category. Their common travail made many of them feel more comfortable with each other than with people who had similar ideologies but had not been through the same kind of personal loss. The most powerful experiences tend to become the common ground of powerful connections with people who have shared the same things.

This is why it is important for us to start connecting with each other around the common experience of aging. People who have not yet reached our stage of life do not know what it is like. We are in crisis. Younger people may view our situation as inevitable, natural, and maybe even fair. And perhaps they are right. But there are dimensions to our situation that cannot be known from a distance. No matter how much outsiders try to sense our mood and offer kind words and helpful actions, they are only observers, not participants.

The Need to Heal, Convert, Fix, or Solve

If you have been on the receiving end of advice given to you when you have been in a terrible state of mind and spirit, then you know that often advisors' attempts at erasing your pain or removing your confusion is worse than doing nothing at all. In part, it is because they do not share our situation, and that fact alone makes us instinctively, maybe resentfully, resist their simplistic words. Their distance makes it impossible for them to understand the complexity and subtlety of our suffering.

In order to make genuine connection with each other, we have to lay aside our eagerness to ease our own discomfort at being unable to remove someone else's distress. Once we admit that much of our rush to help others is to make ourselves more comfortable and more certain of our rightness, then we can approach real connection with each other.

Emptiness is just another word for humility. So long as we have our minds filled with our own concerns and viewpoints, our efforts to connect with anyone else are basically about making ourselves feel better and look better. When we are willing to let go of the illusion that we can fix someone else, then we are ready for community.

TRAITS OF COMMUNITY

The term *community* is used to refer to many kinds of connections from shared ethnic origin to geographical proximity. In this book, we are interested more in the feelings and behaviors that demonstrate unity of people in a group. Unity exists when certain conditions exist between people, when we

- Identify with each other as members of a group,
- Show special concern toward one another,
- Are jointly committed to certain values or goals,
- Are loyal to the group and its ideals,
- Trust each other,[68] and
- Disclose ourselves to each other.[69]

Identification with the Group

In a genuine community, we feel linked to the successes and failures of others in the group. It happens in a close-knit family, where we are affected by the things that happen to parents, children, and siblings. Unity can also be based on a shared ethnic or cultural heritage. It can occur when we believe that we share a similar plight or significant, perhaps life-shaping, experiences. Understanding and empathy grow out of common experiences. We find our own feeling of well-being linked to what is happening to other members of our group. There is a mutual sense of we-ness. The longer the in-group is together, the more experiences we accumulate to reinforce our sense of belonging.

Special concern

Community involves more than mere emotional reactions, whether they are anger against common enemies or sympathy for unpleasant treatment. Unity also requires that we have willingness to come to the aid of others in the group. This kind of concern is beyond doing our moral duty; it is acting because of our sense of we-ness. We may do what is morally or ethically required for those who are outside our group, but by choice we go much further than is required with the in-group.

Shared values or goals

Members of a community also share a set of values, and each person believes that everyone is honestly committed to them. The shared values may be ideals, such as the equal worth of each person, or the inherent right to be treated with dignity. The common values may be rituals or practices that bind us together in familiar behaviors. They may be contained in a body of knowledge that we trust as the accurate story of truth.

Loyalty

One of the most important elements in community is group loyalty. This attachment involves awareness of us versus them; that is, we are the in-group and the rest are part of the out-group. This sometimes creates tension, even controversy. Ideally, people of good will may like to think that creating in-groups is unnecessary. "Why can't we all be equal and part of one group?" may be the wistful goal. However, communities are defined by characteristics that cannot be shared by everyone, even if all people were willing. So, divisions are inevitable. Loyalty to our own group is part of what includes us in the community.

Mutual trust

In a community, we feel that the others will not let us down. We need to believe that others will stand with us in being faithful to our shared values, and they will not exploit or cheat us. We need to believe that when we turn to them, they will be there for us in the same measure that we are there for them.

Demands of Community

These group traits may appear desirable to us. However, they may also seem to be limitations of our personal freedom. And that is true. It is not possible to achieve community without a significant degree of personal engagement with others. We often find ourselves at the threshold of relationships that are ready for more mutuality, but at that moment, we think of the costs, and we draw back.

Being part of a community does not make life simpler. In fact, it may complicate our lives in many ways. We are no longer solitary persons who are completely free to respond to the moment's impulses. We make commitments and keep them. We voluntarily link ourselves to the history and destiny of others, and sometimes this brings upon us consequences that we could avoid if we remained solitary. We feel the benefits of things going well, and we feel the sadness when they do not. The possibility of being deeply connected brings the potential for being deeply hurt.

BENEFITS OF COMMUNITY

When you scan the five characteristics of community listed above, you may be inclined to say, "I don't think I've ever had much of that." If that is true for you, then you are part of the vast majority of people in our culture. Most people get by on some portion of the list to some degree, and many people have almost none of the benefits of true community.

Some of the benefits can be surmised by looking at the list of traits. But we might not know the most profound benefit.

The most common emotional response to the spirit of community is the feeling of joy.

It is like falling in love. When they enter community, people in a very real sense do fall in love with one another en masse. They not only feel like touching and hugging each other, they feel like hugging everyone all at once. During the highest moments, the energy level is supernatural. It is ecstatic. Lily provided one community myth during a workshop in a Knoxville hotel when she pointed to an electrical outlet in the center of the floor and commented: "It's as if we're connected to the entire electrical energy output of the Tennessee Valley Authority."[70]

We are social creatures by instinct and training. To appreciate this fully, we need only to watch television episodes on The Animal Planet channel. Photographic documentaries reveal that each species has patterns of social behavior embedded in their instincts. Lions hunt and relax together in groups that abide by clear structure. Rhinos rarely form groups except for the pairing of cows and calves, and the adult males are usually solitary. Elephants exhibit one of the most complex social patterns in the animal kingdom, often compared to the variety in different groups of humans. The destiny of an individual animal depends on how well it is able to match its life with innate instincts and needs.

We humans need to be connected to other humans in order to be at our best. This is easy to see in infants, when we are completely dependent on adult care for mere survival, and as children when we need adult guidance in forming behavioral habits that will be useful to our safety and well-being. Even young adults do better with the benevolent coaching of people who are willing to share experience, expertise, and access to successful friends.

Our need for human connections may seem to vary greatly with individuals, but normal people will always do better when we have physical and emotional contact with a community. When the people who comprise our birth families and our early years are benevolent, we have a better chance of being healthy and happy.

In the chapter on Fulfilled or Surviving, we saw that one of the basic humans needs is to feel a sense of belonging and acceptance. The need may be below the conscious level, but it is always there. People of all ages are drawn to clubs, office cliques, religious groups, professional organizations, card-playing groups, sports teams, and gangs. All of these help meet a hunger for human contact. The need for more intimacy in contacts explains the importance of family members, intimate partners, mentors, close colleagues, confidants. We need to love and be loved by others. If we do not get the amount of human contact we need, and it varies with individuals, we become susceptible to loneliness, anxiety, and even clinical depression.

As we mature, this need does not decrease, in fact, it may become even more intense. The longer we live, the more separations we have. We lose important people by death, by declining health, or by changes in living situations. But the need for human connection goes on. We cannot store up enough human warmth and contact in early life to take us through a long, cold old age, as if we were hibernating bears. Old photographs of younger faces and happier times cannot replace the regular experience of companionship and good will from other people.

Physical Benefits

The benefits of community are myriad and well-documented. For example, happiness contributes to good health. Studies show that people who are energetic, happy and relaxed are less likely to catch colds. Conversely, those who are depressed, nervous or angry are more likely to complain about cold symptoms.

A team from Carnegie Mellon University, Pittsburgh, found that people who had a positive emotional attitude were not infected as often and experienced fewer symptoms than people with a negative emotional style. The researchers interviewed 334 healthy volunteers three evenings a week for two weeks to assess their emotional states. After their assessment, each volunteer got a squirt in the nose of a rhinovirus - the germ that causes colds. The researchers kept the subjects under observation for five days to see whether or not they became infected and how they manifested symptoms. Tests showed that positive people were no less likely to be infected with the virus. However, infection seemed to produce fewer signs and symptoms of illness. Lead researcher Dr Sheldon Cohen said: "We found that experiencing positive emotions was associated with greater resistance to developing a common cold. But a negative emotional style had no effect on whether or not people got sick."

Studies such as this help us understand that even the body functions better and more strongly when we are doing things that make us happier. Our immune systems work better when we are hopeful and have a sense of well-being.[71] Happiness is a fundamental object of human existence, so much so that the World Health Organization is increasingly emphasizing happiness as a component of health.

Happiness is determined by a complex set of voluntary and involuntary factors. Researchers in medicine, economics, psychology, neuroscience, and evolutionary biology have identified a broad range of stimuli to happiness and unhappiness. The influencing factors include good health, elections, income, job loss, socioeconomic inequality, divorce, illness, bereavement, and genes.

Recent studies have focused on what is perhaps an even more important element that influences your happiness, and that is the happiness of the people you spend time with. Research shows that emotional states can be transferred directly from one individual to another. Is it by mechanisms in the brain that we are not even aware of, but which enable us to copy the emotions and actions that we observe in other people. This contagion can happen anywhere from a few minutes to a matter of weeks.[72]

If we needed more evidence than our own experience of the powerful effect of being in groups of happy people, we now can find it in medical journals and university research studies. No matter what our ages or situations, spending time with people who are hopeful and happy will make us better, too.

Who are the people with whom you spend your time? It seems that the older I get, the more careful I am about where I spend my time. I am less willing to waste time on finishing books that I am not enjoying, staying all the way through movies that are boring or offending me, and being around people whose company leaves me feeling bored, drained, or angry.

People in general tend to think that impatience in mature adults is due to our becoming more crotchety or cantankerous. The implication is that we have lost the ability to maintain mental focus or an attitude of tolerance. The assumption is that enduring unpleasantness is something that we should keep on doing.

The truth is that we have learned some things about life. As we get older, we have more evidence that certain kinds of people and situations generally turn out in predictable ways. Younger generations may maintain hope that everything will turn out just fine and that we should patiently endure all kinds of people. Our experience tells us different. So, we gradually learn not to invest our time in things that do not give us good payoffs.

Also, we become more conscious of the value of time. A friend recently told me why he had made changes in his use of time.

"Think back twenty years. How long ago does it seem to you?" I admitted that it did not seem very long ago.

"Well, that's about all you've got left, if things go really well. Maybe a lot less. So, don't put off what you really want to get done."

So, we can benefit from thoughtful standards for deciding which people and situations that deserve our best investment of time.

PLANNING FOR COMMUNITY

Since we are profoundly affected by the company we keep, it makes sense to stay connected to the people whom we have chosen to be our community. Regular contact is important in order to give mutual encouragement and practical support in following the ways that guarantee the best chances for happiness.

The best scenario is weekly meetings at regular times, so that we can schedule and protect the meetings. Knowing that we have the meetings there tends to make us feel secure. We know that at least once a week we will meet with people of kindred spirits, and that we will listen to each other talk about the spectrum of thoughts and emotions that accompany our aging process. *(**Note**: the Rule of Thirds applies in all settings, so we should not be surprised if not everyone is for us no matter what. However, our percentages will probably be better in a support group.)*

The group may agree to have more than one meeting per week during times when members are going through crises.

Meetings

Throughout the book, suggestions have been made as to how being in an ongoing group can make it easier to develop constructive habits. Here are further suggestions based on what has worked well in mutual help groups.

Meeting Formats

Each group is free to develop a format that best suits their needs as to what is emphasized, the selection of readings, the type of ritual, the meeting philosophy, the emotional tone of the meetings, and the informal group norms.

Suggested Format for Support Groups

For those who decide that their group will be a support group, this format is given merely as a suggestion about the kind of rituals that other support groups have found highly beneficial.

Each group should develop the patterns and rituals that best suit their own group.

- Good Evening ladies and gentlemen. This is the regular meeting of the _____ support group. My name is _____ and I will be your leader for this meeting. Tonight's meeting will be a (open, discussion, speaker, book, etc) meeting.
- Let us open the meeting with a moment of silence to do with as you wish followed by the Serenity Prayer (some groups like to use The Lord's Prayer or the Prayer of Saint Francis of Assisi):

> **God, grant me the serenity**
> **To accept the things I cannot change,**
> **The courage to change the things I can,**
> **and Wisdom to know the difference.**

- This group is a fellowship of men and women who share experience, strength, and hope with each other so that we will all learn how to maintain happiness. (It is often helpful to have the group take turns reading the 10 Choices, though this is a matter of preference.)

Older, Wiser ... and HAPPIER
10 Choices for Rebooting Your Life at 50+

1) **Chooser or Victim**: Making Choices or Feeling Powerless
2) **Adaptable or Rigid:** Adapting to Life's Stages and Circumstances or Being Captive to Futile Habits
3) **Aware or Oblivious:** Fully Aware of Physical and Emotional Realities or Hiding Behind Diversions
4) **Purposeful or Adrift:** Having Satisfying Purpose or Drifting In Search Of Pleasure
5) **Fulfilled or Surviving**: Meeting Basic Human Needs or Settling for Survival
6) **Real or Roles:** Showing True Self in Relationships or Presenting Acceptable Impressions
7) **Peaceable or Contentious:** Contented with Win/Win or Living in a Win/Lose World
8) **Spiritual or Physical**: Attending to Intangible Influences or Heeding Only Physical Reality
9) **Compassionate or Self-Absorbed**: Helping Others or Obsessed by Own Needs
10) **Together or Solitary:** Part of Genuine Community or Emotional Separation

- **Greetings:**
  At this time we will give our names and tell something about ourselves.

- Introduce the Speaker for the evening. If yours is a discussion type meeting, the leader either conducts the discussion or introduces the selected discussion leader.

STUDY QUESTIONS ON TOGETHER OR SOLITARY

1) Who do you trust enough to tell your true thoughts and feelings?
2) Whose presence makes you feel calm and accepted?
3) What kind of gatherings give you the most satisfaction?
4) What groups were you a part of in the past that meant a lot to you? Why was it meaningful?
5) What groups were you a part of in the present that mean a lot to you? Why is it meaningful?
6) Tell about someone who makes you feel great just talking to him/her.

EXPERIMENTING WITH TOGETHERNESS

Choose an action or write one of your own.

☐ I will make a list of the people whom I trust with sensitive information about me.

☐ I will make a list of people whom I can depend on in times of crisis.

☐ I will make a list of people who will be honest with me about my faults and mistakes.

☐ I will make a list of people who make me feel at my best when I am in their presence.

☐ I will make plans to spend time with people on these lists on a regular basis.

OBSTACLES TO HAPPINESS

1) What makes it difficult for me to choose togetherness rather than isolation?
2) Is the obstacle a
   ☐ Thought or belief   ☐ Emotion   ☐ Attitude   ☐ Behavior
   ☐ Consequence/situation?
3) What would I have to do to make a different choice?

Conclusion

We have looked at the ten choices that affect happiness most as we mature. These choices are not surprising; we have seen them made and applied by scores of admirable people in every era and place. And when we make the best choices, we have seen them work for us, too.

As the wheel below suggests, the choices are interrelated. Each one that is wisely made enhances our chances of making others that benefit us.

We have looked at the most effective mechanism for making the choices endure: regular engagement with people with a similar commitment to having life at its fullest.

It is time now to acknowledge that the determining factor is likely to be how much effort we are willing to exert in making the choices and making them stick.

You know what to do, how to do it, and why it will be useful. The rest is up to you!

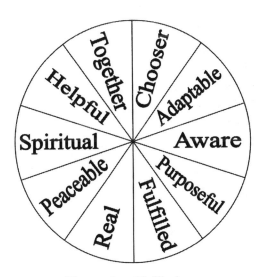

Figure 6 – 10 Choices

Bibliography

Albom, Mitch, *Tuesdays with Morrie*, Random House, New York, NY, 1997.

Allport, Gordon W., *The Nature of Prejudice,* Perseus Books, Cambridge, Mass., 1979.

Beh-Shar, Tal, *Happier*, McGraw Hill, 2007.

Berne, Eric, *Games People Play*, Random House, New York, NY, 1964.

Boulding, Elise, *Cultures of Peace: The Hidden Side of History*, Syracuse University Press, 2000, pg. 90.

Campbell, Joseph, *The Power of Myth*, Doubleday & Company, New York, NY, 1988.

Cohen, Gene D., *The Mature Mind*, Basic Books, 2005.

Coles, Robert, *The Call of Service,* Houghton Mifflin Company, New York, 1993.

Dass, Ram and Gorman, Paul, *How Can I Help?* Alfred A. Knopf, New York, 2000.

Frankl, Viktor E., *Man's Search for Meaning*, Beacon Press, Boston, Mass., 2000.

Fowler, James H. and Christakis Nicholas A, *Dynamic Spread of Happiness in a Large Social Network: Longitudinal Analysis over 20 years in the Framingham Heart Study,*

Published 4 December 2008, doi:10.1136/bmj.a2338, BMJ 2008;337:a2338.

Graybiel, Ann. (2000). "The Basal Ganglia." Current Biology, 10(14), R509-511

Glasser , William, *Choice Theory in the Classroom*. New York: Harper & Row, 1986.

Helmstetter, Shad, *"What to Say When You Talk to Your Self,"* Pocket Books of Simon & Schuster, 1982.

Hillman, James, *The Force of Character and the Lasting Life*, Ballantine Books, New York, 1999.

James, William, *Varieties of Religious Experience*, The Modern Library, New York, 2002.

Jog, Mandar, Yasuo Kubota, Christopher Connolly, Viveka Hillegaart, and Ann Graybiel. (1999). "Building Neural Representations of Habits." Science, 286, 1745-1749.

Jourard, Sidney M., *The Transparent Self,* revised edition, Van Nostrand Co, New York, 1971.

Kunc, Norman, *The Need to Belong: Rediscovering Maslow's Hierarchy of Needs,* Paul Brookes, Baltimore, 1992.

Latner, Joel, *The Gestalt Therapy Book*, Julian Press, New York, NY, 1974.

Luks, Allan. *The Healing Power of Doing Good: The Health and Spiritual Benefits of Helping Others*, New York: iUniverse.com, 2001.

M.A. Shafto, D.M. Burke, E. Stamatakis, P. Tam, G. Osborne, L.K. Tyler. INSULA ATROPHY CONTRIBUTES TO WORD-FINDING DEFICITS IN OLDER ADULTS Program No. 408.2. *2005 Abstract Viewer/Itinerary Planner.* Washington, DC: Society for Neuroscience, 2005. Online.

Maslow, A. (1970). *Motivation and Personality,* 2nd edition, Harper & Row, New York, NY.

Maslow, A. (1971). *The Farther Reaches of Human Nature.* New York: The Viking Press.

Maslow, A., & Lowery, R. (Ed.). (1998). *Toward a Psychology of Being* (3rd ed.). New York: Wiley & Sons.

Maslow, Abraham H., *Toward a Psychology of Being*, Van Nostrand Reinhold, New York, 1982.

Merrill, David W, and Roger H. Reid, *Personal Styles & Effective Performance*, CRC Press, Boca Raton, FL, 1999.

Mitchell, Stephen, *The Enlightened Mind: An Anthology of Sacred Prose*, HarperCollins, New York, 1991.

Mooney, Chris, *Failure to Thrive,* an article by a freelance writer living in Palo Alto, California.

Moyers, Bill, *Moyers on America*, The New Press, New York, NY, 2004.

Myers, Isabel Briggs with Peter B. Myers, *Gifts Differing*: Understanding Personality Type, Davies-Black Publishing, Palo Alto, CA, 1995.

Peck, M. Scott, *A World Waiting To Be Born: Civility Rediscovered,* Bantam, 1993.

Peck, M. Scott, *The Different Drum: Community Making and Peace*, Simon & Schuster, NYC, NY, 1987.

Progoff, *At a Journal Workshop*: *the Basic Text and Guide for Using the Intensive Journal Process*, Dialogue House Library, New York, NY, 1975.

Riso, Don Richard and Russ Hudson, *Discovering Your Personality Type: the Essential Introduction to the Enneagram,* Houghton Mifflin Company, New York, NY, 2003.

Schulz, Mona Lisa. *Awakening Intuition*, Three Rivers Press, New York, NY, 1999.

Shelby, Tommie, *We Who are Dark: The Philosophical Foundations of Black Solidarity*, The Belknap Press of Harvard University Press, Cambridge, Mass, 2005.

Sylwester, Robert, "Mirror Neurons", http://www.brainconnection.com/content/181_1, August 2002.

Tolle, Eckhart, *A New Earth: Awakening to Your Life's Purpose*, Penguin Group, New York, New York, 2006.

Untermeyer, Louis. *Modern American Poetry.* New York: Harcourt, Brace and Howe, 1919; Bartleby.com, 1999.

Subject Index

Author

Dr. Clay Carter's education includes Bachelor of Arts from Georgetown College, Master of Divinity and Doctor of Ministry degrees from Southern Seminary in Louisville, Kentucky. He received post-graduate supervised training in clinical pastoral counseling at Norton Hospital in Louisville. He received two years supervised training in group therapy at the Gestalt Institute of Memphis. He received two years of supervised training in addiction treatment at the Redwood Residential Treatment Center, Redwood City, California. He directed addiction treatment programs in San Francisco and Long Beach, California. Dr. Carter resides in Jacksonville, Florida.

Figures

See "Figures" in the Subject Index for page numbers.

End Notes

1. Burns, David D, *Feeling Good: The New Mood Therapy*, HarperCollins, NYC, 1980, pg. xix.
2. *Ibid.*
3. Jog, Mandar, Yasuo Kubota, Christopher Connolly, Viveka Hillegaart, and Ann Graybiel. (1999). "Building Neural Representations of Habits." Science, 286, 1745-1749.
4. Graybiel, Ann. (2000). "The Basal Ganglia." Current Biology, 10(14), R509-511.
5. Shad Helmstetter, What to Say When You Talk to Your Self, pg. 242-244.
6. http://www.brainconnection.com/content/181_1, Robert, Sylwester, "Mirror Neurons", August 2002.
7. Daniel Gilbert, "Stumbling on Happiness," Vintage Books, New York, 2007, pg 24.
8. (S.E. Taylor and J.D. Brown, "Illusion and Wellbeing: A Social-Psychological Perspective on Mental Health," Psychological Bulletin 1-3:193-210 (1988)
9. R. Schultz and B.H. Hanusa, "Long-Term Effects of Control and Predictability-Enhancing Interventions: Findings and Ethical Issues," *Journal of Personality and Social Psychology* 36:1202-1222, 1978).
10. Gilbert, *Ibid.*
11. Variant on a prayer attributed to theologian Reinhold Niebuhr.
12. Cohen, Gene D., *The Mature Mind*, pp. 3-4.
13. Ibid, pg 4
14. Ibid, pg 5
15. *Failure to Thrive,* an article by Chris Mooney, a freelance writer living in Palo Alto, California.
16. Eckhart Tolle, A New Earth: Awakening to Your Life's Purpose, pg. 297.
17. *Ibid.*
18. Beh-Shar, Tal, *Happier*, McGraw, 2007, pg 34.
19. Moyers, Bill, *Moyers on America*, The New Press, NYC, 2004, pg.196

20. Dan Buettner, "Find Purpose, Live Longer," *AARP,* November & December, 2008, pg. 28.
21. Isabel Briggs Myers with Peter B. Myers, *Gifts Differing*: *Understanding Personality Type*, pp. xi-xv.
22. Don Richard Riso and Russ Hudson, Discovering Your Personality Type: the Essential Introduction to the Enneagram, pp. 5, 183.
23. David W Merrill and Roger H. Reid, *Personal Styles & Effective Performance*, CRC Press, Boca Raton, FL, 1999, front cover.
24. Ira Progoff, At a Journal Workshop: The Basic Text & Guide for Using the Intensive Journal, pp. 10-11.
25. *Ibid.*, 77-78.
26. Sidney M. Jourard, *The Transparent Self,* pg. 32.
27. Stephen Mitchell, The Enlightened Mind: An Anthology of Sacred Prose, p. 55.
28. Viktor E. Frankl, *Man's Search for Meaning*, Beacon Press, Boston, Mass., 2000.
29. Louis Untermeyer, *Modern American Poetry,* pg. 1919.
30. Joseph Campbell, *The Power of Myth,* pp. 120, 149.
31. Abraham Maslow, *Motivation and Personality* (2nd ed.), p. 48.
32. Abraham Maslow, (1954). *Motivation and Personality*. New York: Harper & Row.
33. Mona Lisa Schulz, *Awakening Intuition*, pg. 145.
34. *Ibid.*, pg. 144.
35. Abraham Maslow, (1971). *The Farther Reaches of Human Nature*. New York: The Viking Press.
36. *Ibid.*
37. William James, *Varieties of Experience*, The Modern Library, New York, 2002.
38. William Glasser (1986), *Choice Theory in the Classroom.* pg 23.
39. Cohen, Gene, *The Mature Mind*, pg. 31.
40. Mitch Albom, Tuesdays with Morrie, pg. 10.
41. Joel Latner, *The Gestalt Therapy Book*, pg 130.
42. *Ibid.*, pg. 131.
43. *Ibid.*, pg. 133.
44. *Ibid.*, pg. 133-134.
45. *Ibid.*, pg. 135.
46. Gordon Allport, *The Nature of Prejudice*, pg 25.
47. Eckhart Tolle, A New Earth: Awakening to Your Life's Purpose, pg. 175-176.
48. *Ibid.*, pg 175.
49. *Ibid.*, pg 176.

50. *Ibid.*, pg 137-138.
51. *Ibid.*
52. Danny E. Morris, A Life That Really Matters: The Story of the John Wesley Great Experiment.
53. Abraham H. Maslow, *Toward a Psychology of Being*, pg 71.
54. William James, Varieties of Religious Experience, pg. 76.
55. James, *Ibid.*
56. James, *Ibid.*
57. James, *Ibid.* pg 435.
58. James, *Ibid.*
59. James, *Ibid.* pg 77.
60. Shafto,M.A., D.M. Burke, E. Stamatakis, P. Tam, G. Osborne, L.K. Tyler. Insula Atrophy Contributes To Word-Finding Deficits In Older Adults, Program No. 408.2. *2005 Abstract Viewer/Itinerary Planner.* Washington, DC: Society for Neuroscience, 2005. Online.
61. James, *Ibid.* pg 74.
62. Allan Luks, The Healing Power of Doing Good: The Health and Spiritual Benefits of Helping Others, iUniverse.com.
63. *Ibid.*
64. ebook reproduction of the complete and original 1937 version of *Think and Grow Rich* by Napoleon Hill, originally published by The Ralston Society and now in the public domain.
65. M. Scott Peck, The Different Drum: Community Making and Peace, pg. 86.
66. *Ibid.*, pg. 88.
67. *Ibid.*
68. Tommie Shelby, *We Who are Dark: The Philosophical Foundations of Black Solidarity*, The Belknap Press of Harvard University Press, Cambridge, Mass, 2005.
69. Sidney M. Jourard, *The Transparent Self,* pg. 32.
70. Peck, *Ibid*, pg. 105.
71. Research by James H Fowler **and** Nicholas A Christakis Article URL: http://www.medicalnewstoday.com/articles/4009.php.
72. *Ibid.*

Christ Episcopal
on San Pablo

Topics in this book ⟶